THE AMBASSADOR

by
Terri Morgan

Wudang Research Association

Digital Edition
ISBN-13: 978-0-9672889-6-3
ISBN-10: 0-9672889-6-7

Print Edition
ISBN-13: 978-0-9672889-7-0
ISBN-10: 0-9672889-7-5

An accomplished older woman leads
a tight-knit team to protect the Local Neighborhood.
Together, they must find a way
to stop the invading Olmeri from taking over.

Good friends, good food, good times, and some bad
guys in our Local Neighborhood.

Dedicated to my mom, the lady who raised me and to all
the little girls like me whose dreams are never big enough for
their imaginations
   - Terri Morgan 5/24/2021

WE ARE HERE

The Ambassador presents a grounded vision for a hopeful future and who we could become.

When I first started writing the books, a friend read an early version. He liked the story and characters, but he wasn't quite sure about the location. I explained that we were in the Local Neighborhood. Where's that? he wanted to know. So, I set about creating a map showing the stars and their relative positions. How to orient the map? Where to put the stars? Which stars should be included? I looked at distances and colors. I looked at maps of stars that were a little further away than our closest neighbors but not too far. I found the Pulsar Map Frank Drake created. The stars fell into place.

Now, I had something I could show my friend, point to, and say: we are here.

CONTENTS

CHAPTER 1: DEPARTURE DAY

The wind will tell its story.
Whether you are listening or not.
Where do you want to go? it whispers.
Who are you? it asks.

BEGIN SETUP
SPACE: THE LOCAL NEIGHBORHOOD

Before you and after you
We will remain

We have looked to the stars for 10,000 years. From the time before the early orbiters to the first colonies on Mars and the breakthroughs that let us travel to the nearby stars, we wanted to go. We wanted to go out, to find what we could, to discover what we didn't know. So, we did. We moved out among the stars in our Local Neighborhood. We made friends and discovered new worlds. We learned. We built better ships. We rediscovered ancient technologies. We kept going.

The Central Alliance was founded on Dagon in the Fomalhaut system as a forum to give the Local Neighborhood a way to handle trade issues and to protect each other. As time went by, the Alliance became a federation of systems with a governing High Council. They recognized the need to keep in contact and protect each other. They also needed to reach out to potential new allies and trading partners. They knew the risks of making first contact. They needed special teams and a training program.

So, the Central Alliance High Council asked the Masters of Ras'alhague to create a training program. The Masters were widely known and highly respected as Keepers of the Five Elements: Metal, Water, Wood, Fire, and Earth and as Adepts in the Ancient Arts of healing and fighting.

The Council of Nine agreed to create a program that would both reveal the character of the person and prepare those who could complete it to become one of these specially trained First Contact Ambassadors. It took a generation to develop the program and a few more to refine it. As time went by, the training became quite famous for its rigor and for the respect its graduates earned. Being able to complete the application requesting admission to the program required extensive preparation. Applicants were required to have studied multiple languages, historical perspectives, and all the core philosophies and ideas of at least one civilization, throughout its development. The physical requirements were more demanding. It was expected that these ambassadors be able to evade capture, fight, and improvise as needed. The training to become Keepers of the Elements as well as Adepts in the Ancient Arts would serve them well.

The Masters were selective about who they accepted for the program. It wasn't always the best of the best. It wasn't always by referral either. They looked for the ones who had overcome some difficulty, the ones who knew what hardship was, the ones who had the potential to achieve more and the character, determination, and will to make it happen. Those were the ones they wanted. The program was designed to be hard. If a candidate was not ready for hardship, they could not succeed.

The training was holistic and demanding. Agriculture, food, water, what is needed to grow food, how living things prosper and how they die were all essential parts of the training. How to develop character, courage, and build relationships with others was required learning. The trainees learned what it takes to grow food from seeds, what the land and the plants need to survive, how to make medicines from foods and herbs, how to cultivate a garden. They learned how to find and cultivate themselves, too. Character development was at the core of the training. As they prepared for graduation, some chose to make healing their focus and went on to further studies in medicine. Most of the graduates became trade negotiators and ambassadors.

The graduates were all formidable fighters and clever negotiators. They earned a reputation for being polite, fair, honest, shrewd, and not those to cross. Everyone who completed the program was well-received and well-liked. Being able to walk into a room or situation and have most everyone feel comfortable was something they all learned to do. It was a required skill.

Those who wanted to become ambassadors started out as part of a trade negotiation team to learn the issues for different worlds and what was in the existing treaties. They needed time to build trusted relationships with allies. Among those who became ambassadors, only a few held a First Contact Charter.

A First Contact Charter gave the Ambassador the full backing of the Central Alliance High Council to make whatever decisions were required without consultations. They were careful in their selections with requirements for recommendations from colleagues and one of the Masters at Ras'alhague. After all, the person could be making decisions for the entire Alliance.

INITIALIZING
THE HIGH COUNCIL CHAMBERS ON DAGON

Ambassador Micha Lawrence paced the clean marble floor outside the High Council Chambers. A tall set of ornate doors took up most of the inner wall. Well-spaced woven silk carpets muffled her footsteps. She wasn't tall. She wasn't short either. She was pretty but not overtly so. Her long, dark-blonde hair was braided over her left shoulder. She was dressed in the formal gold and rust color robes of a Keeper of Earth with a simple dark red woven belt wrapped around her waist. Her ambassador's sash with several medals hung across her right shoulder.

She smiled as she looked down at the eight jewels on her First Contact pin glistening in the clear light from the atrium windows above. The pin had a simple, elegant design. The base was flat gold with a ring of gold braid outside the rim. Frank Drake's iconic pulsar map for the Pioneer Plaque was engraved in the center. Eight small jewels were arranged in three dimensions to match the relative positions of the eight original members of the Central Alliance: Sol, Eridani, Procyon, Vega, Altair, Fomalhaut, Ras'alhague, and Aldebaran.

She had been born into a royal family long after the time royalty mattered to anyone. Her family had titles but not much else. She had wanted to be an Ambassador for the Central Alliance since she could remember. In all the videos and stories, it seemed so glamorous and exiting to go to new places and meet new friends. But her parents died when she was a baby and her grandparents didn't have enough money to send her to the special schools. They weren't supportive, either. They didn't think she should aim so high. They wanted her to get a clerk's job or help her grandfather with the printing shop. So, she studied at night, after work, during any free time she had. It wasn't easy helping her grandmother with chores and working with her grandfather at his printing shop. As she had gotten older, her grandfather had let her help make the old-fashioned, elaborate binding books for the Alliance Treaties. She'd ask about the treaties and how the Ambassadors could get them to agree. Her grandfather would scold her. "Leave the questions of how to negotiate trade to others. Don't be so adventurous," he'd say.

She tried several times. Finally, she was accepted by the Masters at Ras'alhague. Life on Ras 2 was primitive. There were few conveniences. That was part of the training. She was selected to join the House of Tu led by Master Tai Aragon, a

Keeper of Earth and Adept of the 9th Level. She became lifetime friends with Sentar, Maru, Galen, and B'ani. She earned the honored place of First Disciple. It meant she would inherit the House of Tu when Master Tai passed away.

She spent time as a negotiator and as an assistant trade ambassador developing her diplomatic and negotiation skills. She received considerable recognition and a few medals for her work in brokering agreements and settling disputes. After she completed several missions that could have turned out quite differently were it not for her skills, she was offered and accepted a First Contact Charter.

She gained quite a reputation for the dinners she hosted and arranged, with attendees talking about the food for weeks afterward. She often managed to get agreements signed quickly and to sort out disputes favorably for everyone. Some of the planetary councils had been hostile. She managed to outwit them, mostly. She had to fight her way out a few times, too.

The inner doors began to open slowly outward.

"Ambassador Micha Lawrence," the clerk called out.

The Ambassador took a breath and straightened, confident and humble at the same time. Her robes swayed gently as she walked into the chamber. She moved gracefully with a traveler's determined gait. Worn, well-polished boots covered the space between her robes and the floor. She walked to the center of the room, crossed her arms to her chest with her fists closed, opened her arms to extend both hands palms up, turned them over, and bowed slightly as she brought her hands down to her sides. It was an old-fashioned elegant gesture the Keepers all used. The original meaning was complicated. The common meaning was simply 'I offer you peace.'

She looked up at the Council members.

The twelve members of the Central Alliance High Council sat on a raised platform in a semicircle around a large, open floor. Carved oak columns supported a curved ceiling. Ebony panels inlaid with mother of pearl fronted the council seats providing an imposing view and a barrier.

Each of the High Council members wore a formal black robe with different colored scarves draped over their shoulders and bands on their sleeves to identify their roles on the Council and their home planets.

High Council President Aliel Smbarak sat in the center chair. Her shoulder-length black hair framed her face. Her antique gold earrings almost matched her eyes. She wore three scarves: dark red, yellow gold, and spring green. The green represented Dagon, her home world; the red and gold her roles in Medicine and Agriculture. Her sleeves were trimmed in gold braid to show her role as High Council President.

A clerk and two assistants sat at tables just below the council members' seats. They were recording the proceedings.

"My greetings, Madame President," the Ambassador said. She looked around the room. "My greetings to the entire Central Alliance High Council. How may I be of service?" she asked.

"We have a problem," Minister Daru said. He wasn't much for pleasantries.

The Ambassador turned to look at him with a questioning gaze and a smile, waiting for him to go on. She wanted to challenge him. 'Ok. Sure. That's why you called me here. Might you be just a little more specific?' she thought. But she didn't say it. It wouldn't help.

President Smbarak frowned at him and turned to look at the Ambassador. "We're getting more reports about the Olmeri. Several of our trading partners are reporting problems with their shipments of grains and other staples," she said.

"What sort of problems, Madame President?" the Ambassador asked.

President Smbarak looked down and shook her head. "Disruptions in deliveries, spoiled containers, booked shipments not delivered. There are too many things that have 'not gone smoothly.' And now, we're getting reports of Olmeri raiders scouting other sectors," she said. She took a breath and sighed.

The Ambassador frowned. "What do our traders say?" she asked.

"They don't," Minister Rang said sharply. "They don't tell us anything. Nothing. They won't give us any details. All they say is they went to pick up the shipment and it wasn't there. They couldn't get the permit to load it. They were delayed and the shipment was sold to someone else. It's always some excuse," he said.

The Ambassador listened carefully. "He is just repeating the problem. He isn't adding anything new," she thought. "Is that what's happening, though, Minister? What have they tried? Why did they fail?" she asked.

President Smbarak turned her head slightly and looked at the Ambassador. "That is the question we want you to answer, Ambassador," she said.

The Ambassador looked at her with concern and raised her eyebrows. "I see," she said.

President Smbarak shook her head and looked down at a small screen. "The latest reports we have are from traders near Ka'len in the Hyades Cluster," she said.

Minister Pargals couldn't resist. "And that is where you are going," he said. He wagged his finger at the Ambassador.

The Ambassador turned, shifted backward, and looked straight at President Smbarak, shaking her head ever so slightly. "Madame President? The Hyades Cluster is well outside the local neighborhood. It will take weeks just to get there," she said. She raised her eyebrows, blinked a few times, and smiled. "Please, oh please tell me that's not where you are sending me," she thought.

Minister Daru shifted forward in his chair. "Well, yes Ambassador. That's why we want you to go there. We didn't give you a First Contact Charter so you could take nice vacations. We'd rather not wait for the Olmeri to come any closer. They have destroyed too many planets already," he said.

The Ambassador straightened and tried not to frown. "You want me to go where and do what?" she thought.

President Smbarak smiled, nodded, and shrugged her shoulders. "We need you to get to Ka'len and broker a treaty with them before the Olmeri arrive. Do whatever you can to stop the Olmeri," she said.

"I appreciate your confidence in me," the Ambassador said with more than a little skepticism.

President Smbarak looked directly at her. She wasn't smiling anymore. "We have assigned the Magellan to be your transport and your over watch. Make your preparations quietly, Ambassador. Don't mention your mission to anyone until you are well underway. Not until you are out of the local neighborhood. Even your team cannot know," she said

"They are used to that," the Ambassador said.

"Whatever you need, Ambassador," President Smbarak said. She looked around the room at the other council members as if to tell them they should all agree.

They all nodded.

"I'll get the preparations underway," the Ambassador said.

"Quietly, Ambassador. Quietly," President Smbarak said.

The Ambassador nodded to her again, pasted a neutral smile on her face, bowed to the High Council members, and turned to leave. "Whoo boy, this is a doozy. But sure. I'll go out there and see what I can do. Thanks ever so," she thought.

CONFIRM SETTINGS
THE AMBASSADOR'S APARTMENT ON DAGON

The Ambassador was sitting in bed with a glass of wine watching an old Earth film, "The Sound of Music." The comm link chimed.

"Micha, are you awake?" President Smbarak asked.

The Ambassador sat up, put the wine glass down on the bedside table, and switched on the video. "Yes, Aliel," the Ambassador replied.

President Smbarak's face appeared on the screen. "What's that in the background? Children singing?" she asked.

The Ambassador smiled. "I'm watching an old Earth film called "The Sound of Music." It's about a wealthy family with quite a few children. The children were singing a song about something called a cuckoo. It's lovely, Aliel, just lovely. You'd like it. You would," she said.

President Smbarak smiled. "I saw that film once. I did like the first part with the children singing. But the next part I didn't like very much," she said. She glanced at the almost-empty wine glass. "How many glasses of wine have you had?" she asked.

The Ambassador raised her hand with the last three fingers up. "Just two. I don't really have anything else to do. We're all packed and well, everything is ready. We're all good," she said.

President Smbarak frowned. "Everything is ready? Is there anything about that everything I should know?" she asked.

The Ambassador blinked a few times and smiled. "No. Thanks for asking though. Everything is good. We're all good," she said.

President Smbarak lowered her eyes, shook her head, then looked up. "Really? All good? Micha, what did you do? No, no, no, don't tell me," she said. She raised her hand palm out, shook her head, and laughed. "I don't want to know. I'm sure I'll find out soon enough. I know you too well," she said.

The Ambassador grinned. "Yes, you do. But that's not why you called," she said.

President Smbarak shook her head. "I wish it was. Traders returning through the Aldebaran system have sent new reports of Olmeri activity along the edge of the Orion Arm. We haven't received reports like this before," she said.

The Ambassador leaned forward. "Like what?" she asked.

President Smbarak sat back in her chair. "Several of our more reliable trading partners for grains and other staples have stopped trading with our buyers. The buyers are unable to pick up their shipments," she said.

The Ambassador nodded. "We knew that was happening. It's part of why I'm leaving in the morning. What's different now?" she asked.

President Smbarak looked down and shook her head. "The traders inquired. The Olmeri replied that it was their choice to trade with others or not," she said.

The Ambassador sat back. "Oh crap," she said.

President Smbarak chuckled. "Well, yes, that's one way to put it," she said.

The Ambassador frowned. "They aren't just scouting anymore," she said.

President Smbarak shook her head. "No. And they are moving more quickly. We received reports from our trading partners in that sector about the Olmeri scouting parties just last year," she said.

The Ambassador sat back a little more and turned to one side shaking her head. "Did they give you any better idea of what the Olmeri are looking for? What do they want?" she asked.

President Smbarak shook her head. "No. We only know that they seem to be, how to say, récolte des planètes, harvesting planets," she said.

The Ambassador squinted and frowned. "Récolter pour quoi? Harvesting for what?" she asked.

President Smbarak shrugged. "Je ne sais pas. I don't know. Once they arrive, we lose trade. Then communications," she said.

The Ambassador shook her head and laughed. "Quelle pagaille! What a mess! And you are sending me to go meet them? Thanks ever so. How is it you always seem to find the very best assignments for me?" she asked.

"You are so very welcome," President Smbarak said. She grinned then shook her head and frowned. "Micha, if anyone can figure out something, it's you. With everything you know about agribusiness and your training, you are the best chance we have at finding a solution. I don't like sending you out there. Other than some traders, we don't have allies in that sector. You'll be mostly on your own. We don't have any good options. We need to find out what is going on and we must find a way to stop the Olmeri before they get any closer." She took a deep breath. "You're scheduled to depart first thing in the morning. Try to get some rest now," she said.

The Ambassador frowned and looked at her sideways. "Like I'm going to sleep well after this conversation," she said.

"Get another glass of wine and go back to watching your film?" President Smbarak suggested.

The Ambassador grinned. "I can do that!" she said.

President Smbarak shook her head and chuckled. "Make sure your alarm is set," she said.

The Ambassador sat up proudly. "Already done!" she said.

President Smbarak nodded. "Micha, I know it won't be easy. Keep your eyes open. Whatever you need...," she said.

"Just ask. Thanks Mom!" the Ambassador said.

They both laughed.

President Smbarak might scold her or question her, but if she needed something, all she needed to do was ask. President Smbarak always found a way.

The Ambassador lowered her eyes then looked up at the screen. "Seriously though, Aliel. Thank you. I appreciate you looking out for me. You always make sure I have whatever I need," she said.

President Smbarak smiled and nodded. "Safe journey, Micha. I look forward to seeing you back here in a few weeks," she said.

The Ambassador nodded. "Thank you, Aliel," she said. She closed the comm link, got up, and poured another glass of wine. She went back to the bed, took a few sips, curled up with a pillow, and fell asleep just as the lead male character in the film was singing a song about a flower that only grows in the mountains and blossoms in the snow, Edelweiss.

GETTING READY
THE AMBASSADOR'S APARTMENT ON DAGON

The Ambassador was curled up on her bed sleeping. The room was quiet and dark. She had a standard garden apartment with a large living room, comfortable kitchen, a bedroom suite, a spare room she used as an office, and a patio. The patio was her favorite place to sit and think.

An alarm chime started, softer at the beginning. She switched the alarm to snooze. It went off again. She switched it off and sat up. She rubbed the back of her neck and the sides of her head. "Red wine" she muttered, looking at the empty glass. "Hmmm. Red wine." She shook her head gently, swung her legs over the edge of the bed, started to get up, and sat back down. She sat there rubbing her knees for just a minute.

"Getting up earlier than usual isn't as easy as it used to be. Maybe I should leave this work to someone younger. Stay home. Putter in the garden. Teach. There are some candidates who showed promise this year. Maybe I should go visit Ras 2 after I get back," she thought. She stood up and put a wrap over her shoulders.

The warm aroma of fresh-brewed coffee drifted into the room. She sniffed the air. "It was supposed to start at 4:00?" she thought. She looked at the clock. It was just after. She let her nose lead her out of the room. She waved her hand across a small panel as she entered the kitchen. Four muted lights came on under the cabinets. The coffee was still brewing.

She picked up a cup and poured just a bit. She liked a little of the sharp bitter taste that only very strong coffee had. Brewed coffee was one of the little things she had tried to keep. So many other things she'd had to give up over the years. This one, this small thing, she wanted to keep. She held the cup close with two hands for just a second. She smiled at the warmth and bittersweet aroma.

She walked through the kitchen and opened the door to go out onto the patio. The before-morning air was cool and crisp. She turned around and went back to her room. She slid her feet into a pair of slippers and picked up a sweater, putting it on as she went back to the kitchen.

She stopped to fill her cup with the now-finished coffee and went out onto the patio. It was quiet in the stillness before dawn. Even the birds weren't up yet. She looked up at the stars and thought back to when she'd first started her training on Ras 2. "The stars aren't so different there. Not that different at all. Maybe after this mission I will go visit again," she said. She looked up and smiled sadly. "I know you're out there," she whispered.

She took a sip from her cup and looked out at the back garden. She started pacing along the low stone wall surrounding her patio. There were more shadows than light. It was a quarter moon night. A few crickets chirped in a bamboo stand. An owl called from one of the tall trees. Several dark birds fluttered in and out among the top branches. "It's too early for birds," she thought. She shook her head. She stopped pacing and watched the movement.

"Not birds. Bats," she said. She looked down into her almost empty cup then out at the garden one more time. She paced a little more and shook her head sadly. "What do they want? What do the Olmeri really want? What they are doing makes no sense. Why destroy whole planets?" she asked.

She sighed and went inside.

INSTALLING
THE AMBASSADOR'S APARTMENT ON DAGON

The Ambassador turned on more lights as she went into the kitchen. She refilled her cup, leaned back against the counter, and took a sip.

A chime sounded and a comm terminal lit up. She left it on audio only. N'amani's clear, resonant voice came through the speaker, "Good Morning, Ambassador," he said.

The Ambassador smiled at the sound of his voice. "Good morning, N'amani. You're up early," she said.

"It's almost 5:30 Ambassador," N'amani said.

"So, it is. Seems I wasn't paying attention to the time. Thank you for the reminder. With all you have to do to get us ready to leave, I appreciate you making time to call me. I have my coffee in hand. I'll be ready in 30 minutes," the Ambassador said.

"You are very welcome, Ambassador. Also, those additional supplies you requested," N'amani said. He hesitated.

"Yes?" the Ambassador said. She was expecting him to tell her there were a few things he couldn't get.

"I have everything you requested," N'amani said quickly.

The Ambassador switched on the video. "You what? You have everything? How did you manage? No, don't tell me. You have everything? Everything? Really?" she asked.

N'amani nodded. "Yes, Ambassador. The last few boxes of dried foods and herbs are being loaded on your shuttle. You have a little more luggage than usual. And, em," he cleared his throat. "A few cartons were included in the stores we already transported to the Magellan," he said.

The Ambassador laughed out loud. "Already on the Magellan? Already on board? Heeee Ha He ho ho!!! Oh

really? You're a magician! What did you do? How did you?"
she asked.

N'amani smiled proudly. "Nothing too much. Some
bargaining here and there. Some of the regular stores the
Magellan requested were increased by just a little. A few last-
minute boxes went in two of the containers. They will notice
the wine bottles in the rice bins eventually. I'm afraid we will
have to find a way to manually repack those," he said. He was
trying not to laugh. It wasn't working. He put his hand over
his mouth and chuckled just a little.

The Ambassador doubled over with laughter. She almost
spilled her coffee. "I'm sure we'll find a way to manage. I'll
help. The Doctor and Beth will, too. And Kell, oh, he's going
to enjoy this! You are amazing, N'amani. Thank you!" she
said.

"You are welcome, Ambassador," N'amani replied. He
smiled bigger.

"Thank you again, N'amani. I'll see you shortly," the
Ambassador said happily. She closed the comm link, picked
up her coffee, and walked back to her room to shower and get
dressed. She'd already set out her travel clothes. "N'amani is
so much more than I could have asked for. Somehow, he just
knows what to do and how to get it done. I wish the Council
had assigned him sooner," she thought.

She thought back to the day she'd learned he was being
assigned to her delegation and their first mission together.

PROGRESS REPORT (RECALL)
PRESIDENT SMBARAK'S OFFICE ON DAGON

President Smbarak was seated behind a large, ornate desk
in an oval office. Ivory slats filtered the light from the tall
windows behind her. Bookshelves lined the walls. A ficus tree

took up one corner. Several plants were set around the room. A plush green carpet with an oval flower medallion had been placed on the hardwood floor in front of her desk. The Ambassador was standing on the carpet.

President Smbarak frowned and shook her head. "You knew we weren't happy with your 'went there did stuff' summaries," she said. She held up a small screen then put it face down on her desk.

"Well, yes," the Ambassador replied.

"So, why didn't you write your reports?" President Smbarak asked. She tilted her head to one side and frowned at the question.

The Ambassador smiled just a little. "I don't like writing reports," she said.

President Smbarak laughed then frowned. "But you are required to write them. It's not optional," she said.

The Ambassador turned her head to one side and pouted. "Doesn't make me like doing it," she said.

President Smbarak chuckled. "I take your point. But we can't let it continue. We're assigning you an acting Chief of Staff until you find someone," she said.

The Ambassador frowned. "I've been looking," she said.

President Smbarak raised her eyebrows. "For almost a year?" she asked.

The Ambassador looked off to one side. "Well," she said.

President Smbarak shook her head. "And your last requisitions report?" she asked.

The Ambassador smiled and shrugged. "What's another case of wine or a few bottles of good sunflower oil among friends?" she asked.

President Smbarak frowned. "It was more than a few," she said. She turned her head to one side.

The Ambassador smiled proudly. "It was for a good cause," she said.

President Smbarak looked at her and shook her head. She picked up another small screen and held it up. "N'amani Anrmlar will be joining your team," she said.

The screen showed a formal image of a tall, well-built, dark brown male with a slight blue tint to his hair and skin, a square face, and kind, thoughtful eyes. He was wearing an impeccably tailored black dashiki with an intricate gold inlay at the collar. He had a subtle smile that hinted he knew what was going on.

The Ambassador was curious and a bit taken aback. He looked like he really could get things done. She liked that very much. "You're assigning an Elronym Administrator as my Chief of Staff? You must really want those reports!" she said.

President Smbarak smiled broadly. "Why, yes. Yes, we do," she said.

They both laughed.

The Elronym were well-known for their administrative, logistics, and organizing skills. They were exceptional at keeping track of things. Their Administrators were some of the most sought after in the Alliance. Having an Elronym Administrator meant all the reports, requisitions, and supplies would be accounted for, reported, and managed. It also meant they'd get their supplies. Besides accounting for things, the Elronym were experts at acquiring whatever was needed.

President Smbarak lowered the screen. "We've already spoken with N'amani," she said.

"Oh," the Ambassador said shaking her head.

President Smbarak nodded and smiled. "Once he gets your backlog cleared and brings your budgets up to date, you can find someone else if you want," she said.

The Ambassador raised her eyebrows. "I haven't met him yet," she said.

President Smbarak smiled. "Tomorrow. You're scheduled to meet him here to start his orientation," she said.

The Ambassador shook her head. "That seems quick. Monday next week wouldn't be late," she said.

President Smbarak sighed, "Minister Pargals has been screaming about these reports for weeks. The only way to shut him up was to tell him we would ask N'amani if he would take this assignment. Luckily, N'amani agreed. So, you got him. Now, please give me something to placate Minister Pargals. Quickly?" she asked.

The Ambassador nodded a few times. "We'll get started in the morning. I didn't realize. Thanks for taking care of it. I'll help N'amani as much as I can. We'll get it sorted out. Don't worry," she said.

President Smbarak looked up and smiled. "Thank you," she said.

The Ambassador dropped her chin, turned her head, and looked up just a little. "Can I go now?" she asked.

President Smbarak giggled and nodded.

The Ambassador grinned and turned to leave.

N'amani had turned out to be so much more than she could have asked for. He naturally took over managing things. He could walk into any room with ease and be at the center of at least a few conversations. He seemed to instinctively know what needed to be done and did it. He was extremely practical, always on time, and he kept track of everything with ease. Better yet, he could fight.

CONTINUE (RECALL)
A RESORT MEETING ROOM ON SIRIUS 7

The Ambassador and N'amani had gone to Sirius 7 the week after he was assigned. She had been told a senior trade emissary wanted a quiet meeting to discuss some local tariffs related to a new treaty. Nothing unusual about that. The Alliance wanted to get the issues sorted out.

The Ambassador and N'amani walked through a set of glass doors that opened to a five-story atrium. Small balconies jutted out from each floor. Long philodendrons hung over the railings.

"This is nice," the Ambassador said. She looked up through the skylights.

"They built a glass mountain and brought the plants inside," N'amani said appreciatively.

They walked across a rustic tile floor to the front desk. The clerk pointed to an open door at the end of a carpeted hallway behind them. They walked down the hallway to the room.

"This doesn't seem right. There should at least be a seating area and a couple of side tables. This room looks like it hasn't been used in quite some time," N'amani said.

"This shelf is a bit dusty," the Ambassador said. She traced a line on top of a cabinet. "What's over there?" she asked. She pointed to a partly-open panel in one of the walls.

N'amani walked over and opened it. He leaned forward to look inside. "Storage," he said.

The Ambassador shook her head. "This room is not set up for a meeting," she said.

N'amani started towards the door. "It's not set up for anything. I'll go back to the desk and check. Maybe we got the wrong room," he said.

"I don't think so. This is where he wanted us to go," the Ambassador said. She nodded then she frowned and looked around the room.

"Why?" N'amani asked.

Just then, another of the side panels in the wall opened. Three fairly large and not-so-friendly-looking males came through the opening. They formed a line.

The Ambassador smiled at them, but her eyes grew cold. "Why indeed? It seems the greeting committee has arrived," she said.

"Ambassador," N'amani said with a warning in his voice.

The Ambassador glanced over her shoulder.

Four more scruffy males were coming in through the door.

"Oh great. We have an escort, too. N'amani, I was told you had some training," she said.

"Yes, I do, Ambassador," N'amani said.

"Do you know how to use it?" the Ambassador asked.

"Yes, Ambassador," N'amani said. He smiled just a little as he set his shoulders. He stepped quickly into the space behind the Ambassador. He stood facing the four coming in through the door.

"Good," she said over her shoulder. "Now would be the time," she said.

The three thugs that had come through the panel started towards the Ambassador.

The Ambassador waited for them to get closer. The one in the center tried to grab her. She trapped his wrist and twisted into him, breaking his elbow and dropping him to the ground. As she moved behind the first one, she kicked the second one in the groin with a back heel kick and broke his knee as she brought her foot down. When the third one tried to grab her, she trapped his arm and spun into him, dislocating his shoulder and breaking two of his ribs.

The four that had come in through the door separated to form a box around N'amani.

N'amani smiled. 'I couldn't have set this up better if I tried,' he thought. He settled into his legs and dropped his shoulders as he picked his targets. He moved before they could react. He turned to his left, stepping into the first thug with a double strike to his ribs and chin that sent him flying into the wall. He spun around to the opposite corner and took out the next one, and quickly spun toward the adjacent corner to strike the third thug. One more turn took out the last one.

The Ambassador saw the last turn. She smiled. "Fair Lady Works the Shuttles," she said.

N'amani nodded. "I like the turns," he said.

"It shows," the Ambassador said. She grinned her Cheshire cat smile.

N'amani looked down a little with humble pride, then he looked up and smiled.

"Seems we may have been in the right place after all," the Ambassador said.

N'amani shook his head and frowned. "Right place for what?" he asked.

The Ambassador shrugged and smiled. "Someone wanted a meeting with us, didn't they?" she asked.

N'amani nodded. "We should go," he said.

The Ambassador pointed around the room at their attackers on the floor. "They will probably need medical attention," she said.

"Let's call from the ship. We should go," N'amani said. He pointed to the door.

The Ambassador nodded.

They left quickly.

FINISHING SETUP
THE AMBASSADOR'S APARTMENT ON DAGON

The Ambassador had showered and dressed. The towels had been hung on the shower door and the sink was clean. She finished tying her hair and stepped back to look in the mirror. She smiled as she fastened her First Contact pin to her collar. She was quite proud of the pin. She'd earned it.

She wore a simple cream color blouse, darker beige tunic, grey pants, and comfortable old shoes. Her favorite red belt was tied around her waist. Some sort of tunic, blouse, and pants were common for travelers on so many worlds. She'd adopted the style. She had long ago learned that if she didn't want to be seen, she should dress simply, in neutral colors. It gave her the ability to blend in with the locals just about anywhere. And that had gotten her out of trouble more than once.

She looked around one more time and turned out the lights as she left. She took a long black cloak off a hook by the door and put it on. She activated a comm link. "N'amani," she asked.

"Yes, Ambassador," N'amani replied.

"Please let the Magellan know we are on our way," she said.

"Yes, Ambassador. The others will meet us at the departure gate. We are scheduled to leave at 10:00 am local time. I received word that the captain would like to see you after you arrive on the station," N'amani said.

"Thank you. I will see you shortly," the Ambassador said. She closed the link, picked up her personal bag, slung it over her shoulder, and walked out into the clear morning light.

BEGIN TRANSIT
DIPLOMATIC COMPOUND GARDEN ON DAGON

The sun was just coming up. A slight breeze brought the crisp fragrance of fresh baked bread and hot cooking oil. The Ambassador lived in a large building complex that was part of the Central Alliance governing compound. It had a mix of comfortable apartments, shops and offices, walled gardens with large shade trees and embedded security. A wide sidewalk circled the flower beds in front of her building. Just beyond the flower beds, the sidewalk split into three directions. One direction led to the center of the compound and the High Council Chambers. Another direction led to more residences. The third direction led to the North Gate.

The Ambassador took the path to the North Gate. She liked walking through the gardens. The gardens were a combination of rocks and flower beds with small pools scattered throughout. Today, the larger roses had been trimmed back and were just starting to get new leaves. The groundskeepers had put fresh dirt around some new peonies. A few miniature roses in the next bed were just starting to open. Trees and shrubs along the back walls of the compound made it seem as if they were in a small village, not the center of Dagon's Capital City.

She frowned a little as she walked through the gate. "This mission is going to be difficult anyway," she thought. "If only I could figure out how to keep Captain Sorrensen occupied with something so she's not always nagging and complaining, looking for something to criticize. It's really going to be hard to keep out of her way on this one. We're going to need her skills. She's so good at extractions," she muttered. She shook her head and sighed. "I don't really want to start out having to argue with her. What does she want to see me about? It can't be good," she thought. She shook her head again.

DEPARTING
TRANSPORT STATIONS AND TERMINALS

Several public transport stations were located just outside the North Gate. The stations were small, open-air buildings with entrances and exits on all four sides.

The Ambassador walked into the station. An array of different- sized platforms took up the center of the floor. It was early and not crowded. Two other travelers were leaving. Three had just arrived.

The Ambassador stepped onto one of the platforms. "Planetary departures," she said. She instantly arrived on a similar platform, this time inside a two-story departure hall. It had wide windows along one wall and shops along another. A few of the shops were open. Travelers went in and out. A young man was sweeping the floor. An older woman was opening one of the shop doors.

The Ambassador stepped off the platform, took her credentials out of her pocket, and walked across a wide floor to the Diplomatic Departures Channel.

The guard looked up from his desk and saw the First Contact pin on her collar. He sat up a little straighter. "May I see your documents, Ambassador?" he asked.

The Ambassador presented her personal identification and health certifications.

"Thank you, Ambassador Lawrence. Your delegation has already been cleared. Good Luck," he said. He handed her documents back to her.

"Thank you," the Ambassador replied. She bowed a little as she took the documents from him.

She turned around to look back one more time, as if to record an image of the departure hall in her mind. She hoped things would go well and she'd be coming home in a few weeks. But there was no way to know until she got there. She shook her head, took a deep breath, squared her shoulders, and walked down a short hallway to the transport platform. She smiled. "It's going to be another adventure. It's always an adventure," she thought.

ARRIVING
SPACE STATION ARRIVALS

The Ambassador stepped off the platform on the space station. The transport area on the space station was secure and well lit. It was surrounded by thick glass walls. Only cleared arrivals were allowed.

The Ambassador went to the Diplomatic Arrivals Lane and handed her identification to the guard.

"Welcome to Dagon 7, Ambassador Lawrence. Will you be staying with us?" the guard asked.

"No. I'm in transit, thank you," the Ambassador replied. "I was told my delegation had already been cleared. We're boarding the Magellan and will be departing the station as soon as our supplies are loaded," she said.

"Yes, Ambassador. Your delegation has arrived on the station. Good luck, Ambassador," he said. He handed her credentials back to her.

"Thank you," the Ambassador said. She put her credentials back in her pocket.

She stepped into the entry scanner and waited for the full-body scan. It only took a second.

She left the arrivals area and walked down a long, carpeted, glass-walled corridor to the departure hall. The space station was much busier than the ground station. Passengers and crews were preparing to leave and others were just arriving. Several ships were docked.

The Ambassador looked up through the three-story windows. The Magellan was tethered to a docking pylon just outside. Her clean, classic lines were part of her beauty. The Magellan was designed for speed and agility with considerable visible and not so visible firepower. She was a warship; one of only five Lewis-class interstellar ships with both light drive and star drive capabilities. It was fine to spend a few weeks on a ship at light speed, but there were times when being able to skip across a few parsecs in short order was very, very useful.

The Ambassador had been on the Magellan for several missions. She was very happy the Magellan was going to be her transport. The Magellan was one of the best ships in the fleet. She smiled a little more remembering that N'amani had managed to get everything she asked for.

A small group in the uniforms of the Magellan were standing off to one side below the windows.

She walked over to them. "Good morning, I'm Ambassador Lawrence. I was told that Captain Sorrensen wanted to see me. Could one of you let her know I'm here?" she asked.

Everyone in the group turned to face her. "Good morning, Ambassador," they said in unison.

A tall, slightly-heavy young woman with pixie cut brown hair was standing just behind the others looking at a small screen. She looked up, stepped forward, and smiled warmly. "It's good to see you again, Ambassador," Commander Brandon said.

"It's good to see you too, Commander Brandon," the Ambassador said.

Commander Brandon shifted her weight to one side, swallowed, and took a deep breath. "Captain Sorrensen was promoted and reassigned. Captain Alexander Logan has been given command of the Magellan. He's waiting for you on the Observation Deck. Up those stairs, second floor, turn right," she said. She pointed towards an alcove with a stairway on the other side of the departure hall.

The Ambassador tried not to let her surprise show. This was unexpected. "Thank you, Commander," she said. She took a deep breath. "Not having to deal with Sorrensen could be a good thing," she thought. She'd heard good things about Logan. He was well-regarded and capable. But this would be their first meeting and their first mission. "Not my preference. Not for this one," she thought, realizing she would need to use the Ancient Arts to find out who he was. She didn't like doing it, but she was being asked to trust him with this mission and the lives of her team. She needed to know more than small talk would reveal.

She went up a short flight of stairs to a landing. She took off her First Contact pin and put it in her pocket. Then, she continued up the second flight.

HELLO
SPACE STATION ARRIVALS MEZZANINE

Captain Logan was leaning on the railing above the main floor, watching the station arrivals platform. He was tall, well-built with sandy hair and a square jaw. He looked up with surprise as the Ambassador came out of the stairwell. She was wearing common travel clothes, neat but not fancy. She wasn't tall, but she wasn't short either. She had dark blonde hair, braided and draped over one shoulder, with a bag on the other.

"I'm sorry, this area is restricted. Can I help you find your transport?" Captain Logan asked as politely as he could.

The Ambassador smiled. "Thank you. Yes, you could help me with that," she said.

Captain Logan blinked a couple of times. She reminded him of one of his training instructors at the academy. She had the same clear blue eyes. Open and bright, as if she were open to letting in the universe. Piercing, as if she could see straight through him. "Perhaps if you tell me where you are going?" he asked.

Imperceptibly, the Ambassador centered her weight and began to slow her breathing. "Yes, I could tell you where I am going," she said. She nodded to him. She focused on radiating calm and trust. Of all the Ancient Arts, this was one of the most intrusive. She began to open her mind, reaching straight into his heart. She could see what he held dear and who he was. He could not hide. He didn't need to say anything. She simply knew. She was pleased. He had courage. He was quick. And he could be stubborn.

Captain Logan shifted back a bit. He looked around, puzzled. He squirmed and tugged at the collar of his shirt to open it. He closed his shoulders a little to the front as if trying to stop a punch to his chest. He began to feel warmer, as if the temperature had just gone up 10 degrees. He felt like every part of him was being examined. Then it was over. He was not quite sure what just happened. Oddly, he wasn't anxious about it. He had a pervasive sense of peacefulness and tranquility. He took a slow, deep breath and turned his attention back to the woman.

"So where are you going?" Captain Logan asked directly. He was beginning to get frustrated with her. He'd like to meet the ambassador he was supposed to transport and get underway. He was tired of playing guessing games with a lost old lady.

The Ambassador's smile got bigger. "I am going there. To visit the stars," she said. She pointed at the stars through the windows.

"Yes, of course you are. And how are you going to get there?" Captain Logan asked with as much sympathy as he could muster. "Her family must be worried about her. How can I get her to tell me something useful?" he thought. He was expecting an ambassador. He didn't want to be minding some old woman.

"I have a ship. A very nice ship," the Ambassador replied.

"Does your ship have a name?" Captain Logan asked.

The Ambassador suppressed a smile. "It's hard to keep this going. He's already told me everything I need to know. Maybe I should, nah, one more," she thought. She frowned. "Of course my ship has a name. And a captain, too!" she said impatiently.

"Could you tell me what the name of your ship is?" Captain Logan asked.

Every time he asked her something, she gave a clear answer. But it wasn't the answer he was looking for or expecting.

The Ambassador glanced down to the departure floor and looked around to distract him.

Captain Logan followed her gaze. "Maybe there's someone?" he thought.

While he was looking away, the Ambassador reached into her pocket, took out her pin, and put it back on. She turned to face him, her pin now clearly visible on her collar. "I could tell you the name of my ship. And so could you," she said with a big smile. She crossed her arms in front of her chest, extended her hands outward with the palms up, and brought them down to her sides. "I am Ambassador Micha Lawrence. I'm pleased to meet you, Captain," she said.

Captain Logan smiled. He recognized the greeting and grimaced a little, realizing she'd just tested him. "Good morning, Ambassador. I'm also very pleased to meet you. Although I wasn't expecting ...," he said. He shook his head and smiled.

They both laughed.

"So, it seems I, um, passed your test?" Captain Logan asked.

"Yes, Captain," the Ambassador replied smiling. She gestured toward a small conference room.

The room was disused but clean. The Ambassador took a seat at a small table on one side of the room. Captain Logan closed the door and sat down across from her.

The Ambassador smiled. "It seems congratulations are in order. The Magellan is a fine ship. You have an excellent crew. Commander Brandon is one of the best resource officers in the fleet," she said.

Captain Logan nodded. "Thank you. Frankly, I wasn't expecting this assignment. But I have to say, I couldn't be happier. Indeed, the Magellan is an excellent ship with a fine crew. I've been handling transport and security for several of the Alliance trade representatives in the Altair and Vega sectors. Their work was mostly focused on maintaining existing relationships. But there were a few times when we, em, unfortunately had to leave on less than friendly terms. I understand you have a First-Contact Charter," he said.

"Yes, I do," the Ambassador said. She frowned. "What have you been told?" she asked.

"Only that I'm supposed to be here, meet you, take you and your delegation somewhere, and bring you home," Captain Logan replied.

"Excellent!" the Ambassador said. She smiled like a big Cheshire cat. "But you don't seem too happy," she said.

Captain Logan frowned a little and nodded. "Frankly, I'm not particularly happy about not knowing where we are going or what we are going to do. But I'm going to do whatever you need me to do and I'm going to make sure we all come home," he said.

The Ambassador smiled. That he was ready to go and didn't know where he was going or exactly what he was going to be doing reflected well on his character. "I hope we don't need the options for leaving on less than friendly terms this time," she said. She turned her head sideways, frowning and nodding with the implication that they could be needed. "We are going to the Hyades Cluster to meet with the High Council of Ka'len to establish a regular relationship, communications, trade, all that. If I'm successful with the first meetings, we will return in a few months to set up the future framework. The Ka'len Council has been mostly receptive to our overtures, but we don't have anything formal yet," she said.

"Okayyyy! So, your first-contact charter really does mean first-contact, doesn't it. The Hyades cluster is almost 60 light years on the other side of Aldebaran. We don't have many partners in that sector," Captain Logan said. He sat back grinning with excitement and just a bit of apprehension.

"Indeed, Captain," the Ambassador said. It was going to take time for him to understand. It wasn't a 10-minute explanation. "We should have a full briefing once we are underway," she said.

Captain Logan nodded. His personal comm link chimed.

"Captain Logan," Commander Brandon said. Her voice came through the comm link.

"Yes Commander," Captain Logan said.

"We have all the Ambassador's supplies loaded. Her detail is waiting at the departure gate. We are ready to depart as soon as you come on board," Commander Brandon said.

"Thank you, Commander. We are on our way," Captain Logan said. He stood up.

"Yes, sir," Commander Brandon replied.

"Shall we go, Ambassador?" Captain Logan said. He gestured towards the door. "Are the other members of your detail as interesting as you are?" he asked.

"I'd say more so, Captain," the Ambassador replied with a wry grin and a twinkle in her eyes. "Shall we go meet them?" she asked.

Captain Logan stepped back to let her go out first. He was even more curious now. It wasn't often that the emissaries he'd transported had a full delegation. This was the first Ambassador he'd transported and she was turning out to be quite a character.

READY
SPACE STATION DEPARTURES

Captain Logan and the Ambassador walked along the Mezzanine towards the departure area at the end of the promenade. Travelers, some in various uniforms, were going in and out of the shops below. The central part of the inside wall was designed to replicate terraces on a mountain side, with stairs and small alcoves with benches for sitting. Vines trailed along rock walls. Trees of various sizes mimicked a small forest. Intricate lighting created the feeling of a cool morning. The sprinklers sprayed a fine mist over rows of spring flowers.

The Ambassador turned her head up slightly and smiled. "It smells nice, here. Almost like my garden. And the spring flowers – peonies and crocus, daffodils and daylilies, and so many different colored tulips. It almost planetary," she said.

"It's some of the best eco-replication I've seen. It looks natural, like the plants just happened to be growing there," Captain Logan said.

The Ambassador looked up at the Magellan through the high windows as they walked into the departure hall. The lights of the station reflected along her sides against the black of space. "The Magellan is a fine ship, Captain. A fine ship," she said quietly.

Captain Logan followed her gaze and smiled. "Yes, the Magellan is a very fine ship," he said. He took a deep breath and squared his shoulders. He looked at the gate and scanned the departure hall for a group that might be her delegation. He spotted a group of four scruffy people standing below the main window. They looked more like not-so-well-to-do tourists with old beat-up luggage. "What are they doing here? That can't be?" he thought.

The Ambassador had spotted them and was half-way across the floor.

Captain Logan hurried to catch up with her.

N'amani was standing with his back to the windows facing into the departure hall. He saw her coming, lowered his chin slightly to acknowledge he saw her, and straightened a little. The others turned around.

"Good morning. I'm very happy to see you all here with your luggage," the Ambassador said grinning.

They all grimaced a little and then smiled as if she'd just given them cookie.

She had standing instructions to either put things in cargo or pack the shuttle but not to bring more than two personal bags. Besides being easier to manage, it helped keep them agile. They weren't bringing anything they didn't need.

"Yes, indeed, we're ready to go. Where are we going again?" the Doctor asked.

The Ambassador smiled and pointed at the ship. "We are going for a ride on the Magellan, Doctor," she said impatiently. She wagged her finger at him. "You know better! However, I do have something we should talk about. Please allow me to introduce Captain Alexander Logan. He's the new commander of the Magellan. Captain Sorrensen was promoted and has been reassigned," she said smiling.

Everyone got a little stiff trying to hide their surprise.

"Thank you, Ambassador," Captain Logan said. He stepped up next to her. "I'm pleased to meet all of you. I look forward to having you on board," he said. He was already a bit in awe of her, a bit nervous about his new command, and not at all sure what he should say.

The Ambassador tried not to laugh. "Captain, may I present my delegation. N'amani is my Chief of Staff, personal bodyguard, and general right hand. He's quite good with planning, organizing, and preparations of all sorts," she said. She extended her hand toward N'amani.

N'amani stepped forward and nodded. He was squarely built and just a little taller than Captain Logan. He was wearing a comfortable dark red shirt and black pants. "Pleased to meet you, Captain Logan," he said. He took a step back.

Captain Logan nodded to him. He wasn't really surprised that she had an Elronym Administrator in her delegation. He'd met the Elronym several times. They were exceptional administrators and could be formidable fighters.

The Ambassador gestured to the Doctor to step forward. "Doctor Marcus Gray. Marc is our team doctor, chef, and all-around good humor guy. He keeps us happy and well-fed," she said.

"I'm quite good with medical things, too," the Doctor said. He grinned playfully and waved. He was slender with a boyish face and a curious sense of enjoyment.

Captain Logan couldn't help but laugh. The only way to describe the Doctor was that he was simply happy.

The Ambassador waved to Beth. "Elizabeth Michaels is our archivist, historian, and cultures expert. Beth is extremely good with all our recording systems," she said.

Beth was standing just behind N'amani. She was the youngest of the group. Her fiery red curls and pixie face made her look even younger. She stepped to one side, nodded to Captain Logan, and quickly stepped back behind N'amani. She was quite shy unless she was behind a camera.

Captain Logan smiled and nodded to her.

"Kell is my pilot," the Ambassador said, a note of pride audible in her voice.

Kell stepped forward and nodded to Captain Logan. He was wearing a dark grey traveler's shirt, tunic, and pants similar to what the others were wearing. He was a little taller than the Ambassador, slender with dark hair.

Captain Logan nodded to him politely as he would to any other pilot. Then, he started sizing him up. "He seems a little young to be her pilot," he thought. His eyes stopped at Kell's hands. Kell had quite open hands with rather long fingers. He looked up at Kell and over to the Ambassador and back at Kell, curious, puzzled, and in awe all at once.

Kell smiled an impish grin and nodded to Captain Logan. "She's done it again. I do so like these kinds of introductions," he thought. He winked at the Ambassador.

Captain Logan turned to the Ambassador and tried really hard not to trip over his words. "You, you, you have an Aldaran pilot?" he asked. His jaw was not quite able to close.

First of all, the Aldarans hardly ever, really never, would pilot for anyone. They didn't want to be bothered with mundane flights and they didn't at all like being told what to do. They were good pilots, really, really good, and rightfully proud of their skills. They mostly weren't braggarts, but they knew they were exceptional. It was just a fact. Nobody, but nobody in the known universe could match the Aldarans for their navigation and piloting skills.

"Yes. Kell has been kind enough to ferry me around to a few worlds," the Ambassador replied. "He's got quite a perspective on this part of the galaxy. He's very good at finding the best places for yangroutang," she said. Yangroutang was a meat soup she'd learned to like on Ras 2. It wasn't really a choice back then. She could eat it or have nothing. She learned to like it.

Kell smiled a bit sheepishly. He liked yangroutang. On more than one occasion, he'd managed to adjust their course so they passed near a planet or a station he knew where they could get it. Even N'amani had acquired a taste for it.

"We have much to discuss, Captain. Much to discuss. Shall we go?" the Ambassador asked.

Captain Logan nodded.

ACCESS GRANTED
SPACE STATION / MAGELLAN GATEWAY

Captain Logan walked over to a large open doorway. It had thick metal doors set into the walls. A palm scanner was set into a metal side panel. Just beyond, a transport platform was visible at the end of a short passageway.

Captain Logan stepped up to the door and put his hand on the palm scanner. "Prepare command transfer. Mark Time. Logan, Alexander. Theta twelve eighteen Gamma three Alpha Mu seven nine," he said.

A purple light came on and began passing over his body.

Maja, the Magellan's AI, appeared in the center of the entryway. She could block or grant access to the ship. She wore a ship's uniform. She looked like a human female in her early thirties with upswept brown hair, light brown skin, clear brown eyes, and perfectly-crafted bright gold earrings. She was not an ordinary AI. She was designed to serve the ship. Every choice she made, every decision to act or not act, was based on the good of the ship, its crew, and anyone or anything else on board. She could not disobey a direct order from the ship's Captain.

Maja looked squarely at Captain Logan. "Voice, palm, DNA, medical records, access code. Match confirmed. Transferring all systems to your authorization, Captain Logan. Welcome aboard, Captain. You have command. Root access granted," she said. She stepped to one side. It wasn't just a formality for her to say this. She was actually giving him full control of the ship, its systems, and all her programs.

Captain Logan took a breath. "I have command," he said. His voice seemed to get a little deeper with the responsibility he just assumed.

The Ambassador turned her head slightly to one side, listening. She heard the change in his voice. She smiled. "Oh, I like him. I like him," she thought.

"I'm sure I have much to learn about the Magellan," Captain Logan said. He looked at Maja.

"Indeed Captain," Maja replied. She smiled. She had been programmed with several types of humor, irony among them. She turned to the Ambassador. "Welcome back, Ambassador," she said.

"Thank you, Maja. I'm happy to be back. It's good see you again, too," the Ambassador said.

Developing a bond with an AI had not been easy. Gradually, as she worked at it, the Ambassador began to understand the practical implications of Maja's core programming. Then, she asked to have Maja modified with new branches for diplomacy. These included assessing patterns of behavior, physical responses, engagement, and cultivating confidence and trust. In addition, subroutines for ethics, rewards, and all sorts of things that supported the Ambassador's missions were added. It took a little training. Maja adapted quickly and progress was rapid. The High Council had been very happy with the modifications. They had added the new branches to the AIs on a few select ships with great success. And, they gave the Ambassador another medal for her initiative.

Maja moved a little closer to the Ambassador. "Does he know?" she whispered.

"No. He will want to see the ship's logs," the Ambassador replied.

Maja shook her head. "It may be difficult for him to understand. He has just come aboard," she said.

"I agree. Not all at once. Give him a day or two to adjust. Maybe you could be just a little slow at finding things. Offer him something similar while you are looking for what he wanted?" the Ambassador asked.

"To distract him. I understand," Maja said.

"For now. Only for now. Once we are underway, I will tell him. He must know everything," the Ambassador said.

"Yes Ambassador," Maja said. She recognized the command to her core programming.

The others had walked past them to the transport platform.

The Doctor waved to them. "Are you coming with?" he asked.

"Of course, Doctor," the Ambassador said smiling at him. "Thank you, Maja," she whispered. She took Maja's arm.

They walked to the platform together.

Captain Logan stood up straight. "Guest Quarters, Section 3, Deck 8, Please Maja," he said.

Maja smiled. "Does he really think I don't know where the guest quarters are?" she whispered to the Ambassador.

"Humor him," the Ambassador said. She giggled.

"Yes Captain," Maja said. She activated the transport

.

NEW SETTINGS
THE AMBASSADOR'S QUARTERS ON THE MAGELLAN

The Guest Section was designed for those times when dignitaries or special guests from a planet might be invited on board. It was secured with restricted access and isolated from the rest of the ship by a system of locks. A network of hallways connected the guest living areas with several meeting rooms. Each meeting room offered a different perspective on the stars or planets outside. The Ambassador and her delegation had quarters in this section of the ship. It was convenient for her to be near any guests. It was also less of a distraction for the crew.

The Ambassador, N'amani, Kell, Beth, and the Doctor stepped off the transport platform into an open foyer with tall windows along both sides of a broad hallway.

Captain Logan remained on the platform. "Ambassador, I'll take my leave for now. There are still a few things I need to do to get us underway," he said.

"Thank you, Captain. When you can, I'd like to have that briefing to go over the details of our mission," the Ambassador said.

"I will let you know, Ambassador," Captain Logan said. He nodded. "Bridge please, Maja," he said.

Maja activated the transport platform.

The Doctor, Beth, Kell, and N'amani started towards their rooms.

"N'amani, may I have a minute?" the Ambassador asked. She motioned to him. She opened the door to her quarters. Her room was standard - a large open living space with a built-in seat along the outer wall, a panel separating the sleeping area from the main room, and an open doorway leading to a sink, toilet, and shower. "Would you sweep the room, please?" she asked.

N'amani took a small cube out of his pocket. He put it in the center of his palm and walked around the room. The cube glowed green. "All clear, Ambassador," he said.

"Thank you, N'amani," the Ambassador said. She shook her head. "All this secrecy, even here. It makes no sense," she said.

"What makes no sense?" N'amani asked.

"All the extra precautions we are taking," the Ambassador said.

"Well, so far, I haven't found any false walls. I will continue looking, of course," N'amani replied. He was referring to their first mission together.

They both laughed.

N'amani held out his palm with the cube on it and did several spins before deftly sliding the cube back into his pocket. "Seriously though, you know you have friends on the Council. You know you have enemies, too. There are those on the Council who would like to see you fail. They may appear to support you and they will rally around you if you succeed. But if you fail, they will be happy to make you a scapegoat," he said.

"I know. I know. I suspect that's part of why Sorrensen was promoted. Not that she didn't deserve it. She did. She's one of the best captains I've ever worked with. She has great instincts and an impeccable sense of timing," the Ambassador said.

"Being careful isn't a bad thing, Ambassador. I have no wish to be pulling you out of any more piles of rubble. That last attempt on your life was much too close," N'amani said.

The Ambassador smiled. "You made the headlines: Unknown Hero Saves Survivors. Nice image of you bringing that old man out on your back. It really was impressive. N'amani, I'm very glad you didn't stop to talk with their press. It could have been a problem," she said.

N'amani smiled. "Their press were happy to talk to the old man's family. He was apparently one of the local favorites. Always a kind word for everyone. There's more to it, Ambassador," N'amani said.

"More than you being a hero?" the Ambassador asked, a mix of pride and kindness in her voice.

"Yes," N'amani said quietly

The Ambassador turned her head to one side and raised her eyebrows. N'amani knew what he could do and he wasn't afraid of it – he embraced it. She liked that part. She liked his modesty even better. He didn't try to make anything about him – it was always about the other person, the one he was doing something for. "What happened?" she asked.

N'amani took a breath. "That old man was really in bad shape when I got to him. I was with the search teams in the second building when I thought I heard a something. I followed the sound. I was clearing the debris to make a way through when I saw the old man huddled in a doorway, the walls collapsed all around him. He was half-buried under the rubble, shaking, afraid. Nothing I said reached him. I kept asking him to come with me. I told him I wanted to help him. But he was too scared. He couldn't hear me. Finally, I told him I was his transport. I was there to take him to see his children and had to get on board right now. When I knelt down to help him get up, he grabbed my shoulders, climbed on my back, and put his arms around my neck like a small child hugging his father. He started shaking and sobbing. He kept hugging me and wouldn't let go. He couldn't talk. Even after I brought him out to his family, he didn't want to let go of me. He finally took hold of his oldest grandson and let me go," N'amani said.

"I didn't know. Why didn't you tell me?" the Ambassador asked.

"You were being treated for your own injuries," N'amani replied with a shrug. "It didn't seem important," he said.

"Sometimes the smallest actions can make the biggest difference. That old man is never going to forget you. I'm more than pleased you found him," the Ambassador said.

N'amani nodded and smiled. "I'm glad I was there to do it," he said.

The Ambassador smiled at him. She began pacing the floor. "What do you know about Logan?" she asked.

"He's seen as a rising star in the Alliance. He was given the Star Cross last year for extracting a trade negotiator from a difficult situation near Epsilon Indi. The team had been told there was an agrarian planet that was interested in trade. What they weren't told was that there were two governments vying for control of the food supply. When the trade negotiator arrived, he and his delegation were taken hostage. One side wanted to force the other side to give them a high-producing hybrid grain they had developed. Captain Logan created a diversion by tricking their weather systems into registering an unusually cold air mass that would freeze their unharvested crops. Then, he offered to send equipment and a team to complete the harvest before the cold arrived. Once the harvesting team arrived, they insisted the trade negotiator and his team were the foremost experts and needed to handle the harvester controls. Once they were all on the shuttle, the cold air mass disappeared... and so did the shuttle," N'amani said.

The Ambassador stopped pacing and turned to face N'amani. "I heard about the rescue, but not how he did it. Clever. Can we count on Logan?" she asked.

"Ambassador? That's not a question you usually ask," N'amani said.

"I need your candid assessment," the Ambassador said.

N'amani frowned at her tone. "I think he will do whatever he believes is the right thing to do. He will protect the ship, the crew, and you, Ambassador," he said.

"Thank you," the Ambassador said quietly. She turned away to look out the window.

"We're going to find out what that means, aren't we?" N'amani asked.

"Yes, we are," the Ambassador replied.

The comm link next to the door chimed and lit up.

"Ambassador, we have left the station. Captain Logan asks if you would join him with your team in the diplomatic briefing room in 30 minutes," Maja said

"Thank you, Maja. We will be right there," the Ambassador replied.

N'amani started toward the door. "I'll go get the others," he said.

"N'amani?" the Ambassador asked.

N'amani turned back. "Yes Ambassador?" he asked.

The Ambassador shook her head. "Never mind. I'll see you in the briefing room. Thank you," she said.

"You're welcome. I'll see you shortly," N'amani said. He walked out.

The Ambassador sat down near the windows. She looked back as the ship moved away from the station. In just a few seconds, she couldn't see the station any more. She turned and looked forward. The Hyades Cluster was just barely visible far in the distance. It would take them just over two weeks to get there. They could go faster, but there were preparations to be made along the way. "It should be enough. It has to be," she thought.

START
THE DIPLOMATIC BRIEFING ROOM ON THE MAGELLAN

The Ambassador was the first to arrive for the briefing. The lights in the Diplomatic Briefing Room came on automatically when she entered. It was the largest of the briefing rooms in the guest section. It had comfy chairs and large windows to watch the stars plus security to protect whatever was said.

"Where should I sit today?" the Ambassador asked aloud. She liked being the first one in the room when she had to give a presentation. It gave her a chance to see the room before anything started. It wasn't as trivial as it might seem. Her position in the room gave her an advantage. It was like that with negotiations, too.

The Doctor came up behind her. "Wherever you like. Daydreaming or planning?" he asked.

The Ambassador turned around. "Both. It's good to see you, Marc. How was your vacation?" she asked.

"It was GREAT! I spent most of the time floating in the Tree Gardens on Qili 7 in the Altair system. Have you been there? They have the most amazing fruit. They call it por'a. It's like a sweet cucumber with a hint of apple. It's wonderful. Here's some for you," the Doctor said. He handed her a small basket.

"Why thank you!" the Ambassador said. She brought the basket up to her nose. "This smells nice. So sweet. It sounds like you found a place to go back to," she said.

"Absolutely. They have several things I didn't get to try," the Doctor said. He pouted and smiled at the same time.

"I'm sure you made an effort," the Ambassador replied.

"Yes, I did. I made a double effort. I went to the buffet every day. Just like clockwork," the Doctor said.

"How many plates?" the Ambassador asked.

"Just three," the Doctor replied. He held up his fist with the little finger up to show the number six.

The Ambassador chuckled.

They both liked to eat. The idea of going somewhere and not making a serious effort to try the local foods would never occur to either of them.

The Ambassador moved to the head of the table and put the basket down. Then, she went to look out the windows.

The Doctor walked over to stand beside her.

Just then Beth and N'amani came in followed by Kell, Captain Logan, Commander Brandon, and a pleasant-looking, medium-built young woman with wavy, shoulder-length blonde hair and bright blue eyes.

Captain Logan walked to the head of the table. He saw the fruit basket in front of what would normally be his chair. He shook his head. "That is not there for me," he thought. He moved to the first side chair. "Ambassador, I'm sure we're all eager to hear about our mission. I understand you know Commander Brandon," he said. He nodded to Commander Brandon.

"Yes, Captain. The Commander and I have had the pleasure of working together a few times," the Ambassador replied. She smiled and nodded.

Captain Logan gestured to the young woman. "Lt. Meredith Katy is our new flight officer. She just completed her training with expert qualifications on three of our fighters. This is her first assignment on a starship," he said.

"Welcome, Lt. Katy. Pleased to meet you," the Ambassador said.

"Thank you, Ambassador. It's my honor to meet you," Lt. Katy replied.

"Shall we get started, Captain?" the Ambassador asked.

"The floor is yours, Ambassador," Captain Logan said. He took a seat and motioned for the others to sit.

"Thank you, Captain," the Ambassador said. She looked around the room. "I appreciate that you have not been briefed until now. I had instructions to keep this quiet. We are going to the Hyades Cluster to meet with the High Council of Ka'len. The Central Alliance wants to establish a treaty." She activated a screen. It showed a star chart of their route to the Hyades Cluster. Then, she activated a 3D model. It showed a system with four planets, two suns, and a heavy asteroid belt just at the edge of the system.

"But why are we going?" the Doctor asked.

"We'd like a treaty, Doctor. Two of the planets and this entire nearby asteroid belt are rich in magnesium and other rare earth minerals," the Ambassador said. She added an overlay to the display that showed what they projected the deposits to be.

"Jackpot!" Captain Logan said.

"Rich seems to be not quite the right word," Commander Brandon said. She smiled.

The Ambassador nodded. "Indeed. The people of Ka'len, the Kora, have been mostly receptive to our overtures. So far, we've only contacted them through remote traders. This is a First Contact mission," she said.

Captain Logan sat up just a little straighter.

The Ambassador pointed to the 3D model. "We know these four planets formed a federation about 300 of our years ago. It appears they have developed slowly. Our traders have talked with the leaders on these two planets. We believe all four planets are receptive to joining the Alliance. They have also told us quietly that the Ka'len Council could be receptive to our plans," she said.

"Our plans???" the Doctor asked.

"I'm getting there," the Ambassador replied. "This asteroid belt...," she continued.

The Doctor wasn't having it. "But why are we going? It's a long way to go for a mining agreement. Even if we are a First Contact team, why do we have to go all the way out there? Can't somebody else go have a look-see? Why are we getting stuck with it?" he asked.

The Ambassador looked at him and then around the room. She took a breath. She pointed to an area just beyond the asteroid belt. "Alliance merchant ships passing through the sector have reported seeing Olmeri scout ships here. They are still far enough away to not be an immediate threat to Ka'len. But they are headed towards the system," she said.

The Doctor frowned and shook his head. "This is not good. Once the Olmeri arrive, they begin taking over any habitable planets. They drain the planet's resources to build their megacities and power their ships. They don't leave anything for the original inhabitants," he said.

"This is really not good. Our early reports are that the Kora are mostly agrarian. They don't seem to have much industry. They seem to have very limited construction abilities. Their planets are heavily forested. They don't have any large cities," Beth said.

Captain Logan looked down and shook his head. "They can't defend themselves," he said.

The Ambassador sighed. "It gets worse. We've just gotten new reports that show the Olmeri are accelerating their timetables. We used to see a few years between the time we got reports of their scout ships showing up somewhere and when that sector would begin withdrawing from trade treaties. Now, it's less than a year," she said.

"Less than a year?" Lt. Katy asked.

Commander Brandon looked at Lt. Katy sharply and frowned. "Be quiet before I come over there," she thought.

The Ambassador continued. "From what we know, it appears the Olmeri are assaying the asteroid belt. We think they want what we want, the minerals. But they don't know what's there. And we want to keep it that way. So, to your question, Doctor. Why are we going? If the Olmeri keep traveling along the belt, it will bring them directly into the Ka'len system," she said.

Captain Logan frowned. "If the Olmeri are able to establish themselves in the Hyades Cluster, they will become an even bigger problem for the Central Alliance," he said.

The Ambassador nodded.

"They're already a problem for the Kora," the Doctor said.

"Exactly, Doctor. So, we're going to do two things. First, we want a treaty that will allow us to set up a monitoring station near Ka'len to give us an early warning about any Olmeri incursions," the Ambassador said.

"Just land and ask them to sign?" Lt. Katy blurted out. She was an exceptional pilot and very good with flight operations. She wasn't deliberately trying to be disrespectful. She was used to saying what she thought during flight briefings.

N'amani frowned and lowered his chin. "Not quite, Lieutenant. This is not a flight briefing," he said.

Lt. Katy bit her lip and looked down.

The Ambassador looked at N'amani and nodded. She went on, "Second, we want the Olmeri to believe that the asteroid belt is not worth their time; that even if they find a few minerals, there's not enough of anything useful to bother about. We want them to go away thinking that whatever they have found isn't worth the trouble," she said.

"How can you get them to do that?" Lt. Katy asked with more than a little disbelief.

The Ambassador frowned at the interruption. "Lt. Katy," she said. She looked around the room. It was clear that question was on everyone's mind. She smiled. "That is a good question. We're going to seed the belt with other minerals to confuse their sensors," she said.

"You want to win without fighting as the old Earth philosopher Sun Zi would say?" Kell asked.

The Ambassador looked at Kell and nodded. "If we can do it. It's going to take quite a bit of preparation and a barrelful of luck," she said.

Everyone looked around the table and nodded.

"Being able to do either one of these seems like a pretty big challenge, Ambassador. What are we actually going to do?" Captain Logan asked.

"If you're asking for an operational plan, I don't have one yet, Captain," the Ambassador replied. She smiled, raised both hands, shrugged, and shook her head.

Captain Logan frowned. He looked down and shook his head.

The Ambassador looked around the room. "We have two weeks. I know it's not much and it's never enough. But it's what we have. If we don't go now, the Olmeri will have enough time to finish their scans. We need them to believe they found nothing and go away. And we need to do whatever we can to stop them from taking over the Ka'len system," she said.

Captain Logan looked up and shook his head.

"You look concerned, Captain," the Ambassador said.

Captain Logan looked straight at her and then around the room. "I am concerned. We are going to a remote area where we have few allies. The Olmeri have been spotted nearby. We have two weeks to prepare. You have some goals but you don't have a plan. So yes, you could say I am a little concerned," he said.

N'amani turned to him and smiled. "Captain, you've not been on a mission with us before. Two weeks is something of a luxury," he said.

The Ambassador's team and Commander Brandon all chuckled. It was true.

Captain Logan leaned forward. "Okay. So, I'm the new guy. I'm still concerned. I was expecting a briefing to cover transport times, official dinners, and how you wanted me to manage any meetings on the Magellan. That's mostly what I had been doing. I'm actually happy about going to the Hyades Cluster. I've not been there. Going somewhere we are likely to meet the Olmeri is, well... em... different," he said.

The Ambassador and her team all laughed out loud.

"Yes. Yes, I'm sure this is very different," the Ambassador said. Her tone was more stern and unforgiving than she wanted. She softened it and went on, "Captain Logan, I am sorry that you have been thrown into this. I'm also a bit unsettled having a new Captain to work with. We are going to have lots of opportunities to get to know each other really, really well over the next two weeks. You will come to understand what my team and I do. But I have to tell you honestly, for this mission, we can't succeed without you, your crew, and the Magellan," she said.

Captain Logan looked at her, questioning her without saying anything. Then, he sat up a little taller, raised his shoulders, lowered his chin, and smiled. The Magellan was his ship now. "Ambassador, I didn't take this commission without understanding what it meant. We will do whatever it takes to help you succeed. But I have to be honest, the High Council didn't tell me any of this. Not even a hint," he said. He shook his head.

"They couldn't tell you, Captain. I told you where we were going because I decided you needed to know at least that much. My team did not know where we are going or what we're going to try to do until just now," the Ambassador said.

Beth and Kell looked at each other, nodded, and shrugged.

The Doctor grinned and nodded.

"We've been on several very quiet missions like this," N'amani said.

The Ambassador smiled. "My entire plan depends on making the Olmeri believe what we want them to believe. We cannot give them any opportunity to find out otherwise. They may come back and try again. That's also why we want a treaty with the Kora. We don't want to walk in the door sounding the alarm bells. But we have to do something. What that something is remains a question." She looked around the room slowly. She knew this mission was going to be a challenge. She needed to get them ready. Sugar-coating it wouldn't help. "Do we know what the Kora want? What do we know about their civilization and history, Beth?" she asked.

Part of Beth's job was to make herself an expert, to learn everything she could about the civilization they were going to visit. She also needed to be able to offer advice and put things in context. That meant reading lots of reports and reviewing any language banks that might be similar to what they could expect.

Beth looked up. "All the reports I've seen are that the Kora don't have much industry. They seem to have very limited construction abilities. Their planets are heavily forested. They don't have any large cities. They have a fusion process quite similar to ours that they use for most of their energy needs. Their ships aren't fast enough to go much beyond their local system. Their culture is focused on providing for their people. Our best guess is that the planets have more than enough magnesium and rare minerals. They don't need them, don't want them, and can't eat them, so whatever's in the asteroid belt isn't something they think of as desirable," she said.

Everyone chuckled a little at that last bit.

Beth continued. "The Kora appear to be interested in seeds and other agricultural help that we might be able to offer. That's been the conversation the traders we have contacted them through have had. The Kora are hesitant to trade, it seems, because they haven't had that much contact with anyone outside their systems. Reports indicated they would be very concerned about any sort of outposts nearby. They would likely be alarmed by the Olmeri," she said.

The Ambassador nodded to Beth. "Thank you, Beth. Very good insights. Do your people know anything about the Kora, Kell?" she asked.

Kell nodded. "My people have met the Kora and have traded with them on occasion. They didn't have much of anything we wanted and we didn't have anything they wanted, so we have mostly left each other alone. They are generally not aggressive, although we have heard reports of some difficulties on their third planet recently. Some sort of civil unrest apparently to try to force a change in their ruling council. I think their Council would like to have allies with big guns and long-range weapons," he said.

Captain Logan and Command Brandon chuckled and nodded to reach other.

Lt. Katy smiled.

"I'm sure they would," Captain Logan said.

"So, Captain, are you ready to get started with the details? We have a lot of material to cover and quite a few scenarios to review," the Ambassador said. She smiled her Cheshire cat grin.

"I need a little time to digest all this. Could we start first thing in the morning?" Captain Logan asked.

N'amani smiled.

"Certainly, Captain," the Ambassador replied. "It is a lot to take in. N'amani, would you give us a quick summary?" she asked.

N'amani nodded and stood up. "Beth will continue her research of what we know of the Ka'len culture and languages. The Doctor will be reviewing plants, foods, and medical topics. Kell is going to make some modifications to his cruiser. The Ambassador will brief you, Captain, on what she needs. I will be working with Commander Brandon and Lt. Katy on possible scenarios. I will also work with Maja to prepare a study plan for you," he said.

The Ambassador smiled and nodded. "Perfect, N'amani. Thank you," she said.

Captain Logan smiled and nodded. "A study plan for me? I need a study plan?" he asked.

"Yes Captain. Time is short," N'amani replied.

Captain Logan frowned and tried not to look puzzled.

"Ok, sure. Thank you," he said smiling.

"Doctor, are you cooking for us today? Or do we have to forage on our own?" the Ambassador asked.

"I was hoping you'd ask," the Doctor replied. He grinned. "May we avail ourselves of the Magellan's gardens and stores, Captain?" he asked.

"Certainly. Commander Brandon, would you help the Doctor get whatever he needs?" Captain Logan asked.

Commander Brandon nodded. "Lt. Katy, come with us," she said firmly. She started toward the door.

Lt. Katy followed.

"You are welcome to join us, Captain. It should only take me about an hour to prepare something," the Doctor said.

"Thank you, I'm going to pass this time. Seems I'm going to have some studying to do," Captain Logan replied.

"Ok, more for me!" the Doctor said. He took Beth's arm and they walked out the door.

"Ambassador, I will take my leave for now," Captain Logan said.

The Ambassador smiled. "Try to get some rest. It really is a lot to take in," she said.

Captain Logan nodded. "Thank you. See you in the morning," he said. He walked out of the room.

The Ambassador turned to N'amani and Kell. "Now then, let's take a closer look at where we're going," she said. She touched a control panel that opened a much more detailed 3D map of the Ka'len system. They sat down and began studying the map.

Over the next two weeks, they studied maps, looked at the history of the Ka'len system, practiced hand-to-hand combat drills, and ran scenarios. Preparations she hoped wouldn't be needed.

CHAPTER 2:
A DINNER PARTY, PART 1:
PREPARATIONS

Each portion in good measure
Each time unto its own
There is more here than is apparent
Look beyond what you know

COFFEE WITH BREAKFAST
THE AMBASSADOR'S QUARTERS ON THE MAGELLAN

The Ambassador was standing next to the coffee maker she had set up in her quarters on the Magellan. She had gotten up early to review the treaty documents. She'd put on a pot of coffee and a flute concerto. The smell of fresh coffee and the sound of a happy flute filled the room. "It's the little things. Always the little things," she thought as she poured a cup and walked over to the window. She blew across the top and took a sip. No matter where she was or what she needed to do, she liked having a few little things. They kept her grounded. Familiar music, the sound of birds in the morning, the stars, and, well, if she was going to be honest, she had to admit she really liked having her coffee in the morning. She went over to her desk, sat down, and picked up a large hand-held screen.

The door chime sounded.

"Come in," the Ambassador said. She didn't look up from the screen.

"Good morning," the Doctor said. He sniffed the air. "What is that? Can it be? Fresh coffee?" he asked.

The Ambassador looked up and smiled. "Help yourself, Doctor. You are always welcome and you know it. You're up early," she said.

"I've gotten used to being up early. We've been working some pretty long hours these past few weeks," the Doctor said.

"And you are supposed to be resting today. We'll arrive at the Ka'len system tomorrow. We need to rest now," the Ambassador said.

The Doctor held the cup under his nose, inhaled, took a sip, and smiled. "I know," he said

"Well, then what are you doing here?" the Ambassador asked.

"Coffee?" the Doctor asked grinning. "I've been conditioned," he said.

The Ambassador laughed.

The Doctor walked over to the bench along the window. A few small cases and one long one were pushed off to the end. "Are you still unpacking?" he asked.

The Ambassador nodded. "I brought a few things from the shuttle," she said.

"So, I see. Is that long case what I think it is?" the Doctor asked. He opened the case.

A long sword in a polished redwood sheath was set on top of a neatly folded set of red and gold formal robes. The hilt was polished mithril. The sheath was inlaid with mother of pearl. The pommel was trimmed with three-color gold that began to glimmer with red, gold, and green lights.

The Doctor turned to face the Ambassador, his eyes wide. "You brought Aladrel? Are you expecting something?" he asked.

The Ambassador shrugged her shoulders. "I don't know," she said.

"So why?" the Doctor asked.

The Ambassador smiled. "Because I don't know," she said.

The Doctor grinned. "You sound like Master Tai," he said.

The Doctor had also trained on Ras 2. He was a Keeper of Water, three generations younger than the Ambassador. He had been selected to join the House of Dui (Water) and had chosen to focus on developing healing skills rather than fighting skills.

The Ambassador bowed. "Why thank you. More coffee?" she asked. She picked up the pot and offered to pour.

The Doctor held out his cup and smiled. "There is no substitute for brewed coffee. This is wonderful. How did you manage it?" he asked.

The Ambassador grinned like a Cheshire cat with a warm bowl of milk. "We're here partly on an agricultural trade mission are we not? And coffee is an agricultural product is it not?" she asked.

The Doctor laughed. "Why yes, yes it is. And yes, we are." He put his cup down on the table, leaned forward, and grinned. "You are really good at this," he said.

The Ambassador smiled bigger and nodded. "Grapes are also an agricultural product," she said.

The Doctor laughed. "Yes, yes they are. We need to have more of those bottled cabernet grapes. They went very well with my rice pilaf," he said. He grinned proudly.

They both laughed. They had spent three hours fishing the wine bottles out of the rice bins.

The Ambassador turned her head slightly. "N'amani is really good at anticipating and being able to acquire what we need," she said. She was trying not to laugh. It wasn't working. She giggled. "Would you like more?" she asked. She reached for the coffee pot again.

The Doctor held out his cup again. "Yes, please," he said.

The Ambassador poured.

The Doctor raised his cup. "To N'amani!" He brought the cup just under his nose and took a deep breath "It's nice to have a few extras once in a while," he said.

The Ambassador smiled at him. "Was coffee the only reason you stopped by, Marc?" she asked.

The Doctor grinned. "No. But it smelled so nice," he said.

"You're welcome to be here just for coffee. You know that, right?" the Ambassador asked.

The Doctor grinned. "What time should I be here in the morning?" he asked.

The Ambassador frowned then chuckled.

The Doctor put his cup down and sat back a little. "You're right. Coffee wasn't the only reason I stopped by. Beth seemed to think that the Kora would be very interested in learning how foods affect the body, using foods for their healing properties, and how they could use some of their native plants, trees, and shrubs. So, I started looking at what they have and what they might need," he said. He leaned forward. "Tell me again. What's your plan?" he asked.

The Ambassador looked down with a puzzled frown. "You know what I have planned, Marc. First convince the Ka'len Council to sign the treaty. I'm prepared to offer them a steady supply of seed grains and a few of the Alliance's newest automated harvesters along with training on how to operate them. Whatever else has to come after. The biggest problem is that we need a way to gain their confidence. But we don't have much information. That makes it difficult for me to figure out what they might want the most and whether or not I can arrange it," she said.

The Doctor nodded then smiled. "I may have found your elusive butterfly – a way to convince the Kora to trust us. What if we could show them that we are willing to help them and do not want to take over or plunder their worlds?" he asked.

The Ambassador turned a sharp gaze on him. "Be careful with that idea. Even stating the negative can be a problem. It opens up too much," she said. She shifted in her seat and turned to one side.

The Doctor nodded. "I take your point. We don't have any sort of relationship with the Kora. They have no idea who we are. We need to focus on what we can do to help them. Keep it positive," he said.

The Ambassador nodded and smiled. "Yes. Go on. Tell me about the butterfly," she said.

The Doctor smiled. "When Beth and I were going through the Kora's main food sources, crops, and historical food supplies, I noticed several plants are very similar to healing plants we have. They can all be quite potent. They could address several of the Kora's most common ailments, including what looks to be a prevalent problem with a disease similar to what we know as malaria. If I'm right, they have a species of tree that can cure it. There is a preparation method and a course of treatment. It isn't too complicated and doesn't require much more than what's needed to prepare a meal," he said.

The Ambassador's eyes got bigger and bigger as he spoke. "You found it! This could be enough all by itself to get the Kora to sign the treaty. Congratulations!" she said. She got up, walked over to him and bro'slapped him lightly on the shoulder. Then she hugged his shoulders, and kissed his cheek. She stepped back and started pacing the floor. "Marc, you just made my day. My year maybe. This is Perfect. Absolutely PERFECT! We host a dinner for the Ka'len Council. You work with their doctors and chefs to prepare the treatment and we include it with the dinner. We record you with their doctors, scientists and chefs, technology transfer, all that – excellent PR, by the way – and they keep a copy for their archives. We take clips from that training and put it together with the finished meal. And, if we are extra lucky, we sign the treaty before we sit down for dinner. Where's Beth?" She opened a comm link. "Beth, could you please come to my quarters. I've got something you need to hear," she said.

"I'll need five minutes, Ambassador," Beth replied.

"Thank you," the Ambassador said. She closed the link. She poured the last of the coffee into their cups. "I'm going to put on another pot of coffee," she said.

"That would be super wonderful fantastic," the Doctor said. He grinned, put his elbow on the table, and set his cheek on his hand. He closed his eyes.

"Marc, did you sleep?" the Ambassador asked.

The Doctor opened his eyes and shook his head. "No, I didn't find the genetic threads until about four. Then, I double-triple checked. I still need a sample to be sure, but ..." he said.

"This could change everything. You know that better than I do," the Ambassador said, finishing his thought.

The Doctor nodded and grinned.

The door chime sounded. A small panel next to the door lit up.

"Come in" the Ambassador said.

"You wanted to see me Ambassador?" Beth asked. "Oh, good morning, Doctor. You're up early. Did you sleep?" she asked.

The Doctor laughed. "Good morning, Beth. Thank you, no," he said.

The Ambassador held out a full cup of fresh coffee, "Would you like some coffee, Beth?" she asked.

Beth nodded. She looked down at the cup and smiled. "Thank you, Ambassador. We were reviewing the files until late or early. I'm not sure which right now," she said.

The Ambassador picked up her cup, went back to the table, and sat down. She pushed a chair out for Beth.

Beth sat down.

The Ambassador took a sip of coffee and smiled. "The Doctor tells me he found something that could be the perfect solution for how we approach the Kora and what we can offer them," she said.

The Doctor grinned playfully. "We're going to cook dinner for them," he said.

Beth frowned and turned her head to one side. "We're whut?" she asked.

The Doctor smiled and nodded. "We're going to cook dinner for them. Remember how excited I was after you showed me the archives on their foods and plants?" he asked.

Beth still looked puzzled but she nodded. "That was right before I left. I thought we were going to start again this morning," she said.

"Yes. Well, I wanted to have another look before I said anything. We don't have samples or a cross-reference. But I'm pretty sure. Some of those plants we were looking at have medical properties. When properly prepared and used, they can treat and cure several diseases. The Kora seem to not know this. I didn't see any references in the reports," the Doctor said.

Beth narrowed her eyes and looked down, shaking her head. "Plants can cure ...?" she asked.

"Sleepiness," the Doctor said. He grinned and pointed at her cup.

Beth smiled. She set both elbows on the table, put her chin on her hands, and closed her eyes.

"How late was it when you stopped?" the Ambassador asked.

"Maybe around two. I was making too many mistakes to be useful. I went to rest and clean up," Beth replied.

The Doctor grinned as if he'd just won an award. "I stayed," he said proudly.

The Ambassador chuckled at his expression. "Would you like more coffee, Beth?" she asked.

The Doctor pouted. "Yes, she would and so would I, thank you," he said. He held out his cup.

The Ambassador grinned. She poured another cup for Beth, then for the Doctor, and finally for herself.

Beth looked down at the cup on the table and smiled. She stood up and stretched. "How are some common plants going to change anything?" she thought. She walked to the end of the room. As she turned around, she saw little colored lights coming from a long bag. She reached out both hands and picked up the sword in its sheath, supporting the blade end across one palm and the hilt with the other. "Ambassador, this is amazing workmanship. Where does this sword come from?" she asked. She started walking back to the table.

The sword began to glow faintly.

The Ambassador looked up at Beth without moving her head.

The Doctor stood up quickly his eyes wide with surprise. "Beth, put that down!" he said.

Beth's shoulders slumped. "I'm sorry. I didn't mean," she said. She turned to put it back.

The Ambassador frowned. "The Doctor is tired and grumpy," she said. She looked at him and shook her head slightly to warn him not to say anything. Then she turned her head to one side. "Beth, how does the sword feel in your hands?" she asked.

Beth's face brightened. She smiled and looked down at the sword. "It feels light, as if there's nothing but I know there is something. It's cool and warm at the same time. It's very comfortable. It has such a fine balance. It fits my hand perfectly," she said. She turned her hand over and closed it around the hilt.

The Doctor looked at the Ambassador.

The Ambassador looked at him, lowered her eyes, and turned her head ever so slightly from side to side. She looked up and smiled at Beth. "That's an old sword from Ras 2. I used to carry it more often. I'm happy you asked about it. If you would, put it back now, please," she said.

The Doctor sat down and looked into his cup.

Beth set the sword back on top of the robes and went back to the table. "I don't remember seeing an inlay like that in the artifacts catalogs from Ras 2," she said.

The Ambassador nodded. "That pattern is quite rare," she said. She set her elbow on the table and held her chin with her thumb, looking at Beth. "Maja," she said, asking for the AI.

Maja appeared. "Yes Ambassador," she said.

"Would you set up an archive with background on these carvings for Beth? Let me review it before you give her access. I may want to add a few things," the Ambassador said.

"Of course, Ambassador," Maja replied.

"Thank you, Ambassador," Beth said.

The Ambassador smiled. "I'm glad you asked. Really. Besides, it's your job," she said. She shrugged and smiled. "You are supposed to make yourself an expert on cultures and artifacts. How can you do that if you don't learn more than what you already know?" she asked. She got up to get more coffee.

"Some for me?" the Doctor asked. He held out his cup.

The Ambassador poured and put the pot down on the table. She turned to Beth. "Now then, back to the plants. If what the Doctor thinks might be possible is actually possible, we will be teaching the Kora how to make their own life-saving medications. That could be enough to convince them to sign a treaty," she said.

"You think that could happen?" Beth asked.

The Ambassador grinned sideways. "The Doctor has to confirm it. But if it is, then yes, I think they will give us a treaty. We need to be ready. That's why I called you. If something is going to happen, it will happen quickly. We will need full documentation of whatever the Doctor does and we need to make sure we have all the appropriate footage for the archives. More than the equipment, I need you to bring your talent for framing and being able to capture the scene," she said.

Beth looked down, took a breath, and smiled. She looked squarely at the Ambassador and sat a little straighter. "I'll be ready, Ambassador. I'm glad you told me. I should bring two more sets of lenses and a few other things," she said.

The Ambassador nodded. "We need to be ready for – cross your fingers – the best of all possible outcomes: a treaty signing right before dinner. Marc, your discovery really does change things in our favor. Both of you have done amazing work!" she said. She raised the coffee pot as if in a toast and freshened their cups.

"This is so nice," Beth said. She brought the cup almost to her nose.

The Doctor nodded. "Fresh brewed," he said.

The Ambassador poured the last of the coffee into her cup. She took the empty pot back to the side table and activated a comm link. "N'amani, are you awake?" she asked.

"Not quite, Ambassador," N'amani replied. "I was sleeping in. You said we should rest today," he said.

The Ambassador chuckled. "That I did. But the Doctor has just told me he may have found something that could convince the Kora to give us a treaty. So, would you arrange a briefing for everyone, including Captain Logan and his team, please? In one hour?" she asked.

"Yes Ambassador," N'amani replied. "What has the Doctor come up with this time? Is it something I'm going to be able to put in a report?" he asked.

"Yes, absolutely," the Ambassador replied laughing. "We're going to cook dinner for them," she said.

"Excuse me?" N'amani asked.

The Ambassador chuckled. "Yes, you heard me correctly. What the Doctor has discovered could be perfect!" she said.

"We're going to cook dinner for them? Seriously? What are we serving?" N'amani asked.

The Ambassador tried not to laugh. "Tree bark. I'll explain in detail at the briefing," she said.

"Tree bark?" N'amani whispered. "A briefing in one hour. Yes, Ambassador," he said firmly.

"Thank you," the Ambassador said. She walked back to the table. She smiled at Beth and the Doctor. "If this works, we could have a treaty and be headed home early. If only things could go as well with getting the Olmeri to leave," she said.

The Doctor stood up. "I'd like to clean up and get something to eat before the briefing," he said.

The Ambassador shook her head and laughed. "Is your presentation ready?" she asked.

The Doctor shook his head. "I didn't know I needed one," he said.

The Ambassador grinned. "You should have eaten before you came to tell me," she said.

The Doctor shrugged and smiled. "I could smell the coffee," he said.

Beth was starting to nod off.

"Beth," the Ambassador said quietly.

Beth opened her eyes and raised her head. "Yes, Ambassador," she said.

The Ambassador smiled gently. "We have a briefing to get ready for. You are tired and would much rather sleep. I know this feeling quite well. You won't get used to it but you will become good friends with it," she said.

Beth giggled.

"You can take a nap after we finish the briefing," the Ambassador suggested.

Beth squinted and frowned. "Take a nap?" she asked.

"That's what I used to promise myself whenever I had to stay awake. After I finish 'this thing' then I'll take a nap," the Ambassador said.

"How did that help you stay awake?" Beth asked.

"It gave me something to look forward to," the Ambassador said. She walked Beth to the door. "Go get some nuts to snack on so you don't fall asleep in your chair and we'll meet you in the briefing room," she said.

Beth grinned. "Thank you," she said. She walked out and the doors closed.

The Doctor watched Beth leave. He shook his head. "Something you weren't expecting? Really? She shouldn't have been able to touch your sword let alone pick it up," he said.

"But she did. And it was effortless for her," the Ambassador said.

The Doctor frowned. "Aladrel should have been too heavy for her to move, let alone pick up. The hilt should have burned her hand," he said.

"But it wasn't and it didn't. Aladrel recognized her. You saw the glimmer," the Ambassador said quietly.

The Doctor turned his head to one side and looked at the Ambassador. He smiled. "Beth doesn't know, does she?" he asked.

The Ambassador shook her head. "Not yet," she said.

"How long have you known?" the Doctor asked.

"Just now. I suspected but I wasn't sure," the Ambassador said.

"Are you going to tell her?" the Doctor asked.

The Ambassador shook her head. "You know better. She isn't ready. She hasn't asked," she said.

"When the student is ready, the teacher will appear," the Doctor said.

The Ambassador nodded. "From the Second Book of the Ancients. What I want doesn't matter. I can't teach her anything until she's ready," she said.

"Then what?" the Doctor asked.

"We will help her find out for herself," the Ambassador said.

"Now you really sound like Master Tai," the Doctor said. He chuckled a little and dropped his head.

The Ambassador nudged his shoulder. "Let's get you a snack, too. We can't have you falling asleep during your presentation," she said.

The Doctor laughed and stood up. "Could I try that?" he asked.

The Ambassador shook her head. "No," she said. She gently pushed him toward the door.

The Doctor grinned and took her arm.

They walked down the hallway together.

DINNER PREPARATIONS
THE DIPLOMATIC BRIEFING ROOM ON THE MAGELLAN

Kell and N'amani arrived at the same time. The lights in the Diplomatic Briefing Room came on as they entered.

"Do you know what's going on?" Kell asked. He sat down.

"No," N'amani replied. He took a seat across from Kell. "She said something about dinner and tree bark," he said.

"Tree bark? For dinner?" Kell asked. He frowned and scratched his head.

N'amani raised his hands and shook his head. "The Doctor has come up with something," he said.

Kell laughed. "Well, there's that," he said.

N'amani grinned.

Kell shook his head and looked over at the door. "Here they come," he said.

The Ambassador walked in followed by the Doctor, Beth, Captain Logan, Commander Brandon, and Lt. Katy. She waited at the front of the room while the others took seats.

"Thank you for coming on such short notice. The Doctor may have a solution that will convince the Ka'len Council to agree to a treaty with us," the Ambassador said. She nodded to the Doctor.

The Doctor smiled happily, stood up, and walked to the front of the room. He activated a screen to show a collection of samples and preparations. "I was reviewing what we know about the Kora's medical history. We don't have much. Of what we do know, they suffer from several diseases similar to those that afflict most of us, including malaria and dysentery," he said. He changed the image to show a small group of trees. "These trees look like what we call cinchona. I need a sample to confirm, but it looks like a match," he said. He looked around the room.

They were all waiting for him to go on.

Lt. Katy turned her head sideways and looked at him.

The Doctor smiled. "Cinchona bark contains quinine. Quinine can be used to treat malaria," he said.

Commander Brandon frowned. "You can make a medicine from tree bark?" she asked.

N'amani sat up and put his hand over his mouth. "We don't have to eat it!" he whispered to Kell.

Kell grinned.

"At least I'm not the only one questioning the idea of making medicines from trees," Beth whispered to N'amani.

N'amani grinned.

The Doctor smiled at Commander Brandon. "From this tree, yes. I can teach their medical teams how extract the quinine, prepare, and administer the treatment. They must be careful. There can be side effects. But if they use the quinine to make a simple, water-based tonic, they can drink it freely. Even children can drink tonic water," he said.

Commander Brandon smiled.

The Doctor continued. "They also appear to have an abundance of what we call chamomile. It can be made into a sedative, used to treat muscle spasms, and it can help with wound healing," he said.

Commander Brandon turned her head to one side and looked at Captain Logan. "It might work," she said.

Captain Logan nodded.

The Ambassador looked around the room. "My plan is to quite literally, invite the Council to dinner. We show them what they have then teach them how to harvest and prepare the treatment. Beth will document the selection, harvesting, preparations and results. With a little luck, we will earn their trust. We'll have a nice meal, some tonic water, a cup of relaxing chamomile tea, and a signed treaty. All smiles and happy toasts to everyone's good health. That would be the perfect outcome," she said. She looked around the room.

Captain Logan shook his head. He looked at his officers, at the Ambassador, at the doctor, and back at the Ambassador. "You make it sound easy. Do you really think you can do all that?" he asked.

The Ambassador smiled. "I'm going to try. It would put us in the position of a high-value, trusted ally. That's exactly where I'd like to put us," she said.

Captain Logan nodded. "Yes, it would absolutely do that. Being able to do it? That's the question, isn't it? I don't see how you are going to do it. Don't get me wrong. It would be great if you can do it. But I just don't see how you are going to make it happen," he said.

N'amani smiled. "Sometimes we don't either, Captain. We look for the possible, not for the impossible," he said.

The Doctor smiled. "Small changes can move a great weight," he said.

The Ambassador nodded. "We may not get all or even part of what I want. That doesn't matter," she said.

"What's the point then?" Lt. Katy asked abruptly.

Commander Brandon glared at her.

The Ambassador looked at Lt. Katy and frowned. "The point is doing what we can do. If we don't look at what we want, if we don't know what to ask for, if we don't have any idea of what the outcomes we'd like might be, how can we possibly get anything we want? Or stop what we don't want?" she asked.

Lt. Katy bit her lip and nodded.

Commander Brandon sat back a little. "What about the Olmeri? Are you inviting them to dinner too?" she asked.

Captain Logan chuckled.

The Ambassador looked at Captain Logan, turned her head, and raised her eyebrows.

Captain Logan nodded.

The Ambassador smiled. "In a way, we are, Commander. Kell, would you review what we have planned?" she asked.

Kell looked at Commander Brandon. "Remember all those times I left the ship, flew around, and came back?" he asked.

Commander Brandon nodded.

"You were testing the new controls you installed on your ship," Lt. Katy said.

Kell smiled and shook his head. He touched a control panel to open a 3D model of the Ka'len system. "Before we leave for the planet, I'm going to seed the asteroid belt with a mix of synthetic magnetite and cobalt. That will create a whole range of false readings for the Olmeri. Actually, their sensors won't be able to read much of anything. If they get too close, the magnetite will, oh let's say, redirect their navigation systems," he said.

Captain Logan grinned.

Lt. Katy sat forward. "Seed the asteroid belt? How are you going to do that? I'm a good pilot and there is no way that anybody can do that. Navigation systems won't work in there. You'd have to use full manual control. Nobody can do that!" she said.

Kell blinked twice and dropped his chin. He looked down for a second, then at the Ambassador. He took a breath and looked at Captain Logan.

Captain Logan looked over at Lt. Katy then at Kell. "Kell, Lt. Katy has never had the privilege of actually meeting an Aldaran pilot. I'm sure she is only concerned for your safety and meant to ask how you planned to manage it. Isn't that right, Lieutenant?" He frowned and looked over at Commander Brandon.

Commander Brandon nodded. With that look, Captain Logan had told her that he wanted her to have a conversation with Lt. Katy and begin disciplinary action. She looked sharply at Lt. Katy with a tight smile that said 'I tried to tell you.'

Lt. Katy dropped her shoulders. "Yes, Sir. That is correct, sir," she said. She sank further into her chair.

Captain Logan looked up at Kell. "Please accept my apologies for the interruption," he said.

Kell nodded to him and went on, "Once I have seeded the belt, we want the Olmeri to continue their surveys. We want them to find the cobalt and magnetite, decide this sector isn't worth bothering about, and move on. We hope they get so frustrated when their navigation systems and other instruments don't work properly that they not only decide to leave, they decide they don't want to come back. After we meet with the Ka'len Council, we will rendezvous with you here or, if that's not possible, here," he said. He pointed to the model. "You'll be able to keep the Magellan at a safe distance outside the asteroid belt," he said.

Captain Logan nodded. "We've been through that part several times," he said.

"What if the Olmeri don't leave?" Commander Brandon asked.

The Ambassador frowned. "Yes, well, there's that. We may have to use, shall we say, less than friendly tactics. But before we consider those, we have another surprise for them. Our ultimate goal is to make them want to go away. We don't just want them to go away. We want them to decide they want to go. We don't want to fight them. That would reveal much more than we want them to know about us. So Kell and N'amani have come up another option," she said.

Kell nodded and smiled. "First, we seed the belt to make them believe they didn't find anything useful. We want to create so many false readings they give up and leave. But what if they don't?" he asked. He smiled at Commander Brandon and went on, "We will arrange for some presents to find them," he said.

"Presents that we will arrange for them to find?" Captain Logan asked.

"No, Captain. These presents are going to find the Olmeri," Kell said. He switched the screen to show a ship covered in space barnacles. "Presents," he said.

Everyone laughed out loud.

Kell continued. "Our scans found quite a few colonies of these space barnacles, as you call them, on several of the asteroids. This particular species is especially attracted to cobalt which we are planning to distribute in the asteroid belt. Maja and I have set up the long-range scanners to send an old-style electric current along the beam. If we need to, we can use the current to magnetize the outer hull of an Olmeri ship. They won't feel it. But the ship will begin attracting the magnetite and cobalt from the asteroid belt. Then, we fire a pulse at the closest group of asteroids, so they collide with each other and break up. The Olmeri won't realize we did anything and won't know what's happening until it's too late," he said.

Captain Logan frowned. "I understand the procedures and what we're doing. I'm still not quite sure how releasing a bunch of space barnacles is going to help us," he said.

Kell smiled. "Their ship will be covered in magnetite and cobalt. When the asteroids break up, there could be several thousand hungry barnacles looking for dinner and a new home. They like cobalt," he said.

Captain Logan laughed and nodded. "Their ship won't be able to move!" he said.

N'amani grinned.

Beth and the Doctor looked at each other and smiled.

Lt. Katy chuckled.

The Ambassador looked over at Commander Brandon and smiled. "To your earlier question, Commander. Yes, we are inviting the Olmeri to dinner," she said.

They all laughed.

BEFORE YOU GO
THE DIPLOMATIC BRIEFING ROOM ON THE MAGELLAN

After the briefing, the Ambassador hung back, waiting for the others to leave. She turned out the lights and went to look out the windows. The stars danced as they sped past.

The Ambassador looked towards the Ka'len system and then, towards the asteroid belt. She shook her head. "Thousands and thousands of moving rocks. All flowing together and all going in different directions. If he misses one turn, one shift, one change," she said. She exhaled, dropped her shoulders, and shook her head. "It's going to be dangerous no matter how good he is," she said.

Kell noticed and turned back. "Ambassador?" he asked. He walked up beside her.

The Ambassador turned to him. "Are you ready?" she asked.

Kell nodded. "Don't worry, Ambassador. I can do this."

"I know you can," the Ambassador said quietly. Her face relaxed into a smile. She slowed her breathing. She was going to use the Ancient Arts to enhance his ability to see what he needed to see. It wouldn't be permanent. It would only last a few hours. But if he needed to see anything more clearly, he would find that he could. She turned towards him. "It won't be easy. It will take all your skills," she said. She put her palms together and began rubbing them slightly. Her palms began to give off a subtle golden glow. She took hold of Kell's shoulders and looked straight into his eyes. Her eyes were fierce and unflinching. "Keep your eyes open. Trust that you can see what you need to see. Miyé wačhínniyaŋpe ló. Niyé héčhuŋ kta okíhi. I trust you. You will succeed," she said. She wasn't being encouraging or kind. She was telling him, with everything she had, that he was going to succeed. He had to succeed. Her expression of confidence in him now might

77

make all the difference. And honestly, he really was that good. She let go of his shoulders and smiled, but her eyes still shone with a warrior's hardness.

Kell stood very still. He bowed his head while she was talking. He raised his head, stood tall, and looked straight at her with the same warrior's spirit. "Miyé héčhuŋ kta okíhi. Waáwaŋlakiŋ ket. I will take care of it. I will protect you," he said.

The Ambassador nodded with respect. He would have to do whatever he was going to do on his own. The Magellan wouldn't be able to help him inside the belt. "See you soon," she said.

Kell turned and walked out.

The Ambassador went back to her quarters. She finished packing, turned off the lights, and sat down on the floor to meditate. "It's taken a lot to get us this far," she thought. She closed her eyes and began to regulate her breathing.

KEEP YOUR EYES OPEN
FLIGHT OBSERVATION DECK ON THE MAGELLAN

Captain Logan, Commander Brandon, and three others were on the flight observation deck looking at an array of control panels.

Kell stepped off the transport platform and walked over to join them.

"Good morning, Kell," Captain Logan said. He turned to one side.

"Good morning, Captain," Kell said.

Commander Brandon looked up from the console. "Good morning, Kell," she said.

Kell nodded to her. "Good morning, Commander," he said.

Commander Brandon took a step back so Kell could see the panel. "We have rechecked all the subroutines that are supposed to work with that new panel you had us install. Everything checks out. But I'm still not sure why you needed another pattern sensor. It took us two days to get all the connections working, even with Maja's help," she said.

Kell frowned a little. He stepped up to the console where the new panel had just been installed. "Thank you for rechecking everything, Commander. This panel is fed by an array of controls I've installed on my cruiser. It will let you know where I am and if there are any Olmeri near me. I may not be able to see them, but with this you can," he said.

Commander Brandon's eyes got bigger. She dropped her chin, looked at Captain Logan, then at Kell. "You had us install an Aldaran navigation relay?" she asked.

Kell nodded.

"You want us to watch your six from here," Commander Brandon said. It wasn't a question and she didn't need an answer. She knew.

"Yes," Kell said. "Captain, who will be keeping watch?" he asked.

Captain Logan motioned to the three others to step forward. "Sgt. Ferrell will monitor your comm links, Master Sgt. Ray will monitor your systems relays and the new sensors. Master Chief Franklin will be on over watch. She will be monitoring your flight path and looking for your exit," he said.

Kell smiled and looked at a screen. It showed a wide view of the asteroid belt. "Thank you, Captain. This won't take long. My timing has to be just right so I'm in sync with the flow of the asteroids around me, especially as I enter the belt. I don't want to hit anything and I don't want any of the asteroids to hit me. It's not the big ones I'm worried about. It's the little ones. I've installed additional forward shields that will take most of the impacts, but there are cross-currents. I need to keep clear of them or risk getting hit from the side," he said. He wasn't explaining this for Captain Logan. He was reviewing it for himself.

Master Sgt. Ray stepped up next to Commander Brandon. "Maja has linked with your ship to assist with the entry timing. But once you enter the belt, you will be on your own. We won't be able to keep the connection," he said.

"That is true," Kell said. He tilted his head slightly to one side. "Does he really think I don't know that?" he thought.

Captain Logan frowned. "Master Sgt.!" He didn't need to say anything more. He turned to Kell. "Is there anything we can do to help you?" he asked.

Kell shook his head. "No, Captain," he said.

"Good luck, then," Captain Logan said.

Chief Franklin stepped up to the display panels.

Sgt. Ferrell took his position at the audio console.

Master Sgt. Ray went to stand at the systems relay station.

Captain Logan and Commander Brandon stepped back to observe.

Kell took a deep breath, nodded to Captain Logan, and walked down the steps to his cruiser.

Outwardly, his ship appeared to be just another very nice galaxy-class Aldaran cruiser. It was quite a bit more. Kell had made a few modifications, mostly hidden and none of them for comfort. He'd added more modifications to his sensors and navigation systems for this flight.

The airlock closed and the hangar door began to open.

FOLLOW THE BOUNCING BALL
KELL'S CRUISER / THE ASTEROID BELT

Kell flew parallel to the asteroid belt looking for the patterns of motion. He needed to harmonize his flight speed and direction with the motion of the asteroids so he could fly with them and between them. He sat back in his chair and looked at the displays on his console.

Maja appeared and activated an overhead display. "The belt changes shape. Once you are inside, you will have to compensate," she said.

"Yes, thank you for the reminder," Kell said.

"Try to keep the cobalt and magnetite along the upper center where it's more likely to attract their attention. We want any readings along the edge to appear to come from the center," Maja said.

Kell tightened his jaw. "Maybe I shouldn't have asked for reminders," he thought. He looked up. "Show map K19," he said. He'd just seen what he was waiting for – a section that was mostly larger asteroids.

A 3D map appeared on a console in front of him. It was oriented to the belt in the same way as the ship.

"Match trajectory and link," Kell said.

The 3D map transformed into an immersive map linked in real time to the sensors on the outside of the ship. It could track asteroids within 5 meters of his ship and show him what they looked like.

Kell sat back in his chair and looked at the asteroid belt. The number and variations of asteroids was daunting. He needed to try to follow the variations and patterns to find an opening. "There," he thought. "Captain, I will be entering the belt momentarily. If all goes well, I'll see you back here in 10 minutes," he said.

Captain Logan stepped up to the comm link. "Understood, Kell. See you shortly," he said.

Kell maneuvered his cruiser into position. He adjusted his speed. He looked at the patterns. He entered the belt. He lost comms. He lost the link with Maja. He lost automated controls. He shifted in his seat. He leaned forward. He took full control of the ship. In half a second, he matched the flow. He began a series of graceful maneuvers, twisting in and out among the asteroids. He rolled over one asteroid and across another, ducking in between the larger ones and coasting deftly around the smaller ones. As he flew, he periodically opened the tanks of cobalt and magnetite. "This isn't too bad," he thought. He smiled. He was actually having a good time. It was a challenge riding the flows as they twisted and turned among the rocks. He liked challenges. He had to stay alert, though. He'd been a little slow in pulling out of one of the turns. A small asteroid had clipped the rear. It could have been a problem.

Kell finished seeding the belt. He started looking for an exit. He cleared two large asteroids. He emerged in a field of small asteroids. He turned to get out of the field. An asteroid struck the tail of his ship. The ship went into a spin. He tried to compensate. He was spinning too fast. He couldn't control the spin. He couldn't see the streams. He couldn't see the openings. He sat back into his chair and set his shoulders. He blinked to clear his eyes.

"Trust that you can see what you need to see," he heard the Ambassador say.

Kell opened his eyes. Everything seemed to slow down. He could see the stream. He could see the flows clearly, far more clearly than normal, even for him. He could see how to harmonize the spin. He pulled in on the controls to spin the ship more. That would let him get control. Fighting it wouldn't help. He touched the wing controls. The inner wings responded. The ship stabilized. He spun into a side-stream. He looked for a way out. He banked to catch an outward flow. He cleared the edge. He took a breath and looked around. He was on the other side.

"I'd rather not have to do that again," he thought.

Kell dropped under the belt and headed towards the Magellan. He was a few minutes late getting back to the rendezvous point. He parked his ship in the hangar, opened the door, and walked down the ramp. He stopped to look at his ship. The back tail section would have to be replaced. Between the damage the small asteroids had done and a chunk bent out of shape out by the bigger one, the outer panels looked more like Swiss cheese that had been nibbled on than a tail panel.

He took a deep breath and shook his head. He turned and walked quickly across the deck.

CODA
FLIGHT OBSERVATION DECK ON THE MAGELLAN

Kell walked up the steps to the Observation Deck. Commander Brandon and Captain Logan were standing off to one side.

"How did things go?" Commander Brandon asked.

Kell smiled a half smile. "Things went well, Commander. I have seeded the asteroid belt," he said. He kept walking. "Captain, I'll let the Ambassador know I've finished. We can leave for Ka'len as soon as she's ready," he said. He stepped onto the transport platform.

Captain Logan nodded, frowned a little, and turned to Commander Brandon. "What do you make of that, Commander?" he asked.

Commander Brandon shrugged and shook her head. "Everything is fine?" she asked.

"I get the feeling he's left something out," Captain Logan said.

Chief Franklin waved to them. "Commander, Captain. There's something you need to see," she said. She pointed to the display in front of her.

Captain Logan raised his eyebrows and walked over to where Chief Franklin was standing.

Commander Brandon followed.

Sgt. Ferrell and Master Sgt. Ray stepped back to make room in front of the screen.

Chief Franking stood aside. "Maja just finished reprocessing the last segment of Kell's flight. It looked like there was something wrong with the sensors. But everything checks out," she said. She touched a control to start the playback.

Commander Brandon looked down, then up, then side to side. "Those twists and turns are impressive. He does make that look easy, doesn't he?" she asked. She shook her head.

Captain Logan leaned in closer to the screen. He shifted back and forth, left and right as he watched the flight patterns. "Kell really is an exceptional pilot," he said with admiration.

Chief Franklin shook her head. "Give it another second, sir. Coming up, right ... here. I have never seen anyone fly a pretzel like that. It's not supposed to be possible," she said.

The screen showed Kell executing a series of intricate loops and turns through the asteroids as he recovered from the spin.

Commander Brandon's mouth fell open. "Did you see that? No. That's not possible. It's just not. No way. Play that back would you, Chief?" she asked.

Captain Logan stared at the screen and shook his head. "Legendary does not begin. What I thought I knew about the skills of Aldaran pilots isn't even close," he said.

ALL PACKED AND READY TO GO
THE AMBASSADOR'S QUARTERS ON THE MAGELLAN

The hallway was quiet and empty.

Kell arrived at the Ambassador's quarters and rang the bell.

The Ambassador was sitting on the floor. She got up. "Come in," she called out.

The door opened and the lights came on.

"Ambassador," Kell said quietly.

The Ambassador smiled happily. She bowed to him. "Háŋ! Chaŋté sutá. Čhaŋté waštéya waŋčhíyaŋke ló. Brave heart! I am so happy to see you," she said, relief audible in her voice.

Kell smiled at her greeting. He looked down and turned his head to one side. "Waŋúŋyaŋkapi. I saw something," he said.

The Ambassador smiled gently. "Niyé ištá kabláye. You opened your eyes," she said.

"Hau. Yes," Kell said. He looked down, frowned and smiled at the same time then looked up, puzzled. "You were there with me," he said.

The Ambassador nodded. "Hau. Yes," she replied. She crossed her arms at her chest, opened them, and bowed again. "I am so very happy you are here," she said.

Kell made whatever he did seem easy. It wasn't. He was one of the best pilots in the galaxy and she was so very lucky to have him with her.

The comm link chimed and lit up.

"Ambassador, we have everything loaded. We are ready to leave for Ka'len 2. I have spoken with their Chief of Staff. They will send a delegation to meet us at the landing site. We will have time to see some of their city before our meeting with their High Council," N'amani said.

"I'm on my way. Thank you," the Ambassador said. She turned to Kell and smiled. "How was the flight?" she asked.

Kell smiled. "Oéčhuŋ kíte šni. Iháŋkeya kítaŋla škiškÁ. Not too difficult. A little bumpy at the end," he said.

"A little bumpy?" the Ambassador asked.

Kell took a deep breath and nodded. "Just a little," he said.

The Ambassador smiled. For him to say 'a little bumpy' meant it was quite rough. "Let's hope the flight to Ka'len is smoother," she said.

Kell grinned and nodded several times.

They walked out into the hallway and turned towards the transport platform.

They would be traveling on the Ambassador's personal shuttle. She had a few things she kept on the shuttle – small gifts for those she was going to meet, her formal robes, and other things. It was easier to pack the shuttle and have it brought on board than it was to try to pack crates and figure out where they had been put. The shuttle was fitted with several recording systems to capture the various diplomatic moments for the archives. And, it looked nice in the backgrounds, especially on her first visit to a planet. Beth had a knack for capturing her walking down the ramp from the ship with the Central Alliance insignia and her personal seal in the frame. She did like making an entrance.

BON VOYAGE
FLIGHT OBSERVATION DECK ON THE MAGELLAN

The Ambassador and Kell stepped off the transport platform onto the observation deck. The Ambassador's shuttle was waiting below. N'amani, Beth, and the Doctor were waiting for them.

They each had a couple of small bags.

N'amani had the diplomatic pouch with the schedules, plans and documents to be signed. He smiled as the Ambassador joined them.

Beth had two bags of recording gear. She looked up at the Ambassador and grinned.

The Doctor had his medical bag, personal bag, and one more thing – his "trip surprise" he called it. He held up the bag, grinned, then put it behind his back.

The Ambassador chuckled.

Kell shook his head and smiled.

Captain Logan, Commander Brandon, Lt. Katy, Master Chief Franklin, Sgt. Ferrell, Master Sgt. Ray, and several more of the crew were waiting just above the steps.

Captain Logan stepped forward. "Ambassador, we've come with an old Earth custom to send you off with wishes for a successful trip and a speedy return," he said. He was holding a large bottle of champagne with both hands. It was tied with a gold and blue ribbon. He extended the bottle to the Ambassador.

The Ambassador stepped up, took the bottle with both hands, and bowed. "We're honored Captain. This portends good things for our mission," she said. She was surprised. "Where did he get this?" she thought. It was quite difficult to get such things. She really wanted to ask but it was not the right time.

N'amani reached out to take the bottle from her.

The Ambassador handed it to him and turned to Captain Logan and his crew. "Thank you, all of you, for your help with the preparations and planning. I know it hasn't been easy. We have studied. We have worked hard. We know what we can do. We are ready. We are ready," she said. She smiled as she thought about how many times the preparations they made had saved their lives. She turned to her team. "Shall we go?" she asked.

The Doctor smiled and nodded. "Can I sit in front?" he asked.

The Ambassador laughed and shook her head. She started down the steps to the deck.

Beth picked up her bags and stood just a little taller.

N'amani looked at the bottle in his hand and at the small bag the Doctor had. He smiled.

Kell took a deep breath and nodded.

Captain Logan and his crew watched as they boarded the shuttle.

The flight doors closed. The airlock opened. Their departure was routine.

CHAPTER 3:
A DINNER PARTY, PART 2:
GUESTS

You have what you need
Light and shadow are one
The way is true

SURPRISE, WE'RE HERE
THE AMBASSADOR'S SHUTTLE

Kell was at the controls of the Ambassador's shuttle.

The Ambassador was napping.

The main display was showing a montage that Beth had created to review what information they had on Ka'len and the Kora.

The Doctor and N'amani were watching, sort of. They'd memorized most of it.

"From what we have, the Ka'len culture is similar to other moderately advanced civilizations. They are capable and not normally aggressive. They are quite keen on improving themselves through study and learning," Beth said.

N'amani smiled and nodded. "Your presentations have gotten much better. You don't ramble so much anymore. But you still make sure you got all the details. Nice!" he said.

Beth smiled happily and looked over at him. "You're a good coach," she said.

"You're a quick study," N'amani said.

Beth grinned.

"We're coming in over Ka'len 2 now," Kell announced.

Beth lowered the arms on her chair and pushed back into a semi-reclining angle. Four arms with screens wrapped around to the front of the chair. She adjusted their positions and switched them on. Two of the screens would show what the outside imagers were recording. The other two would show the inside. "Ambassador, I'm ready," she called out. She set her hands on the controls embedded in the chair arms.

"I'm not sure I am," the Ambassador said rubbing her eyes and sitting up. She looked around. "Ok, then. Are we ready?" she asked.

They all nodded.

The Ambassador nodded to Beth. "Very well. We are recording," she said.

Beth touched the controls and the screens lit up. She would be recording everything for the archives. Having an arrival recording of what they were doing as well as what they were seeing had proven quite useful to the Alliance. It had become standard practice.

"Looks chilly," Kell said. He looked out through the windows at a flat, icy landscape.

"Maybe it's winter here? It seems like everything is covered with snow and ice," N'amani suggested.

"There don't seem to be any people," Beth said.

"Kell, where are we?" the Doctor asked. He looked over at Beth's screens and then through the windows.

"Over Ka'len 2. Where did you expect to be, Doctor?" Kell asked.

The Doctor laughed. "No, no, no. I meant where are we in THEIR geosphere?" he asked.

Kell glanced at one of his screens. "We are over their Northern planetary axis," he said.

"So, ..." the Doctor said. He raised his eyebrows.

Kell grinned. "I'm turning toward their equatorial region now," he replied.

The Doctor got up from his chair and went to stand next to the second chair at the front of the shuttle. From there, he could see Kell's screens and the forward view through the windows. "Kell, could you slow us down and take us just a bit lower. I'd like to try to visually confirm that what we think they have is actually here. I'd also like to get a better sense of their geography. So, as close as you can to the surface," he said.

"You want the up and down?" Kell asked.

"Water flows," the Doctor said.

The Doctor had an uncanny ability to see and feel the flow of a current. Whether it was literally the flow of water, the currents and tides, or the flow of movement, the flow of, well anything. It was one of his gifts. He had cultivated those skills in his training to become a Keeper of Water.

"Maybe not too close. I'd rather have a smooth ride." N'amani said.

The Ambassador smiled. "Marc, remember what we need to do. You and Kell can go exploring later," she said.

"I'm thinking just that. But if I'm going to find what we need, I have to know where it might grow. We don't have time to do a bunch of scans and crosscheck, do we?" he asked. He frowned slightly. "You know as well as I do that the only way we are going to find out quickly is for me to use the Ancient Arts to look," he said.

The Ambassador nodded. "You're right. But can we take it easy? I have to go meet the Kora shortly and I'd rather not be green," she said. She smiled a very twisted smile.

"I will keep us high enough the we don't have all the bumps and low enough for the Doctor to feel the ride," Kell said grinning. "N'amani, Beth, are you ready?" he asked.

They looked at each other and shrugged. "Sure," they said together, pulling their seatbelts a little tighter.

"Doctor?" Kell said. He looked at the empty chair.

"Oh, yes. That would be good, wouldn't it?" the Doctor said. He sat down and pulled the seat belt around his shoulder.

Kell nodded. "Might," he said.

The Doctor settled into the chair. He turned his head toward the center windows where he had the widest field of view, and began to focus on his breathing. He closed his eyes for a moment, then opened them. He adjusted his vision to look at everything all at once. He could see the flow and the contours of the land, the way the plants and trees changed, the groups of similar plants and the ways they grew. It was as if he could see the planet as a full panorama in all its dimensions all at once. As if he was flowing over the planet, touching whatever he saw.

Kell kept the ship high enough that he could smooth out some of the changes for surface height, but not all of them. "They don't seem to have much in the way of mountains. Mostly flatlands with a few hills here and there," he said.

Beth checked her screens. "That's what we expected. They have some hills and valleys. But the planet is mostly plains and grasslands with lots of forests," she said.

N'amani pointed to one side. "There's what looks like a large lake and a river over there. Look at how lush and green those hills are. The water is such a brilliant blue," he said.

The Doctor shifted in his chair and closed his eyes. He opened them, turned and smiled at N'amani. "Those dark green trees are cinchona," he said.

"Are you sure, Doctor?" the Ambassador asked.

"Pretty sure. Can we take one more pass, close to those trees?" the Doctor asked.

"We are expected. The Ka'len High Council is waiting." the Ambassador replied. She shook her head.

"Just one more pass? It will only take a few seconds. I'd rather be certain," the Doctor said.

The Ambassador nodded to Kell. "I wouldn't mind staying here longer, Doctor. This part of their world is quite beautiful. These forests have so many shades of green and the waters are such a brilliant blue. It seems so peaceful. But we have a meeting to get to," she said.

Kell brought the shuttle around and came as close as he could to the tops of the trees.

The Doctor smiled. "Confirmed. Those are cinchona. Thank you Kell. Now, we need samples," he said.

The Ambassador smiled. "Not now, Doctor. We have somewhere to be," she said.

The Doctor grinned. "I had to ask, didn't I?" he said.

The Ambassador laughed.

Beth sat up and pointed out one of the side windows. "Look over there! Those hills are completely covered with wheat and barley. Look at the way the slopes are cut," she said.

N'amani nodded approvingly. "We were told they are a mostly agrarian culture," he said.

The Doctor sighed. "I didn't see much in the way of urban development. I only saw a scattering of structures just outside the forests. I didn't see any large cities. We covered a lot of ground. I'm afraid we might not be having much of a meeting if all they have is a few small villages," he said.

Beth nodded.

Kell turned to look at the Doctor. "Our scanners haven't picked up anything that would indicate concentrations of industrial production or anything that would support urban concentrations," he said.

The Ambassador shook her head. She looked at her navigation screen. "That's not much different than what we expected. We should start getting changed. We'll be arriving shortly," she said.

One by one, they all stepped to the back section of the shuttle and changed into their formal clothes. This was a first-contact meeting. Formal attire was required.

The Ambassador wore the dark gold and deep rust-colored robes of a Keeper of Earth. The Doctor wore the deep turquoise and dark blue robes of a Keeper of Water. N'amani and Kell each wore a simple cream-colored shirt with a round collar, dark gold vest, finely tailored black coats trimmed in dark gold, black pants, and polished black boots. This was standard attire for members of a First Contact Ambassador's delegation. Beth wore a black vest with pockets for her camera lenses over her blouse instead of the outer jacket. It would be a working day for her. She'd be behind the camera.

"Ambassador, we're approaching the coordinates their Council gave us for landing," Kell said.

"There doesn't seem to be much here, Ambassador," N'amani said. He looked out the window. He frowned and shook his head. "There's barely a clearing. The trees are so thick I can't see the ground. How can this be the right place?" he asked.

"I've checked the coordinates three times. We're supposed to set down in that small clearing," Kell said. He circled the area again.

"Come around again a little lower, please Kell. Let's have another look," the Ambassador said.

"The scanners don't show anything except the trees. It seems as if there's nothing here but the trees. How can we have a meeting here?" Beth asked.

The Doctor pointed towards one end of the small clearing. "Over there. There's a small group of buildings," he said.

"That matches the coordinates I have for where we're supposed to land," Kell said. He shook his head.

"You sound concerned Kell," the Ambassador said.

Kell pointed at the display as he came around again. "That little clearing is where we're supposed to land. The approach is going to be steep and short," he said.

"How steep and how short?" the Ambassador asked.

Kell smiled and blinked several times. "30 stories at 70 degrees, just over 2500 meters. I need to be ready to stop just as we come through the lower leaves," he said.

The Ambassador wrinkled her nose and grimaced. "So, we'll be coming to a stop before we land?" she asked.

Kell grinned and nodded.

"Let's go!!" the Doctor exclaimed.

"You would," N'amani chided him.

"I'm ready," Beth said. She tucked her chin a little.

The Ambassador nodded to Kell and sat back in her seat.

Kell brought the ship around one more time, aligned it, and dropped into the gap.

They caught a few glimpses of light through the trees as they were coming in. The canopy seemed more open the lower they got.

Kell stopped the ship just below a cluster of tall trees.

"Ok, then. We are on the ground," the Ambassador said. She smiled and rolled her eyes to one side.

Beth looked out through the side windows. "There's more light here on the ground than seems possible from the readings we had. The canopy should be blocking most of this light," she said.

Kell pointed at the top windows of the shuttle. "Ambassador, I think we may have been misinformed about the Kora and their level of development," he said.

The Ambassador looked toward Kell and then followed his gaze upward.

A graceful city seemed to be floating above them. It wasn't simply a city in the forest. It was the forest. The massive tree trunks supporting the city were cut with stairs leading up to an array of platforms nestled among the branches. They could see people walking along the branches among the leaves. There was a network of rope bridges connecting the platforms. They swung and swayed with the weight of the people moving across them.

The Ambassador chuckled a bit and shook her head. "I think you're right, Kell. It seems the reports we had about the Kora's level of development may not have been, how should I put it? completely accurate," she said. She got up and went to stand at the front of the shuttle next to Kell and the Doctor where she could see out more easily.

Beth and N'amani got up and went to stand with them.

"How did they do that?" Beth asked. "When we scanned, there were only trees. We didn't detect any of this. They have a whole city up there. It's beautiful!" she said.

N'amani pointed to a large central trunk with several smaller, surrounding trees. "Look at that! That's impressive It looks like they are growing a new building complex. They use living trees as the framework and build in harmony with them. This is remarkable. This is not at all what we expected to find. The Kora are more advanced than we thought," he said.

"Over there! They have a waterfall coming from that tree," Beth said. She opened her eyes wide.

The Doctor followed her gaze. "It looks like it could be some sort of irrigation system. The flow has a regular pattern. It's not random like a natural water source would be," he said.

N'amani looked out the window and pointed at a small group coming out of the city. "Ambassador, the Ka'len delegation is here and they are coming to meet us," he said.

"Oh, for another few minutes," the Ambassador sighed. "This is a lot to take in. Ok then. Here we go. Try not to look overly surprised," she said partly to them and partly to herself.

N'amani looked at her sideways. "Right. Like we see floating cities in giant trees every day," he said.

"I know, I know. I want to find out how they did it too. But we can't indulge our curiosity right now. We've got a meeting. And it's walking towards us." the Ambassador said.

"Yes, Ambassador. But can we..." N'amani asked.

The Ambassador nodded emphatically. "Yes, 'Mani. As soon as we get the chance. Absolutely," she said.

N'amani smiled gratefully.

The Ambassador stood up, straightened her sash, and checked her robes. "Here we go. Let's remember what we want to accomplish. Be honest. Don't say too much. Don't reveal anything we don't need to reveal. And most importantly, smile," she said.

Kell opened the ship's door.

MEETING NEW FRIENDS
OUTSIDE THE CITY ON KA'LEN

A wide stone path wound along the edge of the forest and seemed to disappear between two of the largest trees. The Ka'len delegation was moving slowly towards them. Two of the group wore robes not that much different than those the Ambassador and the Doctor wore. The other five wore the same dark green pants with lighter green shirts.

N'amani walked down the ramp with Kell, the Doctor and Beth. He continued towards the Ka'len delegates with the Doctor and Kell.

Beth moved off to the side, taking a position with a view of both the door and the delegates coming to meet them. She began recording.

The Ambassador appeared in the doorway. A ray of sunlight reflected off her medals and the jewels on her pin. Her robes seemed to dance around her as she walked down the ramp.

Beth followed the Ambassador with the camera. As she watched through the lens, it was as if the Ambassador grew taller with each step. A faint purple glow came from within her robes. Beth had the odd sense of being comforted and frightened at the same time. She started moving backwards, staying just a little ahead to keep the Ambassador in the frame. As the Ambassador got closer to the Ka'len delegation, it seemed her stride shortened and she returned to her normal size. Later, when Beth went back to review the footage, none of what she saw was on the recording. It simply showed the Ambassador leaving the shuttle and walking towards the Ka'len delegation.

The Ambassador stopped. She left some space between her and the Ka'len delegation.

N'amani stepped into the space to begin the formal introductions. "Minister Bo'ran, please allow me to present Ambassador Micha Lawrence of the Central Alliance. Ambassador, please allow me to present Minister Bo'ran, Leader of the High Council of Ka'len and Minister Norla, Chief of the Science and Medicine Council," he said.

Minister Bo'ran was just a little shorter than N'amani with a round frame and a little bit of a paunch. He had dark hair, a kind smile, and knowing eyes. "Ambassador, the High Council of Ka'len welcomes you. Que le temps que vous passez avec nous soit fructueux et agréable. May the time you spend with us be fruitful and enjoyable," he said beginning the well- known couplet.

"Que le temps que nous passons avec vous soit agréable et productif. May the time we spend with you be pleasant and productive," the Ambassador said completing it with the standard reply. She crossed her arms and extended her hands. "Minister Bo'ran, thank you for coming to welcome us. I must admit, I wasn't expecting your greeting," she said.

"It is common among many of the traders and merchants who visit us," Minister Bo'ran said.

"So it is," the Ambassador said. She nodded to him. She turned to the young woman. "I'm pleased to meet you, Minister Norla," she said.

Minister Norla was much younger than Minister Bo'ran, tall and slender with wavy dark hair. She had the same curious smile in her eyes as the Doctor and a peacefulness about her that was very pleasant to be near. "I'm honored to be here, Ambassador," Minister Norla said.

The Ambassador smiled and turned to Minister Bo'ran. "May I ask, would it be possible for you to show us some of your city, briefly of course? Your world is most impressive," she said.

"Of course, Ambassador Lawrence. Shall we start with a walk to the Council Chambers where we will be meeting tomorrow? We will pass through a residential area where you can see how we live," Minister Bo'ran offered.

"That would be excellent," the Ambassador replied happily.

N'amani had already set this up, but it needed to be said for the recording. They began walking towards a group of small buildings. Kell, the Doctor, and N'amani followed.

Beth let them all walk away, then stopped recording. She smiled as she put her camera in her equipment bag. "That was perfect. The Ambassador will be pleased," she thought. She hurried to catch up with them.

Minister Bo'ran led them into one of the small buildings. It was clean and well-lit with nice appointments, large windows, and a well-laid stone floor. But it seemed empty. There were only a few people passing through in various directions.

"This is one of our reception halls," Minister Bo'ran said with a broad sweep of his hand as they walked. "We often host traders and other gatherings here." He led them through another set of doors on the opposite side from where they entered.

"This is quite exceptional," the Ambassador said. She looked around the city. It was much more sophisticated than what they had been able to see from the ship. The buildings and trees here weren't separate. Each building was part of the trees around it. "It seems that you have not so much built a city, but you have grown one. We'd very much like to learn how you do it," she said.

"In time, Ambassador," Minister Bo'ran replied. "My people highly value our trees. They give us life and they protect us. We protect them," he said. He extended his hand towards a side street. "This way, if you please, Ambassador. This street will take us through a residential area to the public square. You will be able see how our people live," he said.

"Thank you, Minister, that would be perfect," the Ambassador said. She smiled at his ability to redirect and the Kora's achievements. She had seen so many cultures that had amazing cities. She'd been in the back alleys with cordial shopkeepers and the best foods, the public squares with sellers and buyers looking for whatever is the newest and freshest, and elite shops with everything that could be imagined. The way the Kora had developed their civilization was quite unique. They hadn't tried to remove the trees or use them to make other things. They kept the trees and learned how to make their homes in them.

CITY STREETS
STEPS OUTSIDE THE COUNCIL CHAMBER

The street was quiet with small shops in front and more than a few residences behind. The air was fragrant with spices and cooking. Children played running games. A few adults sat on stone benches that dotted the street. Older adults walked in arm with younger ones. Two women walked together with shopping bags of bread. A small group of men sat around a table playing a game with round discs.

The Ambassador looked at Bo'ran. "Your city feels calm and your people seem comfortable. It seems a pleasant place. It's a remarkable achievement," she said.

"Thank you, Ambassador. We support our people with their basic needs and encourage them to develop their unique skills from early childhood. We consider the happiness and well-being of our people the most important factor in our society. Everyone does something they like. We each contribute our skills to our communities. We don't have to compete with each other for what we need," Bo'ran said.

"That level of social development is quite remarkable." the Doctor said.

The Ambassador walked slowly, savoring the chance to see the people going about their daily lives.

It wasn't long before they came to an open square with a large tree in the center. The High Council Chambers was part of that tree. A grand stone staircase led to arched doorways that overlooked the square. Carvings in the stone and wood seemed to tell a story.

"Minister Bo'ran, the workmanship of these carvings is quite detailed. Your artisans must have spent considerable time creating them," the Ambassador said. She wanted him to tell her what they were without asking him directly.

"These carvings tell our history, Ambassador. Some of them are quite old. And yes, it can take our artisans years just to carve one scene," Minister Bo'ran said. He smiled proudly.

Just as they started up the steps, a small child came running towards them.

N'amani stepped behind, putting himself between the child and the Ambassador.

The Ambassador turned to see a small child. He was neatly dressed and appeared quite happy. He didn't seem to have much energy though. He was limping and having trouble catching his breath.

"Where are you from? You are blue! How did you get to be blue? It's pretty. Can I be blue?" the boy asked. He ran up to N'amani. Despite his limp, he seemed to be enjoying himself immensely.

Minister Bo'ran was annoyed. "How did this child get past security? Find his keeper," he said quietly to one of his aides. Then, he turned to the Ambassador, "I believe this boy is the son of one of our ministers. Please forgive the intrusion. Our children are given quite a bit of freedom when they are young," he said.

The Ambassador smiled. "Minister Bo'ran, I appreciate your concern. I understand the security problem. But I think this time, we can make an exception. He seems so happy to have met us. Would you introduce me?" she asked.

Minister Bo'ran scowled. "Ambassador, we have other things to attend to. This child should not have intruded," he said emphatically.

The Ambassador smiled gently at the boy and looked at Minister Bo'ran. "But he did. And since he's here, perhaps I could meet him?" she asked.

Minister Bo'ran shook his head. "He's merely a child. There is no point," he said.

The Ambassador smiled and stood quite still.

"Young man, come here," Bo'ran ordered.

The boy stopped dancing and went over to where Bo'ran was standing. He looked down and dropped his shoulders like he expected he was in trouble.

"What is your name?" Bo'ran asked.

The boy adjusted himself to stand taller. "I am Relna, son of Make," he said proudly with all the courage and respect he could muster.

"Your parents have taught you well," Bo'ran said approvingly. He turned to the Ambassador. "In our culture, names and lineage are important. Our children learn their family history from the time they can speak. For someone of higher position to ask a person their name is considered a great honor," he said.

The Ambassador nodded. "Our culture is not unlike yours, Minister," she said.

Minister Bo'ran looked surprised. "And you still?" he asked.

"Yes," the Ambassador said. She smiled and turned to the boy. "Greetings Relna, son of Make. I am Ambassador Micha Lawrence. I am very pleased to meet you," she said. Her voice was quiet with a depth that seemed it could reach across ten generations and a low, rumbling vibration that could only be felt. She was a Keeper of Earth, the center, and the grounding element. She wanted him to feel her voice as if the ground was shaking. She wanted him to remember that feeling long after he'd forgotten this day. It might not matter. But then again, it might.

Relna turned his head to one side then the other, listening to her voice. "Your voice is pretty," he said grinning. "Who's that?" He's blue," he said. He pointed at N'amani.

The Ambassador smiled. She was pleased that the boy wasn't frightened. "That is N'amani. Would you like to meet him?" she asked.

Relna nodded several times.

As they turned to walk over to where N'amani was standing, a rather harried middle-aged woman came running towards them.

N'amani stepped between her and the Ambassador.

"Relna," the woman called out. She tried to look around N'amani. She spotted the boy standing with the Ambassador and Minister Bo'ran. She stopped abruptly. She was not of a station to be walking up to them without being invited.

Minister Bo'ran motioned to her to come to get the child. "You are the child's keeper?" he asked sternly as she came close.

"I am his mother, Minister," the woman replied. She bowed deeply as if she expected to be berated and disciplined for allowing the boy to intrude.

"He knows his name. You have taught him well," Bo'ran said.

The woman's face brightened. "Thank you, Minister. That is high praise coming from you," she said. She smiled a little and bowed again, a tear of pride for her son in her eye.

"What is wrong with his leg?" the Ambassador asked. She motioned to the Doctor to come closer.

"He has nang. It's a common problem. Most children recover. But some become extremely sick. If they live, they have problems. He's a happy child. But he has been getting sicker recently. We still hope he might be one of the lucky ones," the woman said. She sighed deeply and looked down sadly.

"Would you allow me to run a small test on your son, madam?" the Doctor asked. He took a small hand scanner out of his bag. "It's just a bit of light. It won't hurt at all," he said. He wasn't waiting. He'd already completed the scan before he finished his sentence. He looked at the Ambassador and nodded.

The Ambassador began slowly. "Minister Bo'ran, we have something we'd like to share with you," she said.

"What might that be, Ambassador?" Bo'ran asked. He was not really interested. "Not some diatribe on health practices or some other uselessness, please," he thought.

"On our way here, the Doctor studied the information we have from our traders about the planets in your system. We didn't have much information, I'm afraid. But we have learned a few things since we arrived. The scan he just did on Relna confirmed that what you call nang is similar to a disease we call malaria," the Ambassador said.

"So, it seems this disease is also something our cultures share," Bo'ran said. He sighed.

"Yes, Minister, our people have this disease, too," the Ambassador said. She nodded to him. Then, she looked straight at him. "We also have a treatment for this disease. As a gesture of our good will, we will show you how to make this treatment and we will help you distribute it to all your people. Your planet has an abundance of the same trees we use to make our treatment. We only use the bark, not the whole tree. You have more than enough trees to supply multiple worlds for a long, long time," she said.

Bo'ran stood absolutely still. His jaw dropped. "Say that again please, Ambassador." he stammered.

"We will show you how to make a treatment for this disease," the Ambassador said. She smiled gently.

She knew it was a big deal. Every time they had been able to do something like this – showing people how to do something they already had the means and ability to do but not the know-how – it had changed the civilization for the better. In the early days, the Central Alliance High Council frowned on any such things. Providing healing medicines and technologies was considered interference. It would affect the entire development of a culture. But as they learned more about diseases and what remedies there were, as well as the damage they did, the policy shifted. They couldn't look away. They didn't want to create long-term dependencies either. Offering medical help generated good will. No question about that. But making an entire civilization dependent on a remote supply of an essential treatment or giving them technologies they didn't have wasn't something they wanted to do either.

The Alliance decided to split the difference. If the natural resources were available and they could show the people something they could do with what they already had using their own technologies, they would. They weren't introducing a dependency and they weren't introducing new technologies. They were simply offering a new way of looking at or working with what the civilization already had. That approach had made them many, many friends.

Bo'ran sat down on the stone steps. "You can treat this disease? You know how to?" he asked. He started crying. "Do you know how many of our people, our children have died from this disease? You, you have a treatment," he whispered. He held his head in his hands, sobbing.

N'amani walked over and put his hand on Bo'ran's shoulder. He just stood there and said nothing.

Bo'ran looked up at him and nodded, grateful for his presence.

"I'm tired. Can we go home now?" Relna asked. He tugged on his mother's arm. He leaned on her a little.

The boy's mother nodded and put her arm around his shoulders. She put her hand on his forehead and shook her head. They turned to leave. "This would be such a good thing for so many of us. If only it could be done quickly," she whispered. She looked down at the boy.

SOMETHING FOR THE BOY
STEPS OUTSIDE THE COUNCIL CHAMBERS

The Ambassador looked over at the Doctor.

The Doctor looked back at her and turned his head with his eyebrows raised, asking her if she was sure. He knew from her asking to be introduced that she wanted Relna to remember this visit. He nodded his agreement and sat down on the steps.

"Relna, could you and your mother please come back for just a minute? There's something the Doctor would like to show you," the Ambassador called out.

The boy ran happily over to where the Doctor was sitting.

"Come here and sit with me," the Doctor said. He held out his arms to Relna.

The boy climbed up onto his lap.

"How are you feeling now?" the Doctor asked. He squeezed Relna's legs to check muscle and joint functions. He pressed on Relna's back to check for kidney damage. "What about here? Does this hurt?" he asked.

"That hurts a little. My head hurts sometimes, too. I don't feel very good. I can't run like I used to. I get tired. So, I have to sit and watch while the others play games," Relna said.

The Doctor looked at the Ambassador and nodded slightly.

The Ambassador smiled at the boy's mother. "Your son is a happy child, so full of joy. The Doctor could help him. It won't hurt and it won't cause any other problems. Would you allow him to try?" she asked.

The woman nodded her head. "Of course, of course. If it will help him. You could help him? Yes. If you can," she said.

The Ambassador nodded to the Doctor.

The Doctor reached into his bag and took out a small, cloth-wrapped packet. He opened the cloth to reveal a large oval amulet with gold backing and a ring at the top. The crystal cut blue sapphire in the center began to glow slightly pink when he picked it up. This was the Ancient Jewel of

Aron. It could only be used by a Keeper of Water. He put the
ring over his middle finger with the jewel over his palm. He
began to move his hand slowly over the boy's body. The
center of the jewel turned orange as he brought his hand over
Relna's shoulder.

"Can I see that? It's pretty," Relna asked. He reached for
the jewel.

"I am doing something with it right now," the Doctor
said. He looked down at the boy and smiled. "When I'm
finished, you can hold it. Would that be okay?" he asked.

"Okay," Relna replied. He pouted, clearly not happy
about having to wait.

The Doctor cradled the boy in his arms, bringing his legs
across his lap. "Are you comfortable?" he asked.

"Yes," Relna said. He tucked himself in under the
Doctor's shoulder.

"Good. Now, Relna, pretend you are going to take a nap.
You want to go to sleep. Close your eyes and keep still. I'm
going to sing a little song. You will feel a little bit warm. I will
be here holding you the whole time. I won't let go. Just relax
and close your eyes," the Doctor said.

Relna curled up in the Doctor's arms and closed his eyes.

The Doctor gently rocked him, holding him with one arm
while he moved the jewel up and down over his body, as if
giving him a bath. He stopped at the boy's right kidney. The
jewel began to change to a dark blue, almost black showing
the kidney was badly damaged. The Doctor regulated his
breathing, began rocking the boy with more strength. He
started to chant in a deep, low tone. He focused on the jewel.
The light slowly began to change to a pale pink white as he
held it in place. He slowed his breathing more and stopped
rocking the boy. In the stillness between each breath, he
focused on the jewel. It began to slowly cycle through all the

colors of the rainbow. Each time it changed, the cycle got
faster until finally it stopped changing colors and glowed
brightly with a clear white light. Then, the light receded and
turned pink again. He moved his hand over Relna's body
again. This time, the glow from the jewel stayed pink. "Relna,
you can open your eyes now," he said gently.

Relna opened his eyes and smiled. "That was nice! It felt
warm," he said. He turned his head upside down and looked
up at the Doctor playfully. "Can we do it again?" he asked.

The Doctor laughed. He removed the ring from his finger,
wrapped it, and carefully put it back in his bag. "Maybe not
today. Your mother may have some other plans," he said.

Relna frowned. "But I'm having a good time. You are
nice. I don't want to go yet," he said. He wiggled a little,
trying to stay in the Doctor's arms. Suddenly, he sat up. "My
legs feel better," he said. He looked up at the Doctor. He slid
off the Doctor's lap and stood on both legs. He bent his knees
and jumped. "Mommy! Mommy! Look at what I can do!" he
screamed. He jumped up and down.

His mother was standing with the Ambassador. She
reached out to grab the Ambassador's arm to steady herself as
she watched Relna slide off the Doctor's lap and jump. "It's
been weeks since .... We didn't think he would ever be able to
do that again. What blessings have you brought us? Thank
you! Thank you!" she said. Tears of joy streamed down her
face. She bowed deeply to the Ambassador.

Relna ran over to her and hugged her. "It's okay Mommy.
I'm better now. Don't cry," he said.

Minister Bo'ran was still trying to compose himself. He
looked up and saw the boy. "What is this? What have you
done?" he asked.

The Doctor went over to him and smiled gently. "I
removed the disease that was harming the boy. He will need

time. He is still weak. But he will make a full recovery. One of
the medicines we will teach you how to make will help keep
him from getting sick again. We will also show you some
ways to prevent this illness," he said.

Minister Bo'ran shook his head. "What you are
suggesting. It's more than," he said.

N'amani pressed Minister Bo'ran's shoulder. "It is a lot to
take in. We're strangers. We've just offered you something
that will benefit your entire planet. Give it a minute," he said.

Minister Bo'ran nodded and took a deep breath. He
looked up at N'amani and smiled. Then, he turned to the
Doctor. "You said we have the plants for this medicine here
on Ka'len 2?" he asked.

The Doctor nodded. "Yes, quite a lot, actually. I was
hoping we might go harvest some while you and the
Ambassador discuss things. Then, I will show your people
how to make the treatment. It's similar to what we would do to
prepare a meal," he said.

Minister Norla had been standing off to one side. She
stepped closer. "Minister Bo'ran, on behalf of the entire
Science and Medicine Coalition, I would like to learn
everything I can about this treatment. We have been trying for
so many years. Doctor, what can I do to assist you?" she
asked.

The Doctor smiled up at her. "First, we need to gather
some samples. I'd like it very much if you would come with
us. I can show you several things on the way. Then, I'll show
you our harvesting technique. We take only what we need and
are careful not to damage the trees so we can harvest from the
same forest again and again," he said.

Minister Norla smiled broadly. "Our people will like this
method of harvesting very much," she said.

The Doctor waved to Kell as he and Minister Norla turned to leave.

"Beth, you should go with the Doctor to document whatever he's doing," the Ambassador said.

Beth grinned and picked up her gear. "Thank you, Ambassador!" she said. She hurried to catch up with the Doctor.

The Ambassador turned to N'amani and smiled. "I will be fine if you'd like to go, too," she said.

"Are you sure Ambassador?" N'amani asked grinning.

"Yes," the Ambassador replied. "Minister Bo'ran and I will be starting our discussions, I believe," she said.

Minister Bo'ran nodded. "It seems we have much more to talk about, Ambassador," he said.

"Indeed," the Ambassador replied.

N'amani bowed to Minister Bo'ran and hurried to catch up with the others.

Minister Bo'ran looked at Relna's mother thoughtfully. "Please keep this to yourself, Madame. We will make an announcement quickly. But we do not want to promote rumors or misinformation, do we?" he asked.

"No, Minister. But everyone will see the change. They will ask questions," the woman said.

Minister Bo'ran nodded. "Yes. For now, just say he is having a good day. After we make the official announcement, well, we may ask you to make a recording," he said.

"Yes, Minister," the woman smiled quietly. She was hardly able to believe what she just heard. "Making a recording would be such an honor. Our position in the community and Relna would have so many more opportunities. Our lives have changed. Everything will be different now," she thought. "Minister, Ambassador, we are forever grateful," she said. She bowed deeply. Then, she took the boy's hand in hers, held her head just a little higher, and turned to leave.

Relna skipped happily down the street at her side.

The Ambassador and Minister Bo'ran headed up the stairs towards a bench in an alcove. They had a wide view of the square. Minister Bo'ran was open to welcoming the Alliance and what they could offer. It certainly didn't hurt that the Doctor had just made the negotiations oh so much easier. By the time they finished their discussions, it was late afternoon.

Minister Bo'ran left to go brief the other Ministers.

The Ambassador went to find her team.

WHAT'S FOR DINNER?
KITCHEN OFF THE COUNCIL CHAMBERS

The Doctor, Kell, and Beth were in a large kitchen adjoining the Council Chambers. The Doctor had set out samples of everything they'd collected on a long table.

Kell was sitting off to one side. Beth was recording.

The Doctor was showing Norla how to prepare the tonic. He was grinning and moving with a flourish at each step. "All the ingredients we are using are common on Ka'len. The key to making the tonic is how we combine them. We start with the cinchona bark, finely chopped. Next, the peel from these lemons, limes, and oranges. And, a bit of lemongrass, allspice, and salt. Then, we fill the container with water and close it. Now, we wait 72 hours for the tonic to cure. Once it's cured, we will add a simple syrup made with sugar and water to give it a pleasant taste," he said.

The Ambassador walked over to where Kell was sitting. "I see the Doctor is in good form," she said.

"Indeed, he is," Kell said. He shifted a little in his seat.

"You're not much interested?" the Ambassador asked.

"We have more modern treatments," Kell said.

"Yes, but they don't," the Ambassador said.

Kell looked at her for a moment. Then, he nodded. "Understanding the old ways has value, too," he said.

The Ambassador nodded. "The Kora learn quickly. It won't take them long. We'll help them as much as we can," she said.

"The Doctor is doing a pretty good job of focusing on the tonic, not that he made it," Kell said.

The Ambassador smiled. "As he should. We have an ethical obligation to not make this about us. It has to be clear to the Kora that they had this treatment all along. It's theirs. We simply helped them find it sooner. That's all. Nothing more," she said.

Kell nodded. "I like your way of doing things. I like him, too. But sometimes he thinks he's the only one who can do anything," he said.

The Ambassador chuckled and nodded.

Just then, Minister Bo'ran arrived with two aides. "Ambassador," he called out. He walked over to where she was standing with Kell. "I am pleased to find you here. And your delegation. I have some news," he said.

Beth had been documenting what the Doctor and Norla were doing to make the tonic. She heard Bo'ran call out and turned just in time to capture the image as he entered the room. She raised her hand to let the Ambassador know she was ready.

The Ambassador nodded to her and turned slightly so that she and Minister Bo'ran were both facing the recorder.

N'amani saw what was going on and ushered the Doctor and Norla into the frame just next to the Ambassador and Minister Bo'ran. Then, he went to stand with Kell.

"Ambassador, I'm pleased to inform you that I have just met with our Council. We originally planned for you to give a presentation tomorrow. Then, our Council would meet. But in light of what you have shown us, the treatment for nang, and the knowledge that your doctor has already shared with us, I called an immediate meeting. We have unanimously decided to accept your Basic Framework," he said.

"Thank you, Minister Bo'ran. This is excellent news," the Ambassador said. It took everything she had to contain her delight. This was so much better than she'd hoped. She could barely keep a straight face.

Minister Bo'ran went on. "The Ka'len Council also welcomes your offer of training and education for our people. To further that, we would like to invite the Alliance to create a research station here on Ka'len 2. We believe that our cooperation will benefit both of us. We are forever grateful to you. Nous vivrons plus longtemps et mieux grâce à vous. We will live longer and better lives thanks to you," he said.

"Minister Bo'ran. We are deeply honored by your decision. Que les étoiles de la bonne fortune et des bénédictions brillent à jamais sur les enfants de Ka'len. May the stars of good fortune and blessings shine forever on the children of Ka'len," the Ambassador said. She crossed her arms, extended her palms, brought her hands down, and bowed.

The Doctor stepped up, crossed his arms, extended his palms, brought his hands down, and bowed. "Minister Bo'ran we are humbled to be a part of the way your ancestors chose to reveal this wisdom to you. Que les enfants de Ka'len vivent toujours dans la santé et le bonheur. May the children of Ka'len ever live in health and happiness," he said.

"Les habitants de Ka'len sont éternellement reconnaissants. The people of Ka'len are forever grateful,"

Minister Bo'ran replied. He turned to the Ambassador. "We understand you are preparing a dinner to introduce these treatments to our Council. Perhaps just before dinner we can have a formal signing? It would make for a very nice celebration," he said.

The Ambassador smiled. "Of course, Minister Bo'ran. That is an excellent idea," she said.

N'amani and Kell bowed their heads and tried not quite successfully to keep straight faces.

"This is so much better than what she wanted to happen," Kell whispered.

"She's good. She's really good at this," N'amani replied. He smiled and stood just a little taller.

The Ambassador motioned to them and to Beth. "N'amani, we'll need two copies of the Basic Framework, folders, and, if you would," she said. She smiled at him. She knew she didn't need to go over the list.

"Yes, Ambassador," N'amani said. He already had everything prepared. He had been working on the presentation folders since they left Dagon. All he needed to do was select which text to use.

"Beth, could you please go with Minister Bo'ran's aides to help set up what we need in the Council Chambers?" the Ambassador asked.

"Yes Ambassador," Beth replied. She smiled a huge grin as she picked up her gear.

"Kell, would you make sure the coordinates and characteristics we were using when we found the plants are transferred to the Ka'len archives so the Kora can use that information to find more," the Ambassador said.

"Yes Ambassador," Kell said. He turned to leave.

"Doctor, I believe you need to remain here to oversee the preparations?" the Ambassador asked.

"Yes, Ambassador. Minister Norla and her teams have already prepared most of the bark and fruit that we are going to need. We won't have enough time for the tonic to fully cure, but we will have containers with all the ingredients for each of the Ministers. We have cut chamomile flowers and prepared cups. All we need to do is add hot water," the Doctor said. He winked at the Ambassador.

The Ambassador smiled at his joke. She wanted to hug him and tell him what a great job he was doing. Now was not the time.

Minister Bo'ran looked at the Doctor. "You have shown us how to produce something in a few hours that will change our world. We are forever grateful," he said.

The Ambassador lost her smile. "Minister, we…," she said.

The Doctor interrupted. "Minister Bo'ran, there is something more you should know about this treatment. Norla has shown me some of her research. She was just on the verge of a breakthrough. The missing piece was how to prepare and combine the bark so it would be safe. All I did was show her our harvesting and preparation methods," he said.

The Ambassador smiled appreciatively at the Doctor. She suspected Norla was several years away from anything. If he could make it seem like it was her work, that would be best. The less it was something he did, the better. She turned to Minister Bo'ran. "I am very happy you and your Council have decided to sign our Basic Framework. It's a good day for both of us," she said.

"Yes, it is. A very good day," Minister Bo'ran said.

"I have a few things to prepare. I'll be back shortly," the Ambassador said. She nodded to Minister Bo'ran, the Doctor and Minister Norla. She turned to leave. She walked back to her shuttle absolutely delighted with the way things were going. There were still several things that needed to go right, no screw-ups. But so far, this was turning out to be an excellent trip.

A LITTLE NAP
THE AMBASSADOR'S SHUTTLE

N'amani was already at the shuttle to get the treaty folders for the signing. He was looking down at a small table. He looked up just as the Ambassador walked up the ramp. He picked up one of the two presentation folders on the table.

It was a folio size binder, covered in a leathery, dark red paper with gold accents at the corners. The edges had a narrow trim of mother-of-pearl that glistened when the books were opened.

"What do you think, Ambassador?" N'amani asked.

"Very nice. Let me see," the Ambassador said. She reached out her hand.

N'amani handed her the folder.

The Ambassador looked at the inlay and bindings closely. "Your workmanship rivals my grandfather's. This is perfect. Do you have the agreements?" she asked.

N'amani grinned proudly. "Already mounted," he said. He picked up and opened the other folder to show her.

The Ambassador opened the folder she had, looked at the agreement, and smiled. "Nice. This is?" she asked.

"The one with everything," N'amani said smiling really big.

"I didn't think we would be using it," the Ambassador said. She shook her head.

"But you wrote it! It was in your archive," N'amani protested.

"Well, yes, I wrote five versions. This is my what if we got everything we wanted and more version. I wasn't really expecting to use it," the Ambassador said. She shrugged, shook her head, and handed the folder back to N'amani.

"You always tell us it's good to be prepared," N'amani reminded her.

The Ambassador laughed. "Well, yes," she said.

"I'll take these with me and go see what I can do to help the Doctor and Beth. I'm sure Kell isn't pleased." N'amani said. He turned to go out the door.

"Likely not. He's not much on chair-shuffling. Thank you. I'll be along in just a minute," the Ambassador said.

N'amani started back toward the city at a brisk walk.

The Ambassador took off her sash and outer robe. If she was going to be rummaging around in storage, they would just get in the way. She went into the storage area in the back of the shuttle and started opening the bins. "I thought we had some," she muttered. She opened another cabinet. "Nope. Hardware. Ah, here we go," she said. She pulled two large bottles of tonic water off the shelf, put them in a bag, looked over at the door, and looked down at her chair. She went over to the chair and sat down. "I'll just rest my eyes. Just for a minute," she thought. She sat back in the seat.

N'amani's voice came through the comm terminal. "Ambassador, the Ministers are almost ready," he said.

The Ambassador sat up abruptly. "Can you give me 10 minutes?" she asked. She knew this was tricky. Delays of any sort always had to be explained. 'I was taking a nap' was not ever going to be on the list of acceptable reasons for a delay.

"Yes Ambassador. Beth has been having a little trouble with the lighting. It is likely going to take her another few minutes to check," N'amani offered.

"Oh, I like him. I really liked him," the Ambassador thought. She took a deep breath. "I'll be there as quickly as possible. I have something else we need to do," she said. She closed the link. She'd need to get a move on to get back into the city in 10 minutes. She stood up, put her outer robe and sash back on, making sure her personal insignia and that of the Alliance were clearly visible. A faint, purple glow came from inside her robes. She picked up the bag with the two bottles in it and walked out. The shuttle door closed.

SHALL WE GO IN?
KA'LEN COUNCIL CHAMBERS

They had set a large table in the center of the atrium for the treaty signing. The Ministers were milling around in the hall and in groups scattered around the Council Chambers. Small jars of the tonic mixture and cups with chamomile flowers had been placed at each Minister's seat. The meal the Doctor had arranged was ready. He and Minister Norla were standing off to one side. Beth had set up just far enough back to get several members in the main shot and not so far as to be too distant from where the Ambassador and Minister Bo'ran would speak. N'amani was standing just inside the entryway with Kell.

"N'amani," the Ambassador whispered. She was just outside the entryway.

N'amani raised his eyebrows and hurried over to her. "That was quick. We are almost ready," he said.

The Ambassador interrupted him. "These two bottles are tonic water from our stores. I need two glasses with a wedge of lime for each," she said. She grinned and turned her head to one side.

N'amani looked at her sideways. "Of course you do," he said. He smiled and shook his head. He looked around. He spotted some empty glasses in the kitchen where the Doctor had been working. He went to get them, scooped up two wedges of lime the Doctor had cut, and hurried back to where the Ambassador was waiting, one glass in each hand.

The Ambassador put down one of the bottles and opened the other one. "Hold still," she said. She poured a little into each glass. She put the bottle down and took both glasses from him. "Can you find a way to get the rest of this into some glasses with a wedge of lime for each of the Council members?" she asked.

N'amani raised his eyebrows and frowned. "Sure. Would you like some nice dinner mints to go with? Can I announce you first?" he asked.

"Thank you, N'amani. Your ability to do the impossible does not go unnoticed," the Ambassador said.

N'amani smiled quietly at the compliment. He moved to the center of the entryway. "First Minister Bo'ran of the High Council of Ka'len and Ambassador Micha Lawrence of the Central Alliance," he announced. His clear, deep voice resonated through the chamber.

Beth had been doing some general recording. She turned to focus on the Ambassador.

The Ambassador walked over to the table and put both glasses down.

Minister Bo'ran joined her. He looked at the glasses and frowned slightly but didn't ask.

The Ambassador smiled and nodded.

Minister Bo'ran looked around the room then at the Ambassador. "Ambassador Lawrence, it is my great honor, on behalf of the people of the Four Planets of Ka'len, to sign this Treaty and to begin a long and fruitful cooperation between the people of Ka'len and the Central Alliance. We thank you for what you have already done for our people. We welcome your friendship and this alliance," he said.

The Ambassador bowed. "First Minister Bo'ran, it is my great privilege, on behalf of the Central Alliance, to sign this Treaty and to begin the exchange of knowledge and cooperation between the Central Alliance and the people of Ka'len. We thank you for your friendship and welcome this alliance," she said.

The folders N'amani had prepared were neatly placed for each of them. These old-style printed folders were rarely used, except for important treaties and signings like this. Each folder carried the Central Alliance seal and the Ambassador's personal seal along with engravings to commemorate the event. Each was unique and highly prized on the black market, too.

N'amani stepped up from behind while they were talking to open the folders.

They each signed.

N'amani stepped up again to switch the copies. They each signed again.

N'amani picked up the Ambassador's folder and walked over to where Beth and Kell were standing. "Keep this for me please?" he asked Beth. "I'm going to go be a waiter now. I need to find some glasses," he said.

"There were several trays of glasses behind the second counter. I'll come with. Kell can keep the folder and my gear. Here," Beth said. She handed Kell her recorder.

Kell smiled. "Thanks. I'd much rather be recording than schlepping," he said.

The Ambassador turned to face Bo'ran and smiled at him. "Minister Bo'ran. I have brought you some tonic water from our stores. It is much the same as the tonic our doctor has shown your people how to make. We would like to offer this small sample as a token of our friendship," she said. She extended her hand inviting him to choose a glass.

Minister Bo'ran hesitated then picked up one of the glasses.

The Ambassador picked up the other glass. "May you and your people enjoy good health and great prosperity," she said. She raised her glass and took a drink.

Minister Bo'ran looked down at the clear, bubbling liquid. He cautiously took a sip. "This is good. I like it!" he said. He raised his glass and took another sip.

The Ambassador raised her glass again. "To a long friendship!" she said.

Minister Bo'ran raised his glass.

They both took another drink.

The other Ministers applauded. They began to migrate to the signing table to extend their greetings. It seemed they all wanted a picture with the Ambassador, too. It took a few minutes for them all to file through.

While that was going on, N'amani and Beth put glasses of tonic water out for each of the Ministers. Then, they went back over to where Kell was standing.

Kell smiled at Beth and handed her the recorder.

"Thanks," Beth said.

"You're welcome," Kell replied.

N'amani moved around a little, trying to get the Ambassador's attention. It didn't take much.

The Ambassador looked over at him.

N'amani nodded.

The Ambassador smiled. "Minister Bo'ran, we had enough of the tonic for all your Ministers to try it. N'amani and Beth have set a glass for everyone," she said quietly.

Minister Bo'ran smiled at her and shook his head. "You are quite amazing," he said. He raised his hand for quiet. "Fellow Ministers, I told you in our earlier meeting about the child, Relna, and the disease nang. I have also told you that the Central Alliance has offered to show us how to make a treatment that can stop this disease that does so much harm to our people," he said.

The Ministers all nodded.

"Those small containers next to your seating places are that treatment. We need to wait three days for it to be ready," he said. He stopped to let them take in what he was saying.

The Ministers each reached for their containers and begin examining them. They began talking excitedly.

Minister Bo'ran held up his hand for quiet. "Our Chief Science Minister Norla has learned how to make this tonic. We can make as much as we need," he said.

The room grew completely quiet.

Minister Bo'ran looked around. He held up the glass the Ambassador had given him. "Those small glasses you now have are this very tonic. Let us celebrate our good fortune and our new friends! A glass of tonic for everyone!" he exclaimed. He raised his glass high. He looked over at the Ambassador.

The Ministers all raised their glasses and waited for him to finish the toast.

"To the Central Alliance!" Minister Bo'ran said. He took a drink.

The Ambassador raised her glass, took a sip, looked around the room, and smiled quietly.

The Ministers each took a sip, looked at each other, and cheered. "To Ka'len!" they cried out together.

The dinner was perfect. They had several lively discussions with the Ministers. It seemed they had quite a lot in common with the Kora.

They stayed a few days to make arrangements for the negotiating teams to return. Then, they headed toward their rendezvous with the Magellan.

TRUFFLES AND CHAMPAGNE
AMBASSADOR'S SHUTTLE

The Ambassador, N'amani, Beth, the Doctor, and Kell were on her shuttle. They were on their way to meet the Magellan. Kell had just set the coordinates for their path out of the Ka'len system. The Ambassador and N'amani were happily reviewing their trip notes. Beth was cleaning one of the camera lenses.

The Doctor picked up his surprise bag. He looked straight at the Ambassador. "We definitely have something to celebrate this time. And I have brought along just the thing. It will go perfectly with that bottle of Champagne Captain Logan gave us," he said.

"Oh really, Doctor? What is it that goes with Champagne?" the Ambassador asked.

The Doctor grinned. "Truffles," he said.

The Ambassador laughed. She stood up, walked over to a side cabinet, and took out some cups. "Yes, truffles go well with Champagne. And where pray tell, did you find truffles?" she asked.

The Doctor smiled. He took a small box out of his bag. "I made them," he said proudly.

"What are truffles?" Beth asked.

"These are truffles," the Doctor said in his best 'you are now going to listen to my lecture' voice. He opened the box.

Inside were 10 small round dark chocolates decorated with pink, blue, green, and rose-colored icing.

"Truffles are an old-Earth delicacy. First, you must start with fine chocolate. It must be blended and warmed just so. Then, you must create the filling," he said.

Beth and N'amani looked at each other.

"Filling?" Beth asked.

"Yes. The filling must be delicate and creamy while the outer layer must be firm and solid," the Doctor said. He grinned as he extended the box to each of them.

"Do you ever sleep, Doctor?" Beth asked. She shook her head.

The Doctor smiled. "Try this one," he said. He pointed to one with rose color icing.

Beth took it gingerly. "It's so light!" she said. She took a small bite. Her eyes got bigger and she grinned. "Oh my, that's delicious!" she said.

The Ambassador grinned. "We should open the Champagne. N'amani, do you want to open the bottle?" she asked.

N'amani shook his head.

The Ambassador smiled and reached for the bottle. She put a small cloth over the top and wiggled it. There was a loud "pop" as the cork came out. A little liquid bubbled out.

"Where's your cup?" the Ambassador asked the Doctor.

"Here," the Doctor said. He put his cup under the top to catch the overflow.

The Ambassador poured more into his cup then poured some for the others. She took one of the truffles. "Cheers and job well done!" she said. She raised her arms, a cup in one hand and a truffle in the other.

Kell had set the autopilot and was standing next to N'amani.

N'amani looked down at his cup. It was bubbling. He looked over at Kell. He shook his head.

Kell looked at his cup and then at N'amani. He shook his head. He started to put the cup down.

The Ambassador frowned. "I know you aren't fond of trying new foods. Just try a little?" she asked.

Kell took a sip and promptly spit it back into the cup. He cringed. "Maybe not this one," he said.

The Ambassador smiled and nodded. "It's an acquired taste. I'm happy you tried it. At least now, you know what it is," she said.

Kell frowned a little.

N'amani looked at his cup again. He took a sip. "What a wonderful thing!" he said. He smiled and crinkled his nose. He took another sip and another. He looked at the box with the colorful chocolates and back at his cup then at the box again. "Doctor, could I try one of those truffle things?" he asked.

The Doctor held out the box and smiled playfully. "Try a blue one," he said.

N'amani took one. As he bit into it, a bit of the creamy chocolate filling oozed out. "Oh," he said, his eyes getting bigger, just like Beth's. "Oh, that is good. Will you show me how to make these?" he asked.

The Doctor laughed. "Sure. I'd be happy to," he said.

Beth and the Ambassador laughed out loud.

"Are you going to practice not sleeping, too?" Beth asked.

N'amani and the Doctor looked at each other and grinned.

Kell stepped over to the controls to check on their position. Their route out of the system was going to take them very close to one of the outer planets. He wanted to make sure they kept a good distance as they went around it.

"Would you try one of these, Kell?" the Ambassador asked walking over to him with the box of truffles.

Kell looked at her sideways. After that Champagne stuff, he wasn't really in the mood to try another new thing. But he couldn't tell her no. He took a breath. He looked at the box. He picked one with the rose color that Beth liked. He took a really tiny bite. He had decided he was going to swallow it, no matter how awful it was. So, smaller was better. "Oh... oh my goodness," he said using an expression he'd learned from the Ambassador. He had the same appreciation in his voice as Beth and N'amani. "Doctor, these truffles are very nice. We should have more truffles," he said. He smiled broadly and reached for the box.

The Ambassador grinned.

Kell took another truffle and went over to sit in his chair so he could watch the controls. He took a bite and smiled. "I didn't expect these truffle things would be so good," he thought.

COMPANY HAS ARRIVED
AMBASSADOR'S SHUTTLE OUTSIDE THE MAGELLAN

Kell adjusted their course just slightly to move them further away from the outer planet. He was at the controls monitoring their route for any stray rocks.

"Ambassador," Kell said, his voice ominous. "We have company."

The Ambassador went over stand next to Kell's chair. She looked out the main viewer. She could barely make out a ship that seemed to be coming towards them from outside the system. She looked at his navigation screen. It was definitely coming towards them. "Have they seen us?" she asked.

"I don't know," Kell said.

"Where's the Magellan?" the Ambassador asked.

Kell pointed at a different screen with a longer range. "There. They are holding in place at the rendezvous coordinates," he said.

The Ambassador looked at the screens and the oncoming ship. "We can't get to the Magellan before they cut us off. Can you get us into the asteroid belt?" she asked. She knew he could and she knew full well what she was asking.

Kell looked at her. "Do you know what you are asking? This ship isn't fitted. I can do it, but it won't be an easy ride," he said.

The Ambassador nodded. "I have a very bad feeling about that ship. I learned a long time ago to trust my feelings about such things. We can't let them take us. We can't fight. The Magellan is too far away. There isn't any other option," she said. She turned around to the others. "Everyone," she said with a serious tone that got their attention. "Put away everything. Tie down anything that might come loose, and strap yourselves in tightly. We need to avoid a meeting and we're going to take a detour. The ride is going to get a little bumpy," she said. She was trying to be lighthearted about it but she was quite serious.

They all saw it and did what she asked.

She turned to Kell. Miyé wačhíŋniyaŋpe ló. Niyé héčhuŋ kta okíhi. Oéčhuŋ kte héčha. I trust you. You will succeed. Do whatever you must," she said. It was more of a command than encouragement. She turned to the others. "Prepare yourselves," she admonished them.

Kell maneuvered behind the outermost planet and used it to increase the speed of the shuttle. He plotted the shortest path possible towards the asteroid belt. If they were lucky, the approaching ship would see them as a wayward asteroid and not bother with them. He looped around the planet and had covered about half the distance to the belt when he noticed the other ship increasing their speed to overtake them.

"Ambassador, they have started trying to overtake us. But they are too far away," he said. He aligned the shuttle with the asteroid belt and slid into a stream.

The ship came up alongside where they entered the belt, slowed and began to follow them from outside the belt.

Kell made the twists and turns seem effortless. But it was more than a bumpy ride. The turns tossed them back and forth, side to side. Sometimes, there were up and down turns too. Vertical was not something any of them often felt on a starship or even smaller craft. The stabilizers took care of that. Usually, they weren't flying patterns, either. Kell was pushing the shuttle well beyond its design specs. He found a sub-stream and turned into it. He followed it to the inside edge of the belt and started looking for an exit. He found a path and emerged from the belt. The ship that had been following them was on the outside.

"Captain Logan, are you there?" the Ambassador asked into the comm link. She was a bit dazed. Kell had been with her a long time and she'd flown on some wild rides with him. This was going to be one for the storybooks.

"We're here, Ambassador. We will be ready to receive your shuttle shortly," Captain Logan replied.

"Ah, Captain, sooner would be better. We are closer than you think. We have some new friends in a ship on the other side of the belt looking for us and we'd rather not meet them on my shuttle," she said, quickly giving him the situation.

"I understand, Ambassador," Captain Logan said. He signaled to his officers to scramble. "We have received your new flight path from Kell. We will be ready on this side in .... just under 20 seconds," he said.

"Ambassador, they are trying to block us," Kell said. He pointed at the other ship. It had just dropped under the asteroid belt. It began to accelerate rapidly and aggressively toward the shuttle.

"Captain, can you paint them and open up one of those asteroids without them realizing it was you?" the Ambassador asked.

Captain Logan turned his head to one side quizzically and looked at his screens. "Yes, Ambassador. We can absolutely do that. Lt. Katy, please acquire the targets and fire," he said. He smiled at the usefulness of their preparations and drills. He'd been against seeding the belt. It seemed like something they would never use. Now he had an entirely new appreciation for her planning skills. How she'd seen this coming, he had no idea.

"Targets acquired. Target 1 painted. Target 2 destroyed, Captain," Lt. Katy said.

The other ship began gradually slowing down and kept slowing until it was barely moving at all. The ship's hull had immediately started attracting chunks of asteroid along with the cobalt they'd sprinkled in the belt. The barnacles followed and they were hungry.

"Ambassador, we have another problem," Kell said. He pointed at a long-range screen showing a larger ship coming towards them.

"We need to get back to the Magellan," the Ambassador said. A note of determination and anxiety came through in her voice. She hadn't recognized the first ship. It was a design she'd not seen. She recognized the second. "That's an Olmeri ship," she said.

Kell accelerated towards the Magellan, slid into the docking bay, and parked the shuttle.

As soon as they stopped, the Ambassador got up, pulled her formal robes out of her bag, and started putting them on over her travel clothes. "Doctor, please get dressed and come with me. I will need your help. Beth, set up three stations. Just show a treaty signing. You know what we need. N'amani, take care of background. Use the oldest approach footage we have. Kell, tactical flight auxiliary," she said. The Olmeri were a surly lot that wanted to argue about every little tiny thing. She wanted to bypass the arguing and get straight to the part about them leaving.

AN INVITATION TO DINNER
BRIDGE ON THE MAGELLAN

The Ambassador and the Doctor stepped off the transport platform onto the bridge of the Magellan. The Ambassador was wearing her formal gold and rust color robes with her sash and medals. The Doctor wore his formal turquoise and dark blue robes. Everyone, including Captain Logan, turned to look at them. They didn't often see Keepers wearing their colors.

The Ambassador took a position directly in front of the main screen. "Captain, I've asked Kell to go to auxiliary flight control. I hope we don't need him. Beth, are you and N'amani ready?" she asked.

The comm links on the wall behind her lit up.

"Yes Ambassador," N'amani replied.

"Yes Ambassador," Beth replied.

"Captain Logan, would you please hail our friends, with video. I'd like to speak with them," the Ambassador asked. She turned to face the screen and took a fighting stance, her feet well placed and apart.

"You want to speak with them? They just tried to hijack your shuttle. They've not been friendly. Why are you even?" Captain Logan asked.

The Ambassador turned to face Captain Logan. She looked directly at him and said nothing.

Captain Logan wasn't sure what happened, but he knew, with complete confidence, that he was going to do exactly what she asked. "Yes, Ambassador," he said.

She turned back to face the screen. She signaled Beth and N'amani.

The Doctor stepped behind her. He took a position just behind her left shoulder and set his foot outside hers – joining Earth and Water. He was going to help support her weight and add his skills to hers while she focused on misdirecting the Olmeri. What they were doing was barely visible outwardly. They didn't want it to be. They wanted it to appear as if they were simply standing close to each other.

The comm link opened.

The Ambassador could see the bridge of the Olmeri ship. She closed her right foot and stood straight. She crossed her arms, extended both hands, palms up, closed to the center, and bowed. "I am Ambassador Micha Lawrence, Daughter of Tor E'ran of Vega 9, and First Disciple of Tai Aragon of Ras'alhague. I offer you greetings on behalf of the Central Alliance," she said. She opened her stance, turning just slightly so the back of her shoulder rested against the Doctor's chest.

The Olmeri Captain and his officers were clearly surprised to see her and couldn't hide it. They knew about the Masters of Ras'alhague. Their expeditions had met a few of the Keepers and they would prefer to not meet any of them ever again. Every time they met one of these Keepers, they had to retreat. Every time. They didn't like it. Not at all.

"Greetings Ambassador," the Olmeri Captain replied. "We had no idea you were aboard. From the erratic way that shuttle was flying, it seemed to us it was lost and did not have an adequate pilot. We were only trying render assistance," he said.

The Ambassador smiled politely. "He's deliberately being insulting by not giving his name and his ship's name. It's standard protocol for a Captain to identify himself or herself. He can't possibly expect me to buy the 'render assistance' line. They were far too aggressive. Plus, a scan would have picked up the signal from my personal seal on the shuttle. They knew there was an ambassador on board and they came after my ship anyway. This isn't good," she thought. "Thank you for coming to our aid, Captain. Luckily for us, the Magellan was close by," she said.

As the Olmeri Captain was talking, Beth put a clip of a treaty signing on a distant planet on a screen he could clearly see. If they were going to make the Olmeri believe the treaty signing happened elsewhere, showing them footage from somewhere else was a good way to start.

On another screen, N'amani put up some archive footage of a trade mission they completed two years earlier to the Elnath system on the opposite side of the local neighborhood. The footage showed them entering the system.

Beth began to bring the footage together on a third screen as if she was going about her normal duties.

The Ambassador noticed the Olmeri Captain had changed his focus. She turned slightly to where she could see Beth working with the clips. She signaled Beth to turn it off then she turned back to the video link. She frowned and shook her head, looked back again, and frowned. She turned to face the main screen. "Hardly, Captain. We are returning from some trade meetings. I'm sure you know how those go. Signing agreements, recordings, and dinners. We took an unplanned detour. Then we had some trouble with our navigation systems and ended up off course. We had to call the Magellan to come get us. Did you have trouble with your navigation too?" she asked. "Is he going to admit they had problems or not?" she thought.

"No. We have no problems with our navigation. We never have problems with our navigation," the Olmeri Captain replied.

The Ambassador smiled broadly. "That's good to know, Captain. I'm happy to hear it. Since you are here, perhaps you would like to join us for dinner? I'm sure we could find many things to talk about," she said.

"Thank you for the invitation, but no, Ambassador. Perhaps another time," the Olmeri Captain replied.

"Very well. Another time, Captain. I look forward to it," the Ambassador said. She bowed slightly and signaled Captain Logan to close the comm link. She took a deep breath and centered herself.

The Doctor slowly moved away from her.

The Ambassador was finding it harder and harder for her to recover after she did something like this. While she was talking, she had used her skills to plant several ideas the Olmeri Captain would believe were his own, including that she was very upset about his seeing that signing, that he could not trust his own navigation systems, and there was nothing in this sector they might possibly want. It took quite a bit of effort to hold those thoughts, transfer them, and have an ordinary conversation. Having the Doctor's support, literally, made it easier.

"Where did you send them?" the Doctor whispered.

"I was thinking of Rigel," the Ambassador said quietly.

The Doctor chuckled.

The Ambassador turned to face Captain Logan with a tired and grateful smile. "Please take us home, would you Captain?" she asked.

Captain Logan smiled and nodded with new-found respect. "Yes, Ma'am," he said.

The Ambassador paused at a comm link as she and the Doctor left the bridge. "Kell, N'amani, Beth, all of you, good job. Very good job. We're going home," she said.

Captain Logan watched her leave. He shook his head. He was still trying to take in what just happened. The Olmeri were ready for a fight. They wanted a fight. He was ready to fight. If that's what they wanted, he would be happy to oblige. And she did what? She stood there calmly and invited them to dinner. And they left? He saw it. Front row seat. He still didn't believe it. "This is most definitely not going to be just another diplomatic ferry assignment," he thought. He smiled to himself and sat up just a little straighter in his chair. "Set course for Fomalhaut. Let's go home," he ordered.

The crew began going about their regular duties. The ship turned gracefully and accelerated.

There would be time for debriefings and reports and all the things that had to be done later. For now, they could all sit back and enjoy today. Today was a good day.

CHAPTER 4:
INTERLUDE

The space between is not empty
Truth is found on the middle ground

ANYWHERE ELSE
A LOCAL SHUTTLE

The Council Chambers on Pelscara were in a large central city that was not that much different from the large cities on Dagon. Open walkways lined with trees led to and from well-kept, modern buildings. Local travel was a problem. They didn't have a transport system. It wasn't easy to get around unless you could fly one of their local craft. They had a pretty good system for managing low-level flights. Altitudes and speeds were restricted by craft and flight plan. Navigation routes were well-managed. Otherwise, there weren't many options.

Kell was outside the Council Chambers building in a small, local shuttle waiting for the Ambassador. He watched as the Ambassador came out of the building. She strode down the walkway with far more determination than usual. She was clearly not happy.

"Where to, Ambassador?" Kell asked as she got in. He was trying to humor her by pretending to be a taxi driver. It didn't work.

"Not here. Let's be somewhere else," the Ambassador said.

Kell deftly moved the small craft into the express departure lane. They were on their way.

"Could you find us a place to have something to eat? Where there aren't going to be onlookers? Somewhere quiet? And obscure?" the Ambassador asked.

"It went well, did it?" Kell asked. He knew full well from her demeanor and her request that it didn't. The only time she was on a mission and wanted to go somewhere she wouldn't be seen was when there'd been a problem.

"Swimmingly," the Ambassador said. "We were discussing the seating arrangements for the reception that is supposed to follow the Treaty Signing next month. The First Minister for Culture suggested that rather than attending the reception, I should make a few remarks then leave. After all, it was going to be a gathering of dignitaries to celebrate the treaty signing and why did I need to be there," she said.

Kell's mouth dropped open. His eyes got big. He couldn't restrain himself. "He said what?" he asked. He was laughing and crying and worried all at the same time. "Oh dear, I wonder if she...?" he thought. "And may I ask...," he said aloud not intending to finish the sentence.

"Yes. Why, yes, yes I did. I most definitely did," the Ambassador replied.

"Oh, the Council will not be pleased," Kell said. He shook his head. He knew full well what an understatement that was.

"Y'think?" the Ambassador said sharply. She looked down. "I'm sorry, Kell. That came out very rude. I'm still fuming over this. It's not your fault. I shouldn't snap at you. I am sorry," she said.

"Don't worry, Ambassador. I'm not fragile," Kell said. He nodded and smiled.

The Ambassador chuckled. "No, you are not. And I am grateful for that every day," she said.

Kell shook his head. "I still remember that general assessment we went out to do a few years ago. The one that really didn't go well. We left the same day we arrived. When we got back, the High Council summoned you. They weren't happy," he said.

The Ambassador nodded. "No, they weren't. Neither was I. The introductions had just started when their Regent decided he wasn't going to speak with a mere ambassador. He told me

I should go ask his clerks for copies of the documents if I wanted to review their application. I tried to tell him that I wasn't there to review documents. He proceeded to tell me that if I wasn't there to review their application documents I could leave. I agreed and told him exactly what I thought. We left. The Regent didn't realize what he'd done until he got the rejection notice. He filed a whole series of protests. That's why the High Council summoned me. After they reviewed my recording, they agreed with my decision. They did tell me I could have made my points without quite so much clarity," she said.

"So, I'm guessing you ...?" Kell asked.

"Why yes. I was quite clear. Very, very clear," the Ambassador said. She smiled.

"You do have a way of cutting straight to the point when you want," Kell said.

The Ambassador smiled. "Thank you," she said.

Kell laughed and looked over at the navigation-search screen. "Ambassador, there's a place showing up in a local area search that seems to have good reviews. Not so many guests right now," he said.

"That sounds perfect. I don't want to be seen. I'll get changed," the Ambassador said. She slid to the back seat and took off her outer robe, sash, and belt. She put on a travel tunic and tied her belt around it. She folded her robe around her sash and put them in her bag.

Kell brought the craft down on the roof and parked it in a marked space. A few other craft were scattered in other spaces. He opened the hatch and stepped out. "Ready when you are, Ambassador. Bring your sunglasses. It's bright out here," he said.

"Thank you. Very smooth landing. I didn't feel it," the Ambassador said. She grinned at Kell as she walked out.

"Timing. If I break to slow down and then, just before we stop release the brake just a bit, the craft will gently glide to rest. Mostly. Makes the landing barely noticeable," Kell said.

The Ambassador shook her head. "Whatever it is, you are extremely good at it. Thanks. It is a bit toasty out here. How do we get inside?" she asked.

Kell pointed. "There's a stairway in that direction," he said.

SOMEWHERE QUIET
A SMALL CAFE ON PELSCARA

The Ambassador and Kell walked across the roof to a wide stairway.

Two floors down, they entered a small restaurant. The entryway was cool and not brightly lit. Most of the light came from a bank of fish tanks that took up one wall.

"Much cooler here," Kell said. He looked around. "It's very much like the pictures," he said.

"It's not crowded," the Ambassador said. She sighed happily. She looked at the fish tanks. "They have a fish special on the menu?" she asked.

Kell turned his head and smiled. "Actually, that is the menu, Ambassador," he said.

"Oh. Maybe not today," the Ambassador said.

Kell laughed. "How about over there?" He pointed to a table about halfway towards the back.

The Ambassador nodded. "Good," she said.

Kell took a seat with a view of the door. He liked to be able to watch the doors, especially when they were off somewhere.

The Ambassador took the chair next to him with her back to the wall.

A waiter came over with a small plate of pickled cabbage.

They each ordered a bowl of the 'house special' soup and a tall glass of the 'house special' beer.

The waiter came back quickly with the beer.

"Cheers?" Kell asked. He raised his glass. It was more of a question.

"Not really. But sure, cheers," the Ambassador replied dryly with a bit of resignation in her voice.

They both took a sip, looked at each other, shrugged, and drank more.

"Not bad," the Ambassador said. She sipped a little for the taste.

"It's pretty good," Kell said. He took a long drink. "So, em... are you going to tell me what happened? How did they get to where they were telling you not to attend? I thought you were close to a final treaty?" he asked.

The Ambassador scowled. "I did too. We had finished all the text changes. It finally seemed like we were past the whole 'beneath my station" snobbery. Then, when we started talking about the seating arrangements for the signing ceremony, it came roaring back. They don't think of me as an emissary or our negotiating teams as diplomats. We are considered servants in their culture, so why should it be any different in ours," she said.

"How did they expect to deal with the Central Alliance Charter of Rights?" Kell asked.

The Ambassador shook her head. "That was always going to be a problem. They didn't seem to take the Charter seriously. It was just another one of the 'negotiating points' they tried to make go away," she said.

Kell frowned. "The Charter of Rights is what holds the Alliance together. It sets out the framework for the rights guaranteed to the people on all the planets in the Alliance," he said.

The Ambassador nodded. "It's one of the keys to the Basic Framework. I'd finally gotten them to agree to a provisional signing. We started talking about the signing reception. The First Minister decided he was going to take the center chair for the ceremony. He then proceeded to tell me that I didn't need to attend but if I wanted to make a few remarks before leaving he would allow it. I checked him twice. I asked him to consider carefully what he was saying. He was adamant. He didn't want me there. So, I told him that I accepted his decision, congratulated him on having completed the seating arrangements, and conveyed my certainty that his dignitaries would enjoy all the wonderful food he had arranged for the reception. He seemed surprised that I wasn't making a bigger fuss. He was immensely pleased that I was leaving. Then, he demanded I tell him who was going to come to sign the treaty for the Central Alliance. I carefully explained to him that as a First Contact Ambassador and Leader of the Alliance Delegation, signing the treaty was my charter. And since he didn't want the signatory for the Central Alliance at the reception, there would be no signing. I went on to inform him that I would be reconsidering all the trade terms we had agreed, the agricultural support teams we had planned to send would not be coming, and that if he ever thought about dismissing any of our emissaries again, I would be pleased to ensure he was no longer First Minister of anything but his own ass. Then, I took my leave," she said. She took another drink and shook her head. Her jaw was tight and her shoulders tense.

Kell's jaw dropped when she said 'carefully explained.' He'd only seen her 'carefully explain' things once or twice before. She wasn't playing. He knew the level of trust the Alliance placed in her. It was well deserved. She would not have her charter otherwise. This level of insult was beyond anything he could have imagined. He had seen her tolerate all sorts of slights and stalls to try to get a better negotiating position. Someone was delayed. Another had an unforeseen issue. The documentation isn't quite ready. Slights like those were common. But to come out and directly tell her that she would not be welcome to attend the signing dinner for a treaty she was instrumental in brokering and would be the primary signer for was beyond anything he could imagine. "The only reason there is any treaty to be discussed at all is due to your efforts. And you are the one who is supposed to sign it!" he said.

Kell motioned to the waiter to bring more beer. He looked at the Ambassador and shook his head. "There's more to it, isn't there? There's something you're holding back," he said. They'd been on too many missions together. He knew when something was wrong.

"Yes," the Ambassador said. She took a long drink.

The waiter brought the beer and soup. He also brought some small plates with breads and crackers. They stopped talking while he put the glasses and dishes on the table.

The Ambassador looked down and blew across the soup bowl. Steam rose up. "During every meeting, the First Minister picked at the smallest details. He ranted that we were inept and incapable of typing correctly. He twisted the simplest statements into something that needed hours to resolve. At every step, he looked for another way to create some issue, some problem, some "one thing" that had to be solved before anything else could be discussed. And when we finally resolved 'that one thing,' he found something else. I finally realized he wasn't interested in actually brokering the deal or in making sure everything was well-designed. He was interested in making me jump through hoops," she said.

"I don't understand. Jump through hoops?" Kell asked.

The Ambassador nodded. "It's an old-Earth expression. It means to set up obstacles to make someone work harder. He wanted to set things up so he was always in charge, always telling me what to do. Then, he'd make it as difficult as possible to do whatever it was. He twisted whatever I said into something else, using the smallest variations to make his point. He made it clear that he thought I was intellectually and otherwise inferior. He doesn't have much use for Terrans," she said.

Kell could see something was very wrong. "Ambassador, you've run into this sort of thing a few times. It always makes your negotiations more difficult. But you managed it. You're still not telling me something. What else happened?" he asked.

The Ambassador looked down sadly. "We were talking about trade dispute rules. He kept interrupting. I finally had to ask him to let me finish before he made his objections. He went on a tirade. He shouted. He accused me of insulting him by insisting he listen to me. Then, he told me that Pelscaran females learn from childhood to be quiet when a male is speaking and that I needed to learn from their good example," she said.

Kell's jaw dropped open. "He said THAT?! He actually said that to you?" he asked.

The Ambassador nodded and took another drink.

"He didn't stop there, did he?" Kell asked.

The Ambassador shook her head. "No. He started ranting about minor imperfections in the drafts. I tried to explain that everything we had agreed was included. The only difference was that we had formatted the pages to include more signatures. He refused to look at any of it. I tried to tell him that the terms needed to be reviewed and each page signed before the treaty could be signed. That's when he told me that as a mere ambassador, my views on the terms or the treaty were of no consequence," she said. She took another long drink.

Kell shook his head. "Does he have any idea what being a First Contact Ambassador for the Central Alliance means?" he asked.

The Ambassador looked up at Kell and smiled. But her eyes weren't smiling. "He's about to find out. Here's to more beer!" she said. She raised her glass.

Kell looked at her. He heard the warning in her voice but he wasn't sure what she meant. It was never easy watching her try to do what some said was impossible. She'd done it so many times he'd gotten used to her succeeding. It was hard to watch her go through all of what she'd been through in trying to get this one done and have it come to this. "The soup smells good," he said. He pulled his bowl closer and leaned over it.

The Ambassador took a spoonful. "It is pretty good soup," she said. She smiled, took another spoonful of soup picked up a slice of bread, and took a few bites. "We've been trying to get this treaty signed for 2 years. It would have been a good thing all around. The Pelscarans would get badly needed expertise on land use and planting for increased harvests plus some new equipment. The Alliance would get a preferential price on some of that harvest. But during every negotiation session, the Pelscarans found issues with petty things, such as whether or not a trade negotiator was wearing proper attire or telling the agriculture experts they should be sure to clean their shoes. They went out of their way to be insulting. But if anyone on the Alliance side said anything about their fair-use terms being too vague, they would take umbrage claiming it was insulting their integrity to ask such questions. They pressed for full schematics and complete training on the new equipment we were giving them so they could repair everything themselves. They didn't want to be able to repair it. They wanted to steal it. It was so tiring. Every time we'd give them something they wanted, they'd demand something else, something that they hadn't mentioned previously but claimed they had and we had left it out. Before they sent me, the Alliance had already been through seven teams of negotiators. The insults took a toll. The Pelscarans just kept doing whatever they could to demean and diminish. Then, they started harassing some of our...," she said. She stopped.

Kell looked down. He brushed his cheek with the back of his hand.

"Kell?" the Ambassador asked. She didn't need to.

"Yes. Every day since we've been here," Kell said. He dropped his chest a little to compose himself.

The Ambassador shook her head sadly. "Why didn't you tell me? I am so sorry. No one should have to..." she said.

Kell looked up and shrugged his shoulders. "I'm Aldaran. I've heard worse. My people have long been known for our piloting and navigation skills. Our expertise and our confidence make others envious and afraid. We're treated like outsiders who don't belong. That's why we try to keep to ourselves," he said.

The Ambassador frowned. "I know some of your history. Your people were out here exploring and escorting traders long before mine. You should have told me. You should not have had to endure it," she said.

Kell shook his head. "If I had, you would have stopped it. And that could have jeopardized your mission and the treaty. I could manage. It wasn't too bad," he said.

The Ambassador shook her head sadly, held up her hand, and looked at Kell harshly. "Don't you ever let something like that go again. I won't tolerate you being mistreated. Not now. Not ever. It. Should. Not. Have. Happened," she said.

Kell nodded with appreciation. "Pilamayaye. Thank you," he said.

The Ambassador sighed. "Well, the Council sent me to sort this out. The discussions needed to be concluded and so they have been. Cheers!" she said. She raised her glass.

Kell chuckled and raised his glass to meet hers. As much as the taunts and snide remarks hurt him, he knew she was much more deeply hurt than she was going to let him see. She had an incredible pedigree. She was actual royalty and exceedingly well-respected at home. She'd spent countless hours in study and practice, always looking for a way to turn around a difficult situation that would create benefits for everyone. For them to treat her so disrespectfully was more than wrong. "So, what are you going to do?" he asked.

The Ambassador grinned and pointed at the empty beer glasses. "Go back to my quarters and check in with the Council. Then, I'm going to take a nap," she said.

"That's not quite what I meant," Kell said.

"Yes. I know. But it is what I'm going to do," the Ambassador said.

Kell chuckled and shook his head.

They got up to leave.

"Really though, what are you going to do?" Kell asked again as they were walking across the roof.

The Ambassador looked at him for a minute. She'd known what she was about to do might need to be done before they left for Pelscara. "I'm going to get dressed. Then I'm going to have a conversation with the First Minister and the Pelscaran Council. I'd be pleased if you would attend," she said.

"Thank you, Ambassador," Kell replied. He nodded. He was intrigued. She didn't 'get dressed' very often. Getting dressed was her way of saying that she was going to present herself as a First Contact Ambassador for the Central Alliance – with all that her title represents. Besides that, she'd invited him. He'd been present for many high-level meetings, but this was the first time she'd made a point of inviting him. He had no idea why she was inviting him now. He would find out soon enough. He took off in a slow curve towards their accommodations. He was still puzzling over what she was going to do. He both wanted to know and he didn't.

GETTING DRESSED
THE AMBASSADOR'S ROOM ON PELSCARA

The Ambassador picked up her bag and set it on the bed. She opened it, looked at it for a minute, then went over to a small desk and activated her personal relay. The signal was encrypted and encoded with her personal ID. It would be relayed with priority by any ship that picked it up. She paced the floor as she waited for the connection.

The screen lit up. "Ambassador Lawrence. This is a pleasant surprise," President Smbarak said.

"No, it's not. I wish I had better news, Madame President," the Ambassador said.

"What happened? Micha. Micha? Es-tu là avec moi? Are you there with me?" President Smbarak asked.

"Oui. Je dois te dire..., Yes. I have to tell you.... The First Minister disinvited me from the signing, said women should shut up, and Kell has been harassed," the Ambassador said. She spoke quickly not wanting to say any of it. Her hands were shaking. She was more than annoyed. She caught her breath, trying to keep back her anger and her tears.

"Mon Dieu! Quelle un diable! Que vous et Kell allez bien? My god what a devil! Are you and Kell alright?" President Smbarak asked.

"Allez bien. N'avons pas été physiquement attaqués. We are okay. We were not physically attacked," the Ambassador said.

"Il y a au moins ça. At least there's that," President Smbarak said.

The Ambassador shook her head and looked down. "The Pelscarans have repeatedly and deliberately insulted everyone from the Alliance. They have been rude and condescending. I tried to get them to look at us as partners, as friends. They could only see us as servants who must cater to them. I couldn't get past that," she said. She didn't have to report this sort of thing very often. She had almost always been able to find a way. Not this time.

"Micha, no. This is not your fault. You can't make them see what they don't want to see. We knew they were being difficult," President Smbarak said.

The Ambassador looked down and shook her head. She took another deep breath. She clenched her fists and released them. She was sad and angry and this was all just so wrong. "C'est pire. It gets worse. They wanted to exclude our Charter of Rights. I thought they understood the Charter of Rights was fundamental and they would have to accept it if they wanted to become members. But they looked at it like it was just another bargaining point," she said.

"Mon Dieu! Did you find that out before or after they disinvited you?" President Smbarak asked.

"Before. That's been the sticking point. The Pelscarans made it plain that any agreement they are going to sign is for show. They aren't going to comply," the Ambassador said.

President Smbarak sat up straighter. "For the records then, what have you decided, Ambassador?" she asked. She didn't need to ask. She knew.

The Ambassador nodded. "Madame President, the Pelscarans are not ready to join the Alliance. They are too full of themselves and too busy trying to tell others what to do. They don't want to get along with others unless the others are servants who must take their orders. Even the basic idea that abusing those who are of a lower station or different is wrong does not appear to be something they are ready to consider. They see everything as a power game. Whoever has more, gives the orders," she said.

"I agree. They are not ready," President Smbarak said firmly.

The Ambassador shifted back a little. "There's one more thing I need to tell you. I am getting dressed to go meet with their Council," she said.

"You're getting dressed?" President Smbarak asked.

"Yes. I have something to say to their First Minister before I leave," the Ambassador replied.

"Normally, I'd ask you to explain. Not this time. You have my full support for whatever you are going to do. They need to understand that what they have done is not acceptable. They also need to understand what the Central Alliance and our ambassadors represent," President Smbarak said.

"Thank you, Aliel. I'm grateful for your support. It helps. It really does make a difference," the Ambassador said.

President Smbarak nodded and then frowned. "You will be called to appear before the High Council," she said.

The Ambassador sighed. She dropped her shoulders. "I understand. I failed," she said.

President Smbarak tightened her jaw, slapped the table in front of her, and pointed at the Ambassador. "No, you didn't fail Ambassador Lawrence. You did not fail. You have done exactly what we sent you to do: resolve the issues and come to a decision. You did more than that. You have provided us with valuable insights. Now, we know who the Pelscarans are and what they will do. You have our thanks and our gratitude," she said.

The Ambassador smiled slightly and nodded. She'd not seen her friend quite this upset before. "Thank you, Aliel," she said with gratitude and appreciation. If there were any issue about this when she came before the Council, she had no doubt that Aliel was going make it crystal clear where she stood.

"Be careful, Micha. Be very careful. This is going to cause a stir," President Smbarak said.

"Probably. Thank you, Aliel," the Ambassador said. She closed the comm link.

SMALL AND LIGHT (RECALL)
THE TRAINING COMPOUND ON RAS 2

The Ambassador was resting in her guest room on Pelscara. She had packed. Her bags were next to the door ready to go. Her robes were draped over the end of the bed A small packet wrapped in gold cloth lay on top of them. She had already notified other members of the delegation that they would be leaving immediately. She and Kell would leave right after her meeting with the Council. She sat up and stretched. She looked over at her dark gold and deep red robes and smiled a little. She picked up the packet, held it in one hand, and gently peeled open the worn gold cloth. "What has it been? Thirty years?" she thought.

She remembered the day Master Tai gave it to her.

She had been training all day. It was hot. The ground was dry. She left tracks as she moved through the sets, over and over again. None of them were easy to do. She had stopped to rest.

Master Tai came over to her with a small package in his hands. It was wrapped in a simple, gold-colored cloth and tied around on all sides with a red ribbon. He held the packet with both hands and extended it towards her. "Here. This is for you," he said.

"Thank you, Master Tai," Micha said, surprised and bewildered. She took the packet with both hands. She had learned it was the polite way to give or receive anything. "What is it?" she thought. She squeezed the packet as she put it with her things.

Master Tai had taught them that opening a wrapped gift immediately was impolite. The package should be put away and opened later, in private.

So, it wasn't until later in the day, after she went back to her room, that she opened the packet.

She held the packet with one hand and pulled the knot in the center. The ribbon fell away. She took each of the corners and laid them back. Inside was what looked to be a small square of cream-colored fabric. She recognized the cloth immediately. It was legendary. When she picked it up, it unfolded to reveal an inner shirt of the most elegant silk and mithril weave. It glimmered with tiny rainbows even in the dim light. "Oh my. Oh my! I... me? I've been...!" she said. She started crying and laughing at the same time.

Master Tai giving her the shirt had a deeper significance. Only those accepted for inside training were given such things. It was both an acknowledgement of her work thus far and an invitation for her to begin the next level of training.

She put it on. It was an amazing cloth; light and heavy at the same time. It seemed to change colors in the light, sometimes silver, sometimes white, sometimes whatever was nearby. It was as if it became part of her, like another layer of skin, moving as she moved. She'd never seen a shirt like this up close before. She looked down at the shirt. "It fits me perfectly," she whispered. She smiled. A tear welled up in her eye. She sat down and hugged her knees, rocking back and forth rubbing the sleeves. "It fits me. It fits me," she repeated.

She always kept the shirt with her. She didn't wear it often, only on certain occasions. This was going to be one of them. As light and airy as it appeared, the cloth was almost impenetrable.

FINISHING TOUCHES
THE AMBASSADOR'S ROOM ON PELSCARA

The Ambassador had almost finished getting dressed. It took a few minutes to put on all the various layers.

She fastened her Family Crest to her collar. It was another of those things she only wore on certain occasions. Her ancestors had been among the first to leave the Sol system. Her family were among those who led the effort to unite the systems and create the Alliance. She looked at her bags, opened one, and took out a smaller bag. She pulled a small belt out of the bag and set it on the bed next to her outer robe. She was going to wear it. But putting it on could wait a few minutes more.

It wasn't an ordinary belt. It was the Belt of Orion. It was made of cream color braid interlaced with gold and rose crystal threads. The front clasp was three-color gold with a fire opal in the center, the Ancient Jewel of Alnilam. She was only the third adept to be able to wear it. The first time Master Tai suggested she try she could barely pick it up. It was too heavy. Only those who had the strength to see and fully accept themselves as who they are could wear it.

She put on her outer robe with the Insignia of the Alliance, pulled her Ambassador's Sash with her medals and awards over her shoulder, and fastened her First Contact pin on her collar.

Finally, she picked up the belt and put it on. The opal began to glow. The gold and red fire inside became stronger and more insistent. She closed her robes to hide it. "After all I have put up with, it's time to put a stop to their insults. This is going to be fun," she thought. She was half trying to convince herself and half knowing she was going to enjoy it. She picked up her plain travel cloak and took a deep breath. "Kell, ..." she said into the comm link.

"Yes, Ambassador. I'm parked out front," Kell replied.

"Thank you, I'll be right out," she said. She stood for just a second behind the closed door, lowered her head, and took one more deep breath. "Here I go," she thought. She opened the door and walked out.

Kell looked up just as she came out. He had only seen her fully dressed like this a few times. She seemed to be floating more than walking, the layers of gold and rust swirling around her. There was something about the way she moved that made him was happy he was waiting for her and not trying to stand in her way. "Good afternoon, Ambassador," he said. He eyed her robes as she got in.

The Ambassador smiled. "This is more or less what I look like when I go to meet the High Council," she said.

"Impressive," Kell said. He nodded.

"I'm going to meet the Pelscaran Council as a First Contact Ambassador and a Keeper of Earth. If they want to insult me, I'm going to make sure they know who I am," she said. She raised her back, dropped her shoulders, lowered her chin, turned her head just slightly to one side, and smiled.

Kell grinned.

"Let's go," the Ambassador said.

Kell adeptly moved the small craft into the local lane. It wasn't far.

WHAT IS TRUE
THE COUNCIL CHAMBERS ON PELSCARA

The Ambassador and Kell arrived at the building, parked and walked up the wide steps to the Council Chambers together. An open landing led to a set of tall glass doors. The doors opened as they approached. Inside, the large hall was mostly quiet.

"We've spent so much time here. The trade teams have all worked so hard. I wanted to have a nice, quiet signing, celebrate a little, and go home. Ah well...," the Ambassador said.

"We get that last part, don't we? The going home part?" Kell asked.

"Yes. We do get that," the Ambassador replied with a grin. She had asked for the meeting. She told the Pelscarans that she had spoken with the Alliance and now, she needed to speak with them. She fully expected the Ministers to believe she was going to apologize after having been chastised by their Council. They would be eager to let her know what a mistake she had made to say such things to their First Minister. She was counting on it.

Most of the Pelscaran Ministers were already in the Council Chambers. A few were standing just to one side of the entrance. They all had snide expressions as if they were jackals waiting for the chance to berate her again.

"She's here to beg us to forgive her," one of them said.

"I bet their Council President had a thing or two to say to her," another said.

Kell heard them and looked sideways at the Ambassador. She seemed to be smiling just a little. Not much. But there was a hint. "She set this up! She is going to do something. And she's enjoying it!" he thought.

The Ambassador walked over to a landing just above three wide stairs leading to the main floor. She stood there quietly as she waited for the Pelscarans to take their seats.

Several of the Ministers kept talking. Finally, one by one, they moved to their seats.

The Ambassador looked around the room. She was still on the landing and still wearing the plain cloak over her robes. "Good evening, Ministers. I thank you for agreeing to meet with me on such short notice," she said.

"If you wanted a meeting with us, you should at least be dressed properly," the First Minister said.

The others all nodded. "Not even dressed properly," they echoed.

The Ambassador took a step back and motioned to Kell. "Do not come onto the floor. Watch from over there," she said sternly. She pointed towards an anteroom with an open viewing area where visitors could watch the proceedings. She twisted slightly removing the plain cloak and handing it to Kell with one broad sweeping motion. The Pelscarans liked showy and dramatic presentations. She was about to give them one they would remember for some time.

Kell nodded and went over to where she'd pointed.

The Ambassador started down the steps.

Kell turned his head from side to side. He wasn't quite sure what he was seeing. She seemed to get taller as she strode out to the middle of the floor. Her robes floated around her.

But she seemed to be getting heavier, as if with each step she took, she carried more weight.

The First Minister squinted as he stood up. "Well, at least you look more like an ambassador now," he said.

The other Ministers laughed.

"We only agreed to this meeting so you could apologize to me and beg our forgiveness. Hurry up and get on with it," the First Minister said.

The other Ministers nodded. "Shameful," one said.

"How undignified," another said.

"Calls herself an ambassador, ha ha," another said.

The Ambassador kept walking. She stopped in the center of the floor. The fire from the opal got stronger and deeper until it began to radiate a deep red all around her. The dark light from her belt grew stronger, pervasive, penetrating. It seemed to flow around her and through her. For a brief moment, she seemed to disappear into the darkness. Then, a bright light started to radiate around her. A dark puddle appeared below her feet. It was as if she was not standing on anything. It was as though she was suspended somewhere in-between.

The Ministers had been so busy repeating their chastisements of her to each other they hadn't noticed the light. First one, then another saw it. They stopped talking.

The Ambassador took the opportunity. "Thank you for agreeing to meet with me," she said.

"Yes, well, get on with it. We have things to do," the First Minister said.

The other Ministers all nodded.

"Yes, yes, get on with it. Hurry up," a few of them muttered.

The Ambassador smiled and deflected the insult with a polite, deferential tone. "Thank you for your indulgence, First Minister. I will be brief," she said.

"As well you should," the First Minister sniped at her.

The Ambassador looked around the room. "Over the two years of our negotiations, our teams have had some productive exchanges," she said.

The Ministers all muttered a version of "not really" and "not so much" to themselves, shaking their heads.

The Ambassador smiled quietly. She had expected them to be contrary. What she was saying was not for their benefit. It was for the official record. "The Central Alliance includes many worlds and many cultures. We recognize that we don't always agree and that we must learn about and try to respect the customs of other cultures. That is the basis for our Charter of Rights. We have worked very hard to develop this understanding and encourage all our member worlds to do the same. Over time, we have learned that it is important for those who want to join the Central Alliance to both understand why it was formed and to support the principles on which it is founded," she said. As she spoke, the light around her intensified, becoming deeper and more penetrating. The pool under her covered the entire floor.

The First Minister scoffed. "We really don't care that much what you think is important. The Central Alliance has told us for two years that they want this treaty. You have caused this problem with your attitude and your bad manners. You need to admit your mistakes and apologize. You are nothing but an ambassador. You deliver messages. You don't speak for the Alliance. We don't need to listen to you. Where's the President of the Alliance? Maybe we should talk to him," he said.

The Ambassador smiled. "He is going to walk right into it," she thought. "First Minister, speaking with the President of the High Council won't do you any good in this matter," she said.

"I don't care what you think will do me good. I want to talk to the President. You go call him and tell him to come here himself if he wants any treaty with us," the First Minister shot back.

The Ambassador smiled. "He's hooked," she thought. "First Minister, I would be extremely happy to go call President Aliel Smbarak. In fact, I spoke with her just a short time ago. She and I are good friends. However, it seems a waste of your time and hers to call her just so she can tell you that you should listen to what I am about to tell you," she said.

They all stopped chattering and looked at her again.

"How dare you! No woman can be the President. What is this?! Who do you think you are?" the First Minister demanded. He puffed up his chest. His face turned purple.

Kell shook his head. He could not remember ever having seen someone treat her this badly. As he watched, a faint golden spiral began to turn inside the dark red light around her.

The Ambassador looked straight at him. "I am Ambassador Micha Lawrence, daughter of Tor E'ran of Vega 9 and First Disciple of Master Tai Aragon of Ras'alhague. I hold a First Contact Charter and I speak for the Central Alliance. You have made every effort to make these negotiations as tedious and difficult as possible. You have been abusive. You have treated our teams as if they are your servants," she said. Her voice seemed to penetrate every part of the chamber.

The First Minister shouted back, "No. We did none of those things. Your side was constantly whining about the details. You never did anything we told you to do. You didn't want to cooperate," he said.

This was the Pelscarans' standard negotiating method – to make up something or find some small thing to use to lay blame. They used it as a bargaining ploy. The natural response for someone who did want to cooperate would be to offer more concessions as a way to demonstrate a desire for cooperation. The Pelscarans got quite a few concessions that way. Not this time.

This time, the Ambassador shook her head. "You have done all those things. You are doing the same thing now," she said. She was offering the First Minister the opportunity to wag his finger in her face in front of all the other ministers. She didn't expect him to pass it up.

"I am doing no such thing. I said no such thing. You are trying to cause another problem," the First Minister shouted. He pointed his finger at her.

The Ambassador smiled. "I can't hear you. Why don't you come out here and tell me to my face instead of shouting at me? Come out here and tell me how it is you think I'm causing a problem," she said.

The First Minister huffed and puffed again. "If you can't hear me that's your problem. I don't need to do anything. It's all your problem. You started it," he said.

"Are you afraid to step into the light, First Minister?" the Ambassador asked suppressing a grin.

"If you can stand there, so can I," he said. He puffed up arrogantly and walked out onto the floor.

STEP INTO THE LIGHT
THE COUNCIL CHAMBERS ON PELSCARA

The Ambassador was standing in the fire of the Ancient Jewel of Alnilam. It radiated a deep red that was equal parts light and dark. It revealed everything about anyone who was in the light to anyone who was touched by it. She would see exactly who he was. Since she was also in the light, he would see her. But it was more a mildly perceptual thing for the receiver, something they could dismiss as a brief feeling or an odd thought. Anyone who stepped into the light would be instantly confronted with all her memories, as Tor E'ran's daughter, a princess of the Alliance, as a Keeper of Earth, and as an Adept in the Ancient Arts. It would not be pleasant for them. Even when she kept control of her thoughts, it would be a lot for the other person to deal with. But if she was careful, the damage could be kept to a minimum. "Was there something you wanted to say, First Minister?" she asked. She tilted her head to one side.

The First Minister started towards her. The floor under him seemed to be disappearing into a dark puddle and he was sinking deeper and deeper into it. The light around her poked his skin like sharp needles. He looked the Ambassador, bewildered and awed. He could see her as she was. She wasn't the small, inept creature he had been taunting. She was so much stronger than he had even thought to imagine. He was afraid of her now. He tried to take a step back but he couldn't move. He tried to open his mouth, but he couldn't.

The other Ministers had been laughing and talking. They noticed the First Minister, struggling to speak and unable to take another step. They grew quiet.

The Ambassador looked around the room. "I now speak for the Central Alliance. We seek peaceful relationships and trade. We have spent countless hours trying to negotiate a

trade agreement with you. At each step, you found something
to fault us for yet never once suggested you were in error. We
had many discussions over things that shouldn't have been an
issue, but were. You have been all too ready to disparage us
and make us the brunt of your jokes," she said.

The First Minister waved his hands. He was still trying to
open his mouth.

The Ambassador looked down at him. "The light you are
standing in is the Fire of Alnilam. While you are in it, you can
speak only if what you will say is true. You cannot speak now
because what you want to say is not true. You have ONE
opportunity to say something truthful. Is there something you
want to say, First Minister?" she asked.

The light around her dimmed slightly.

The other Ministers all looked at the First Minister,
nodding and waving to encourage him to say something.

The First Minister began slowly. "Ambassador Lawrence,
we regret giving you the impression...," he said.

"What impression?" the Ambassador interrupted sharply.
"Be careful what you say," she said.

The light above her turned a brilliant fire red, filling the
entire room. The golden spiral took on a clear bright white hue
and wrapped around her. The pool below her turned such a
deep red it was black.

"We ... em... we regret giving you the impression that we
were ungrateful to you and to the Alliance. We did some
things we should not have done," the First Minister said.

The other Ministers nodded and looked contrite. There
was clearly more to this Ambassador than they thought and
they would rather not find out what else she could do.

"Yes. You did," the Ambassador said in a flat, matter-of-
fact tone. The light around her became less intense. The pool
below her took on a reddish hue again. "There is no excuse for

what you did. It created problems no one needed and made for a difficult negotiation. The way you have treated our teams is completely unacceptable. I was planning to return for the treaty signing next month, but you disinvited me," she said. The light around her grew more intense, sending out a volley of sparks like porcupine needles.

The First Minister winced in pain as they struck him.

The Ambassador looked around the room. The light changed again, becoming less intense. "You will learn our Charter of Rights and you will prepare a plan for how you are going to address these rights in your society. In two months, an emissary will return with a new framework that requires you address the manner and the types of communications we will have. At the first sign of anything like what I or my team have experienced, we will end the negotiations. Permanently," she said. She looked around the room again. "I see that you all understand. Good," she said. She turned to leave. The light began to recede.

IN THE SPACE BETWEEN
OUTSIDE THE COUNCIL CHAMBERS ON PELSCARA

The Ambassador walked up the steps.

Kell had been watching from the viewing area. He stepped out of the anteroom and handed her the plain cloak he'd been holding for her.

She paused to pull it over her shoulders and close her robes as they walked outside. As long as she wore the belt, the jewel would glow. "Let's go." she said. She smiled at Kell as gently as she could.

Kell hesitated. He had seen her too. Powerful, with a will that would not be stopped; a deep pain he could feel but not fathom, and a grim resolve that gave her command. As much as he had seen and appreciated her quiet approach and efforts to be kind, he now understood where that strength came from. It was dark, very dark, that part of her. As if she stood between, neither in the darkness nor in the light, and yet part of both; as if they were pulling her apart.

The Ambassador stopped and touched his arm gently. "I know what you saw. I invited you to see it. Sometimes I'm afraid of who I am, too," she said softly. She looked down for a minute. Then straight at him.

Kell looked at her with a new understanding and a new level of respect. Her eyes had a clarity and a depth he had not seen before. It was as if she was looking through him, to who he was inside, straight to all he kept hidden. He was afraid.

"There is as much darkness as there is light. To stand in the fire is to be pulled in both directions and to risk being pulled too far in either direction. The mind must be quiet and the spirit strong. There can be no doubts," she said. She could see his fear. It wasn't the right time. She stopped. "You have a clear mind. Your spirit is strong. You know how to stand. I've seen your courage many times," she said.

Kell took a deep breath and pulled himself up just a little straighter.

"Having this very nice inner shirt helped," the Ambassador said changing the subject. She opened the sleeve of her outer shirt to show him the fabric.

Kell smiled with appreciation and relief. "It's beautiful. What is it? The way it shines, as if the light is coming from within," he said.

The Ambassador nodded. "It was a gift from Master Tai. I don't wear it often. It protects me. It's made of a silk and mithril cloth that makes it almost impenetrable," she said. She looked at Kell thoughtfully. Her expression changed to one much more serious. "We have something to do. It won't be easy," she said.

"Ambassador?" Kell asked.

"We have something we are going to do. It will require all our skills, even the ones we keep hidden. We can have no doubts. Today, I invited you to see something that few have ever seen. Miyé wačhíŋniyaŋpe ló. I trust you," she said.

"Pilamayaye. Iȟámayaye." Thank you. You make me smile." Kell said. He realized fully for the first time that she wasn't using his language to be polite or to encourage him. She was trying to reach him on a much deeper level, as if she wanted to talk to his grandmother. Somehow, he knew his grandmother wanted to hear her. She knew. She understood. He didn't know how, but she did. He smiled.

"Kell, could we take a scenic route home? I'd like some time to think," the Ambassador asked quietly.

"Of course, Ambassador. We can skirt the Eridani system. There's a place I know where we can get some fresh soup." Kell said. He looked at her sideways, grinning.

"Yangroutang?" the Ambassador asked.

Kell nodded.

The Ambassador's face brightened "Let's go!" she said.

CHAPTER 5:
ENDINGS AND BEGINNINGS
PART 1: CONSULTATIONS

Before the ending of one, two begins
It contains the beginning of the next one
And decides the ending of the last one

PRELUDE
AMBASSADOR'S QUARTERS ON THE MAGELLAN

The Ambassador and her team had gone out on a routine meet and greet mission to the Altair system. She was in her quarters on the Magellan struggling to prepare her mission report. "Record. When we arrived, the ... No. Scratch that. We arrived in the morning. The ... Now what? They don't want a weather report," she said.

The comm chime sounded.

The Ambassador looked up at the screen and smiled a huge smile. "President Smbarak, good evening. I'm so glad you called," she said.

"Good evening, Ambassador. You are working late," President Smbarak said.

"Not sure if working quite captures it. I've been trying to put something together for N'amani. The best I have so far is a weather report," the Ambassador said. She dropped her head, frowned, then looked up.

President Smbarak laughed. "That's why you seemed so grateful when I called," she said.

The Ambassador nodded. "I took notes from the private meetings to give to N'amani," she said. She grinned, shifted her shoulders, and sat up a little taller. She was clearly trying for an ata-girl.

President Smbarak frowned a little. "And?" she asked.

The Ambassador dropped her chin and looked up. "I can't read some of my notes. I tried though," she said.

President Smbarak tried not to laugh. "So now you are?" she asked.

"Trying to record the summary that N'amani needs to make sense out of what I have so he can prepare a full report," the Ambassador said.

"Great. When can we expect the report?" President Smbarak asked.

The Ambassador laughed. "You want miracles, Aliel? I took notes," she said.

"Yes, Micha. I'm happy you took notes. Next time, maybe, I don't know, something you can read?" President Smbarak said.

They both laughed.

"Can't you clear N'amani so he can come with me?" the Ambassador asked.

"He's on the short-list," President Smbarak said.

"Make it shorter?" the Ambassador asked smiling.

President Smbarak nodded. "I'll try," she said.

"Thank you. So, why did you call?" the Ambassador asked.

President Smbarak frowned and sighed. "We just received a new batch of reports. They are grim. The Olmeri incursions have started again. We are getting more and more reports of trade suspensions and environmental damage, but this time on a much bigger scale. They have started going after entire systems, not just a few outlying planets here and there. They have been spotted much too close to several systems with planets that are critical to our most widely used medicines. We can't let them continue their expansion projects. I don't have an answer. We have to find a way to stop them," she said.

"Stop them? How!? We don't even know what they really want. All we know is that once they pick a target, they are relentless. They won't stop. They may change their focus for a short time, but they continue to press for whatever it was they wanted until they get it. The best we can hope for is to slow them down.... or divert them," the Ambassador said.

"Divert them? Mon Dieu! Micha, we can't send them somewhere else!" President Smbarak said.

"We can't let them keep coming either. If we could somehow find a way to limit where they can go, maybe give them something else to do and somehow set up a 'no pass' zone, we could at least buy ourselves time to find a solution. They are not benevolent overlords. The damage they do is massive. When they take over, they destroy the existing civilization and all of the planetary ecosystems," the Ambassador said.

"Yes. And that's exactly what will happen inside this 'no pass' zone you are talking about. Micha, do you understand what you are suggesting? We can't... We can't do that! We simply can't," President Smbarak said. She was not one to get excited or become emotional about much. But the idea of sending the Olmeri somewhere else was so repugnant she had to make it clear.

"I don't like it either, Aliel. I wouldn't even consider this if I thought we had any alternative. I've seen their destruction first hand. They don't leave anything of the original world alive. They put the food, water, and mineral supplies, no, the very existence, of every system in the Alliance at risk. We can't let them keep coming. We have to find a way to stop them. But for now, diverting them is our best option. Que pouvons-nous faire d'autre. What else can we do?" the Ambassador asked.

"Je ne sais pas. On est tous inquiet. I don't know. We're all worried," President Smbarak admitted.

"Il y a plus n'est pas là? There's more, isn't there?" the Ambassador asked.

"Oui," President Smbarak said. She sat very still and looked at the screen. "This is not easy for me to say and it won't be easy for you to hear. The Olmeri are actively looking for you. Everyone with you is at greater risk now. You have to be more careful, Micha. Why in all creation did you think introducing yourself was a good idea?" she asked.

The Ambassador shrugged and shook her head. "I know. I know. It couldn't be helped. They would have found Ka'len. The Kora can't protect themselves yet. I had to do something," she said.

"But now the Olmeri know who you are. You and Kell both took great risks. Lucky for all of us they couldn't figure out where you had been. You sent them to Rigel?" President Smbarak asked.

The Ambassador grinned. "They needed to go somewhere far, far away," she said.

They both laughed.

"Alright Micha. I'll get the Council to agree to your plan. We know we need more time. This could give us that. What do you have in mind for the diversion? How are you going to get them to go wherever it is you are going to send them?" President Smbarak asked.

The Ambassador smiled. "I don't know yet."

President Smbarak frowned. "That does not fill me with confidence," she said.

The Ambassador shrugged. "It's the best I can do," she said.

They both laughed at what they just said. That direct honesty was something they valued and respected in each other.

President Smbarak grew serious. "Micha, this is one of those rare times when the High Council is unanimous. You have full authorization and approval to use, find, or acquire whatever resources you need. We must find a way to stop the Olmeri," she said.

The Ambassador nodded. "I understand, Madam President. Thank you," she said.

"Don't thank me, Micha. Whatever you are going to do, I know it won't be easy, not for you or anyone with you. I will be here, awaiting your plan and your safe return. To use an old Earth expression, Godspeed, Micha. Godspeed," President Smbarak said.

The comm link faded and the screen went dark.

The Ambassador turned away from the screen, shaking her head from side to side. She didn't want to do this, not any of it. She didn't want to be dealing with the Olmeri. But here she was. "So it begins," she thought. She knew more than she wanted to know about what they were going to face. It would take all of her team and a few more. "Tomorrow will be a long day," she said. She laid down on her bed, curled up with a blanket, and went to sleep.

A NICE RECEPTION
LARGE DINING ROOM ON PROCYON 5

The Ambassador and Kell were at a reception on Procyon 5. The Pyr had been allies of the Central Alliance for several generations. They were capable fighters and shrewd traders. If there was information to be had, they likely had it. Dinners and lots of toasts with a pungent local liquor were customary and often the best way to find out what they knew.

The Ambassador was standing next to the main table in the dining room with a small group of Regents. It was quite an opulent table. Bowls of fruits and vegetables, platters of roasted meats, and steaming plates with so many tasty little things she'd quite lost track.

"To what was, what is, and what will ever be!" the Ambassador said. Her voice carried across the room. She raised her glass for a toast. She drained the small glass and turned it upside down to show it was empty.

The Regents all did the same.

Kell walked up beside her. He pointed to a tray of tiny meat pastries. "Ambassador, have you tried these?" he asked. He'd been sticking a little closer to her since the meetings on Pelscara. They'd been traveling almost non-stop for three weeks. She'd told everyone on the ship they were going out to have 'consultations.' Like that was supposed to mean something. Mostly, she'd just gone to dinner parties with the various leadership groups, taken a couple of tours of planetary facilities, and held a few meetings. She'd brought three people on board. Oddly, she had not introduced them. She had set them up with dignitary quarters and asked they not be bothered. They kept to themselves. This was supposed to be their last consultation. She had told them that much. She did like the dinner parties, though.

The Ambassador smiled with admiration. "Yes. I had several. They were nicely seasoned," she said.

Kell chuckled a little, happy to see something that pleased her.

"Ambassador Lawrence," an overly stiff, very formal voice said from behind them.

The Ambassador turned around and grinned. "Galen! Oh my! Galen. It's been too long. Far too long!" she said. She reached out towards the tall, lanky man, arms open.

Galen reached out to pull her close.

They embraced the way old friends who have been through too much together embrace. It was at once a recognition of where they had been and who they had become.

Kell smiled a little more. She was clearly very happy to see this person. He was about her age, well-built with a kind face and streaks of white in his blond hair. He wore a plain suit with an inner shirt that buttoned to the neck. There was something else about him, too. Something deeper. It wasn't a passing thing. There was a pervasive peacefulness coming from him. Just standing next to him was quieting.

"It's very good to see you again, Micha. Very good, indeed. It's been too long." Galen said. He stepped back to look at her.

"Indeed, it has been far too long. I'm so happy you could be here," the Ambassador replied.

Kell was surprised and puzzled. She planned to meet him but had not mentioned it? This was very strange. Once they were underway, she was usually very open with the whole team about what they were doing. Not this time. She'd not told them much of anything beyond the next destination.

The Ambassador noticed Kell's curiosity. She motioned for him to come closer. "Kell, please let me introduce you to my old friend, Doctor Galen Bontire. Galen is a professor at the Planetary Sciences Institute and is giving some lectures here. We trained together on Ras 2. Galen, this is my pilot, Kell," she said.

Galen blinked a couple of times and looked at the Ambassador. "Your ..." he said.

"Pilot," the Ambassador said. She nodded and smiled.

It was a big deal. They both knew it.

Galen had recognized Kell as Aldaran. He thought Kell might be an advisor or some emissary with the Alliance. Not her pilot. He knew the Aldarans' skills and their hesitancy to use them in the service of others. She must have quite a charter. "I'm pleased to meet you, Kell," Galen said. He crossed his arms, extended his palms, closed them to his sides, and bowed slightly.

Kell bowed. "Hau, čhiyé." It means "I am happy meet you, older brother," he said. He smiled at Galen.

Galen smiled at the level of respect. For Kell to call him 'brother' at their first meeting was remarkable. She and Kell must be close. "Hau, misúŋka." Galen said and bowed.

"You speak my language?" Kell asked.

"Only a few words," Galen replied.

Kell smiled. "I think more than a few," he said.

Galen grinned.

The Ambassador tilted her head back slightly and raised her eyebrows.

Kell realized she wanted to speak to Galen alone. "Ambassador, I'd like to check a few things on the shuttle and then get some rest. We have a full day tomorrow," he said.

The Ambassador smiled. "Thank you. I'll see you in the morning," she said.

"Goodnight, Ambassador, Goodnight Doctor," Kell said. He turned to leave.

Galen frowned a little. "I hope we meet again. I'd like to have a chance to actually talk with you," he said.

Kell nodded. "Another time, Doctor," he said.

The Ambassador turned to Galen and smiled one of her 'I have something to tell you and oh just wait 'till you find out,' smiles.

"I know that smile. Something I should know?" Galen asked.

"Of course. We need to catch up. I have so many stories to tell," the Ambassador joked, smiling wryly at first. Then, still smiling, the expression her eyes became deadly serious. She said nothing.

Galen saw the change and smiled bigger. "I see," he said.

"Let's get a little something more to eat. Then we can go sit on the patio. It's stopped raining. It will be refreshing," the Ambassador said.

Galen scratched his chin and raised an eyebrow. "I don't know about that. But I am hungry. We could reminisce about being at the cabin after a rainstorm instead of sitting comfortably in that nice alcove over there. I wonder if the coffee is fresh?" he asked.

The Ambassador laughed. "Not really a question, is it?" she asked.

The Pyr were fond of several beverages. Coffee was not one of them.

Galen laughed. "No, not really," he said. He picked up a plate.

The Ambassador shook her head. "Get one of those trays," she said. She pointed to a stack on the end of the table.

Galen picked up two trays and handed one to her.

They spent a few minutes loading their trays with small plates, got some coffee, and went outside.

DRINKS ON THE PATIO
AN OUTDOOR PATIO OFF THE DINING ROOM

It was a large house with a grand entrance and a large dining room. The wide patio running along the back of the house was set with small tables. A few potted plants were set around the outer edges. The air was fresh and just a little chilly. Galen and the Ambassador walked out onto the patio.

"Over there looks to be mostly dry" Galen said. He pointed to a table near the outer wall of the house. Beyond that was a little garden space, behind that, a large stone wall.

The Ambassador kept her head down as she set her tray on the table and removed the plates. "We are being closely watched," she whispered. Then, she quickly looked up and smiled brightly as if she had just said something funny and perhaps just a bit embarrassing.

"Yes, of course. I wouldn't have thought any differently!" Galen said. His voice was a little louder than necessary. "What did you do about the soup? That had to have been! Ha ha ha!! Oh, I wish I had been there!" he said.

The Ambassador started laughing with him. "I'm actually rather glad you weren't. You'd have been spending the night in the same quarters with my delegation. And you would have smelled awful!" she said.

They both laughed out loud again. Not quite as loud. Just loud enough to be heard by the guards on the other side of the patio. Two old friends catching up. Nothing to bother about.

The Ambassador held out a small plate of tiny pink and green pastries. "Try one of these," she said.

Galen took one. He bit into it. "Such interesting layers. So small and light," he said. He put the rest of it in his mouth and reached for another.

The Ambassador laughed. "It takes quite the hand to make these. My aide, N'amani can make something quite similar," she said. She pointed at the plate and wagged her finger. She took one and held it in front of her mouth, turning it from side to side as if to admire it before taking a bite. "We went to Ka'len near the Hyades Cluster. We met the Olmeri on our way home," she whispered. She took a bite. "But instead of this plain crème, he uses his grandmother's recipe with genuine maple syrup," she said.

Galen sat back and shook his head. "No way! I haven't seen real maple syrup since we left Ras 2. It's too hard to get. What the trees can produce isn't always reliable. Where did you find a supply?" he asked.

The Ambassador smiled. "N'amani is Elronym. The land has been in his family for generations. After his mother passed, the land rights went to his older sister. Sadly, she died in an accident a few years ago, so they went to him as his mother's first son. They keep three forests," she said.

"That explains it!" Galen said. He raised his hand with an a-ha gesture and brought it over his mouth. "How did you get away?" he asked. He smiled and reached for another plate.

"Why I invited them to dinner, of course!" the Ambassador said.

Galen looked skeptical. "Did you now? And what did you serve?" he asked.

"Fresh barnacles," the Ambassador said if it were a delicacy.

Galen tried not to laugh. "You will have to share the recipe," he said.

The Ambassador chuckled, shrugged her shoulders, and pouted. "As it turned out, they couldn't stay. But I made sure to invite them to come back another time. It seems they may be planning to take me up on my offer," she said. She turned her head to one side and smiled.

Galen waved his hand over the plates and shook his head. "It's really too bad they couldn't stay. I'm sure they would have enjoyed anything you prepared for them. But you say now it seems they are going to take up your invitation?" he asked.

"Yes. It looks like it will be quite soon. I've been told they are already making travel plans," the Ambassador said.

Galen was smiling but his eyes were quite serious. "Well then, it seems we need to be making some preparations of our own," he said.

The Ambassador grinned. "Indeed. I think it will be quite an event. Would you care to join us?" she asked.

Galen already knew he was being invited to go somewhere. That's why she was here. "That sounds like a wonderful party! I'd be happy to attend. Do you think your aide can make some of those pastries?" he asked in a very loud voice.

The Ambassador nodded. "That is a great idea! I will ask him. We'd have to go to the Altair system to collect the syrup. It would be, maybe a 2 or a 3-week trip from here," she said. She blinked a few times and smiled.

Galen picked up on the ruse. "Could I come with? It's been some time since I've been out. I've gotten to be something of a homebody. This would be an amazing chance to see original biodiversity. Please let me come with!" he said.

"Of course you can come with. We will be pleased to have you," the Ambassador said.

Galen grinned. "When do we leave?" he asked.

The Ambassador scratched her nose. "First thing tomorrow," she whispered. She stood up. "I could stretch my legs a bit. Why don't we walk around," she said.

They walked around the patio slowly, looking at the potted plants. A few branches from the trees along the wall hung over the patio.

Galen reached up to take a leaf. His back was to the guards. He looked at her and held the leaf for her to see. He wanted the guards to believe they were talking about the leaf. "Sure, of course. Dream on. How are you going to get us passage on a ship leaving tomorrow? I'd like a reclining seat please. Even with top credentials, it will take a week or more to even make the request let alone get it approved," he said.

The Ambassador looked at him and grinned.

Galen smiled. "You know something, don't you? Give," he said.

The Ambassador grinned bigger. She looked at the leaf and held out her hand.

Galen handed her the leaf.

The Ambassador took it and held it up in front of her face. "I have my own ship," she said.

Galen dropped his chin and opened his eyes wide. "You have whut? Holy crap! You must have one hell-of-a-charter," he said. He immediately realized he'd said that a bit too loud. He started laughing, as if she'd just told a joke.

The guards started moving towards them.

The Ambassador saw them. She grinned, took Galen's arm, and started back inside.

"Oh my! No?! Really?" Galen said with a bit of feigned disbelief. "No wonder it's going to take us a month!" he said as they walked past the guards.

"We'll have plenty to do along the way to Altair 2. You said you wanted to learn how to make those pastries," the Ambassador said.

They kept laughing as they walked into the reception hall.

"It seems I need to go prepare a few things," Galen said. He patted her arm playfully.

The Ambassador smiled. "You won't need much," she whispered. She walked over to the main table. "I really like these cookies," she said. She picked up a napkin and wrapped a few of the cookies in it.

Galen smiled and held out his hand. "I'd like some too, please," he said. He understood exactly what she meant. She wanted him to bring only essentials. One bag. Two at most.

The Ambassador handed him the cookies.

Galen put them in his pocket and walked out. "This is going to be interesting. It's going to be a challenge to get ready to leave so quickly," he thought. He'd grown accustomed to the slower pace of a quiet, scholarly life. Going out again wasn't something he relished. He had promised himself he would keep to his studies and not get involved in any interplanetary troubles. But this was Micha asking. She rarely asked for anything. There must be more to it. Much more.

SOMETHING TO GO
LARGE DINING ROOM ON PROCYON 5

The Ambassador had stayed back. She wanted to give Galen time to leave to and see if he was followed. She picked up a plate and stepped over to another table with small pies. She stood there as if trying to decide which of the pies she was going to take.

Vice-Chancellor Wiren came up beside her. "How do you like the truffles, Ambassador?" she asked.

The Ambassador turned and smiled. She found the Vice-Chancellor unpleasant. Nothing she could put her finger on. Just an odd feeling. She didn't want to be anywhere near her. "Those are excellent, Chancellor. But these are the most delicious I have ever had. How do your chefs manage such beautiful detail and flavors? I also have to say, the plates are beautiful. The detail on these birds and flowers you have painted along the edges is exceptional," she said. She traced the edge of the plate in her hand.

Chancellor Wiren smiled and squared her shoulders. "It took a few weeks of planning and several days of preparation. We always appreciate your praise and appreciation of our cuisine, Ambassador. We're happy to offer you a few small delicacies from our world," she said. She picked up a plate of gold and cream-colored pastries and offered it to the Ambassador.

The Ambassador smiled politely, took the plate with both hands, and bowed. "Thank you, Vice-Chancellor. I was just getting ready to go to my quarters. If you will give me leave,

I'll take these with me. Having them with my coffee in the morning would be quite nice," she said.

"Of course, Ambassador. As you wish. I look forward to our meeting in the morning. Goodnight," Chancellor Wiren said.

"Goodnight, Vice-Chancellor," the Ambassador replied. She smiled and walked out of the room.

Something wasn't right. She'd heard something in the Vice-Chancellor's voice. There were now three guards in the hallway instead of two. She smiled at them and at her plate as she walked out. No, something was very wrong. She could feel it. She had learned to trust her feelings.

SOONER WOULD BE GOOD
GUEST HOUSE ON PROCYON 5

The Ambassador walked back to the guest house as quickly as she could without raising suspicion. She gathered her things. She hadn't brought much. Everything fit in her diplomatic bag. She was just about to walk out the door when her personal comm link chimed. She took a small screen out of her pocket.

Lt. Katy appeared on the screen. "Ambassador, we need to move up our departure," she said.

The Ambassador frowned. "What does that mean, Lieutenant? You aren't giving me any information," she said.

"Captain Logan ordered me to contact you. He said to tell you and Kell to get back on board as quickly as possible. He didn't explain. That's all I know," she said.

The Ambassador nodded. "I see. Tell Captain Logan we have one more. Where is N'amani?" she asked.

Maja took over the link. "N'amani is on board. Kell is waiting on your shuttle," she said.

"Thank you, Maja. Let Kell know to be ready. I'm leaving now. We will meet him as quickly as we can," she said. She closed the comm link. Her instincts had been right. The fact that Logan had not offered an explanation meant they needed to move quickly. She opened a local comm link. "Galen Bontire," she said. It took a few seconds for the directory to find him.

"Micha?"

"Now. Southeast gate. Quickly," she said. She closed the comm link without waiting for him to say anything. She picked up her diplomatic bag and opened the door.

There was now a guard in the hallway opposite her door. He stepped forward and blocked her exit.

"I have orders that you should not leave your room tonight, Ambassador. If there is something you need, tell me and I will arrange to have it delivered," the guard said.

The Ambassador smiled at him and stepped back just behind the threshold. "Through or around?" she thought quickly sizing him up. She smiled bigger and shook her head. She pulled her bag to the front. "I must go speak with my aide about these agreements. We have to review some things. There are details of our meetings. The Alliance expects my report. I won't be long. It will only take us a short time. It must be done tonight. We have meetings in the morning. I'm only going to the next floor. Surely my going to visit with my aide on the next floor can't be considered 'going out.' The High Council is waiting for my report. Do you want to keep the High Council waiting?" she asked. As she was speaking, she shifted back and forth with emphasis. Each time she talked about the reports, she shifted forward. When she talked about the time, she shifted back and to the side. Gradually, she moved out into the hallway. She kept talking until she was just outside his reach but not far enough away to cause him to react. He'd have to lean or take a step to grab her.

The guard didn't have an answer.

The Ambassador didn't expect him to answer her. She smiled at him and pointed up. "I don't want to keep them waiting either. I will return shortly," she said. She disappeared before he could blink.

The guard stood there for a second and then followed her. He stopped at the stairwell and turned his head to listen. He looked up then down and shook his head.

The Ambassador was already out the door. Among the skills she'd mastered were moving quickly and being quiet. It would take an equally skilled adept or a thermal camera to track her.

DANCE WITH ME
OUTSIDE THE DIPLOMATIC COMPOUND ON PROCYON 5

Evening had turned into night. The amber lights along the walkways gave them a warm glow. It was quiet. There was a faint smell of fresh-watered plants.

The Ambassador walked away from the guest house deliberately but not too fast. She wanted to appear as though she were simply going out to take care of something. But it was late. And there was something else. She felt it. Her intuition was telling her that she needed to leave. She made herself lighter. She lengthened her step. She saw someone moving towards the gate from the West. She recognized Galen's long stride. She glanced around. She didn't see anything. She picked up her pace. "We'll be fine. We get inside the gate and use the hoverpeds to get to the hangar. Kell is ready. We'll be on our way in just a few minutes," she thought. She heard something. She shifted her weight slightly and kept walking, listening closely. She shifted the shoulder strap holding her pouch over her head so it went across her chest. Her steps became more deliberate. Someone was nearby. She could feel it.

A figure stepped out of the shadows directly in front of her. "Why Ambassador Lawrence, what a surprise to meet you here. We weren't expecting anyone to be out this late," Vice Chancellor Jervis said.

Two guards stepped up just behind him.

"Chancellor Jervis, good evening. Yes, this is a surprise," the Ambassador said a bit louder than necessary. She smiled at him. She did not want to have to deal with him. She'd learned he had become a little too friendly with some traders who were scouting for the Olmeri. She shifted a little to where she could see past him to where she'd seen Galen. It was too late.

Two more guards had Galen. They were all walking towards where she and the Chancellor were standing.

The Ambassador smiled as if saying goodbye. "I see your men have met Dr. Bontire. We have just been discussing a trip to Altair. My shuttle has archives from some of the farms we might visit. We won't be long," she said. She took a step towards Galen.

Galen nodded to her and closed the gap. He smiled. "Indeed Chancellor. I'm quite excited to have the chance to visit Altair 2. I need to see what I should prepare. We appreciate your concern in coming out to meet us. I'm certain we will be fine. We'll only be a few minutes. I'm fascinated by any biology archive. Most find them rather boring. But if you want to come along, you're welcome to join us," he said. He smiled broadly and turned his head. He knew this was a problem and pretending it wasn't would not make it go away. He looked at the Ambassador.

The Ambassador tilted her head slightly to the right.

Chancellor Jervis shook his head. "Dr. Bontire, Ambassador. It seems you don't quite understand. We would prefer that you return to your quarters. Your shuttle will still be here in the morning. Besides, you have an important meeting in the morning, don't you Ambassador? Why don't you and the Doctor go get some rest. You can look at the biology archives in the morning," he said. He took a step back and motioned to the guards to take them.

The Ambassador and Galen had been moving around. A shift here, a step there. Closer to the inside. On the same line. Moving in time. They put the guards in a box.

Two guards in front. Two behind. They started to move.

Galen took a small step forward.

The Ambassador took a small step back.

With that, they changed the time each guard would arrive. Now, one would arrive before the other.

The Ambassador set her shoulders. She shifted her weight back. She waited. The first guard reached her. He grabbed her left wrist. He stepped around to take her shoulder. She tightened her arm. He tightened his grip. She shifted, brought her arm up and out, slammed her elbow into his ribs, used the recoil to break his nose, trapped his leg, and broke his knee. She shifted back, dropped lower, turned and sent him flying into the second guard. They both went down.

Galen set his weight. He waited. The first guard grabbed his wrist. He struggled. The guard held tighter. He snap-turned his arm and broke the guard's thumb. He grabbed the guard's hand and twisted it backward and down, then behind. He applied more pressure. The guard's arm went limp. He caught the guard under his ribs and tossed him into the second guard. They weren't going to get up anytime soon.

The Ambassador picked up her bag.

Galen picked up his bag.

Chancellor Jervis cowered behind a tree.

The Ambassador looked at him and shook her head. "Chancellor Jervis, I will file the appropriate protests. We are leaving. You shouldn't try to stop us," she said. She nodded to Galen.

They ran to the gate. The Ambassador entered her access code. Galen pushed the gate open. She ran through. He hung back to cover her.

The Ambassador ran to the mechanics' shed. She grabbed two hoverpeds. She stood on one and held the handle of the other.

"Guards!! Guards!" Chancellor Jervis called out.

"He's recovered his voice," Galen said.

"Yes well, let's go," the Ambassador said. She pointed to a bank of hangars.

Galen took the handle and jumped on.

They were in the open, visible, and they weren't moving that fast.

NEED A RIDE?
THE AMBASSADOR'S SHUTTLE

Kell had gone out to check the shuttle earlier. Maja had called to let him know that the Ambassador and someone else were on their way. He had finished his preflight checklist. He was starting to get concerned. "She should have been here by now," he thought. He looked out the window again. This time, he saw two hoverpeds coming towards the hangar followed by several more. The first two would be overtaken in a few more seconds. "Oh crap." he said. He set the controls to full manual and moved the shuttle out of the hangar. He brought the craft around and came up parallel with the first two hoverpeds. He slowed, almost to a stop, and opened the side door. With what seemed no more than a breath, he turned the craft so it was in front of them capturing both of them mid-flight.

"GO!" the Ambassador shouted as she and Galen fell through the door.

Kell started up over the city as he waited for the door to close. Then, he accelerated on an 85-degree ascent. It would have been hard to follow them, but possible. He confirmed they weren't being followed, slowed, and leveled off in the upper atmosphere. "Are you alright Ambassador?" he asked. He turned around to look back at her.

The Ambassador smiled. "Yes. Thank you Kell. I'm okay. You were right on time, as usual. Remember Dr. Bontire?" she asked. She got to her feet, brushed off her clothes, and sat down. She frowned as she moved her left arm into her lap.

Kell smiled. "I was hoping to meet you again, Doctor. But I didn't expect it would be quite this way," he said.

Galen laughed. "Me either. How did you do that? I mean how did you get the ship to go that slowly and stay airborne? And that turn! It was almost like falling into cotton cloud. Well, maybe not quite that soft..." he said. He rubbed his elbow and sat down.

Kell smiled. "Manual controls," he said.

Galen chuckled. Only an Aldaran could have done anything like that. It could only be done with perfect timing and manual controls.

The Ambassador pressed the link on her comm panel. "Captain Logan," she said.

"Ambassador, it's good to hear from you. We were a bit concerned," Captain Logan replied.

"Indeed, Captain. We have much to discuss," the Ambassador said.

"More than you think, Ambassador. We need to leave as soon as you are on board. I'll explain. Sooner is better. Kell?" Captain Logan asked.

"We will be in range in just under two minutes, Captain," Kell replied.

"Cut that to one," Captain Logan said.

"Understood Captain. Have the hangar ready," Kell said. He turned to the Ambassador and Galen. "Sit back and buckle up," he said. He punched it.

"You are going to tell me what's going on eventually, aren't you?" Galen asked.

The Ambassador nodded. "You won't like it," she said.

"I'd figured that out already," Galen said.

"I have coffee," the Ambassador offered.

"Real coffee? As in actual real ground coffee beans?" Galen asked.

The Ambassador nodded.

"I'm really not going to like this, am I?" Galen asked.

"Probably not," the Ambassador replied.

Galen chuckled and shook his head.

FREE PARKING
FLIGHT DECK ON THE MAGELLAN

Kell slid the shuttle into the hangar and locked it in place. The outer hanger door closed. They had just started to get up when the star drive pushed them back into their seats.

The Ambassador looked at Kell and raised her eyebrows. "Seems we really don't want to be here. Maja, what's happened?" she asked.

Maja appeared. "The High Council received word that Procyon 5 is cooperating with the Olmeri. A small group of Olmeri ships were spotted heading this way. The Council also received a message from one of our traders that the Olmeri want to bring you to Olm for questioning," she said.

"Oh great. I'm willing to bet that was the meeting Chancellor Jervis wanted me to stay for. I'm so glad we didn't stay. Maja, please arrange a briefing with everyone, including our guests, as soon as possible," the Ambassador said.

"Yes Ambassador," Maja replied.

Kell stood up. "Ambassador, I'll meet you in the briefing room. I have something to take care of," he said.

The Ambassador nodded. "Thank you," she said.

"Any chance you are going to tell me what's going on?" Galen asked.

The Ambassador shook her head. "Not right this minute. I'll explain everything in the briefing. Your sleeve seems to not be quite connected to your shirt anymore," she said.

Galen looked at his torn sleeve. "Yes. That is true. Your pants have some extra ventilation," he said. He pointed at the torn knee of her pants.

The Ambassador looked down at her pant leg. She tried to reach her arm to her knee. She couldn't.

Galen frowned. "What's wrong with your arm?" he asked.

The Ambassador wrinkled her nose. "Elbow to the ribs. I think he was wearing body armor," she said.

"Let me see," Galen said.

"I can't move it," the Ambassador said.

"That's because it's broken in three places," Galen said.

"Oh," the Ambassador said.

"I don't have anything with me that can treat this," Galen said.

"My team doctor is a Keeper of Water. He can treat it. Can you get me fixed up so I can get through the briefing?" the Ambassador asked.

"I can set the breaks so there's no more damage. But I can't repair them," Galen said.

"Do it," the Ambassador said.

"It's going to hurt," Galen said.

"I can't feel it now," the Ambassador said.

"That's a bonus. I need something to wrap your arm," Galen said.

The Ambassador nodded towards a side storage bin. "That cabinet. There's a long scarf," she said.

Galen got the scarf. "Okay then. Sit still," he said. He held her shoulder and pulled down just above her elbow. The bone snapped into place. He gently wrapped the scarf around it. Then, he took her forearm in his hands and pulled. The bone snapped into place. He wrapped the scarf around it. He gently bent her elbow and moved her arm to just under her ribs. Then he wrapped the scarf around her waist.

"I can't move my arm," the Ambassador complained.

"You couldn't move it before I wrapped it," Galen said.

"Well," the Ambassador said.

"Not moving it is the point," Galen said.

The Ambassador nodded. "It doesn't hurt," she said.

"It will," Galen said.

"How long?" the Ambassador asked.

"Maybe thirty minutes," Galen said.

"Then we should go," the Ambassador said.

"Are you sure?" Galen asked.

"The alliance with the Pyr is a problem. There's a lot to cover. The sooner we get started the better. I'll be okay for now. Besides, I'd really like a cup of coffee," the Ambassador said.

Galen grinned. "Real coffee? Lead me to it!" He reached out his hand to help her get up.

The Ambassador got up slowly. "Nope, still doesn't hurt," she said. She grinned.

Galen shook his head. "Let's go before it starts," he said.

They hurried down the ramp and across the deck.

CHAPTER 6:
ENDINGS AND BEGINNINGS
PART 2: THE OLD GUARD

In the time before, there were heroes

HELLO AGAIN
THE DIPLOMATIC BRIEFING ROOM ON THE MAGELLAN

Kell, the Ambassador, and Galen had returned to the Magellan. As soon as they were on board, the ship engaged the star drive. Kell went to make a call. Galen set and wrapped the Ambassador's broken arm. Then, they transported to the guest section for the briefing.

The Ambassador and Galen stepped off the transport platform and walked down the hallway to the briefing room. They were still a bit disheveled from the fight.

Galen sniffed the air. "Coffee!" he said.

The Ambassador grinned. "Told you," she said. They walked a little faster.

Lt. Katy and Commander Brandon were standing near one of the projector screens. Captain Logan, Beth, N'amani, and the Doctor were standing near the coffee table off to one side. N'amani had just made a fresh pot of coffee.

Three others stood with their backs to the door at the far end of the room looking out the windows. There wasn't anything to see. They were going too fast.

Captain Logan looked up. "Ambassador, it's good to have you safely on board," he said. He looked at her arm and turned his head to one side.

The Ambassador nodded. "Thank you, Captain. I appreciate you getting us out of," she said. She stopped and smiled. Galen was going to need a minute.

The three at the far end of the room had turned around when they heard her voice. They were all grinning. Even their eyes twinkled.

Galen had started toward the coffee table. He looked up at the movement. His jaw dropped. He started laughing. He slid over the conference table, landed perfectly, and opened his arms. "Sentar, Maru, B'ani!! I never imagined I'd see all of you in one place! It's so good to see you again," he said.

"Ho! Galen!" Sentar called out. His great booming voice filled the room. "Seems you are the mystery passenger we had to pick up," he said.

Sentar was tall, about the same height as Captain Logan and N'amani, with broad shoulders and a square build. A few curls of his short brown hair were brushed with grey. He took a step, reached out to grab Galen by the shoulders, and slapped him on the back.

Galen stepped forward, returned the hug and the slap. He turned around his hand still on Sentar's shoulder. "Micha! Seems there was something else you weren't sharing!" he said.

The Ambassador smiled her Cheshire cat grin. She looked at Sentar and winked. "Wouldn't be complete without him, would it?" she asked. She grinned a little bigger.

Sentar smiled and shook his head. He and Galen had shared a room during their training years. They had been best friends. They'd tried to keep in touch, but it wasn't easy.

Maru and B'ani were standing just behind Sentar. They stepped forward to Galen with Maru on his right and B'ani on the left.

Maru's dark brown hair fell in curls to her shoulders, complimenting the light gold of her face. She had an openness about her that was almost childlike. She seemed much younger than she was.

B'ani was still as slender as ever. She had always kept her straight black hair short so it framed her face. She wore a cream color shirt that seemed to give her rich dark gold skin an even deeper hue.

Maru and B'ani had been close friends since their early days on Ras 2. They were training partners. They both liked traveling. They had been security for more than a few trade delegations. They'd gotten into and out of a few scrapes together. Their negotiation skills were quite good. Their fighting skills were better. It was rare to see either one of them without the other.

"It's so good to see you again!" Maru said quietly. She took Galen's arm.

B'ani was still laughing as she came up to take his other arm. "The expression on your face when you saw us was priceless! Can we do it again?" she asked.

"How did you get here?" Galen asked Sentar.

Sentar pointed at the Ambassador. "Same as you," he said.

"I hope not. We had to insist on leaving Pelscara. They made sure we had souvenirs, too. See?" Galen said. He held up his torn sleeve.

"You mean a ripped sleeve is not the newest fashion?" B'ani asked.

Sentar laughed. "Alright, so maybe not exactly the same. I did not have to give up a good shirt. Micha just dropped by and invited me to come along," he said.

"She's good at that," B'ani said.

"Indeed," Maru said.

"What about you and Maru?" Galen asked. He looked at B'ani.

"We arrived together," they replied in unison.

Sentar chuckled. "Of course you did. When have you two not traveled together?" he said.

"It's so good to see all of you. I missed you," Galen said.

They had trained together, eaten together, lived together, and kept each other company for three years on Ras 2. After they graduated, they all went in different directions. They'd kept in touch more or less. But other than an occasional visit, they had not spent time with each other in many years.

Everyone had been paying attention to Galen, Sentar, Maru, and B'ani. It was hard not to. Their presence filled the room. They were all Adepts and Keepers. Sentar was a Keeper of Metal, Maru was a Keeper of Water, B'ani a Keeper of Fire, and Galen was a Keeper of Wood.

Sentar grinned at Galen and looked over at the Ambassador again. He looked down at her arm and frowned. "What happened?" he asked.

Galen pointed to his sleeve. "We declined an invitation," he said.

The Doctor stepped up next to the Ambassador. "You broke your arm?" he asked.

The Ambassador nodded. "Galen set it. It doesn't hurt," she said.

"Yet," the Doctor said frowning at her and nodding to Galen.

"We'll have a short briefing?" the Ambassador said.

"Very short," the Doctor said. He looked at her arm.

"She has always been like this," Galen said. He smiled at the Doctor and winked at the Ambassador.

The Doctor shook his head and sighed.

The Ambassador smiled at them. "Thank you for taking care of me," she said quietly.

The Doctor grinned and nodded to her.

Galen smiled.

The Ambassador moved to the front of the room. She grinned at her old classmates. She looked at her team, Captain Logan, and his officers. "Okay then, we should get started. We can have lunch tomorrow to catch up. And make proper introductions. We have a lot to cover and some new developments to discuss. Maja, would you summarize what we know up to now?" she asked.

Everyone sat down around the table. The four old friends on one side, Captain Logan, Commander Brandon, and Lt. Katy on the other. N'amani, Kell, and Beth sat around one end. The Doctor took a chair in front near the Ambassador.

A large screen on one side of the room lit up. It showed footage of the Olmeri destruction on several planets along with various maps showing their known paths and path projections.

Maja appeared. "The Olmeri have accelerated their 'enter-and-leave' incursions. They enter and leave, enter and leave until finally, they don't leave any more. We don't really know where they are going or why. We do know if we allow them to continue, they will cut through wide areas of Central Alliance-protected planets as well as currently occupied non-treaty worlds. The Council received word that the Olmeri were exploring another system near the Hyades Cluster. So far, they have not found Ka'len," she said.

Captain Logan looked at the map. He frowned. "This is worse than we suspected," he said.

The Ambassador nodded.

The Doctor shook his head and turned his palms up. "But what are we going to do? What can we do? We're supposed to be a diplomatic team. What are we going to do?" he asked.

The Ambassador looked around the room. Her eyes were cold. "We are going to stop them," she said.

The Doctor stopped fidgeting.

Beth and N'amani looked at each other and frowned. They were not used to hearing this tone from her.

The Ambassador dropped her chin and set her shoulders. "We cannot allow them to continue on any of their current paths. During the past two years, they have poisoned the food chains on twelve worlds that used to be among our most productive trading partners," she said.

The screen behind her showed images of the worlds before and after.

N'amani lowered his head. "I can't. This is worse than anything we've seen. We can't let them keep coming. My people are tied to our ancestral homes and the natural environment. We are willing to fight, but we are mostly administrators. We're accountants. Many of us are farmers and growers. We are no match for the Olmeri. Please. The Alliance has to do something," he said.

The Ambassador nodded. "I know. That's why we're here, N'amani. We are going to do two things. First, we're going lure the Olmeri away from the local neighborhood. Second, we're going find out as much as we can about them," she said.

Sentar blinked. "We're going to do what?" he asked.

"Are you serious?" Maru asked frowning.

"You're nuts," B'ani said. She looked at the Ambassador and shook her head.

Galen shook his head. "I knew I wasn't going to like this," he said.

Commander Brandon looked at Captain Logan and raised her eyebrows.

Captain Logan shook his head, smiled, and leaned in closer to Commander Brandon. "Whatever she has in mind has the full backing of the High Council. I've been told to make sure she gets whatever she asks for," he whispered.

Commander Brandon shrugged and nodded.

The Ambassador pointed to the display. "This outlying area between the Orion Spur and the Perseus Arm is the Perseus Transit. We are going to lure as many of the Olmeri as we can out there and trap them so they can't leave," she said.

Sentar frowned. "Seems a bit remote," he said.

The Ambassador nodded. "That's why I chose it," she said.

Sentar shook his head. "We'll be out there all alone," he said.

The Ambassador smiled. "Not entirely alone. We're going to put a string of magnetic field generators along a pretty wide swath on this path. Once we get the Olmeri past the threshold, we turn on the generators. The Olmeri ships will lose navigation if they try to leave," she said.

Kell grinned. "A honey pot?" he asked.

The Ambassador nodded.

Galen shook his head and looked down. "Micha, what about the systems in that sector? The Olmeri are not much on sharing. Those worlds. We can't. We just can't," he said.

The Ambassador shook her head sadly. "I know. We've asked quietly. We understand most of these systems are not occupied. What's another option, Galen? I'm open to anything. Anything," she said.

B'ani nodded. "I'd like another option, too. The Olmeri are relentless. Sending them somewhere else isn't what we need to do. We need to find a way to stop them," she said.

The Ambassador shook her head. "I don't disagree. For now, we need to distract them to buy ourselves some time. We want to keep them busy preparing to extract resources that aren't there from planets that aren't occupied while we look for a way to stop them permanently," she said.

The Doctor and Galen looked at each other.

"You're going to use bio-injections, aren't you?" the Doctor asked.

The Ambassador smiled and nodded. She pointed to the display. "Yes. Maja has identified roughly 200 systems around these stars which we believe are unoccupied. They can't support life as we know it. That's where we want to lead the Olmeri. We've picked these three systems to seed. We expect it will take the Olmeri about a year to complete their colonization. We are also going to arrange for them to discover readings indicating there could be more. We want them to be so distracted by the anticipation of what they are going to find that they don't notice of a few ships having a bit of engine trouble. We're also going to put sensor arrays along the same path as the field generators. When they experience engine trouble, we're going to plant a virus to mask the location of the problem along with readings showing they encountered some natural event. Perhaps they were too close to a nearby star? At the same time, we're going to trigger their sensors so they pick up new readings of a wealth of resources nearby," she said.

Sentar looked down and shook his head. "We're going to do all that? Where are we going to get the ships?" he asked.

Captain Logan raised his hand.

Sentar grinned and nodded.

The Ambassador took a breath. "It won't take them that long to figure out what is happening. But even just a few months delay could be enough for us to find a way to stop them," she said.

"Couldn't we find some way to keep them busy longer?" B'ani asked.

"How?" Sentar asked.

"I don't see how we can do all this quickly enough. We need more time," Galen said.

"The average time it takes the Olmeri to destroy the ecosystems on a planet is three years. Then, they move on. If we had some sort of magic regeneration dust to sprinkle over the planets they have destroyed and then trick them into thinking they are new worlds, maybe they'd be happy to stay in their own part of the galaxy," Commander Brandon said.

"Ah, the magic pixie dust solution. It's something I've been looking for, too. If you can tell me where to find some, I will happily fill and carry bags of it on board," Galen said.

"Shush Mister Ecosystems expert," Maru said. "You know better than any of us that it's not as far-fetched as it sounds. With the right combination of compounds, we can shorten the growing time to 5-8 months for plants that would normally take 10-12 years to mature," she said.

Galen grinned playfully.

"Something like that might give us a longer-term solution," B'ani said. "For now, Micha, how are we going to get the generator and sensor arrays set up, complete terraforming the planets, and find a way to get the Olmeri to follow us all the way out to the Perseus Transit?" she asked.

Beth smiled. "Getting them to follow us is easy. We just let them know the Ambassador is on board," she said.

Galen grinned. "Oh yes, they'd very much like to talk with Micha. They'd really like to talk with her," he said.

The Ambassador smiled. "Yes, well... Everything is more of a challenge now. We need to avoid the Olmeri and any contact with those who are friendly towards them. They can't find out what we're up to," she said.

Sentar leaned forward. "Don't you think "challenge" is a bit of an understatement? It is going to take an army to get this done," he said.

The Ambassador smiled at him then looked at Maru, B'ani and Galen. "I have one," she said.

Sentar sat back in his seat, nodded, and laughed. "So that's why you invited us," he said.

The Ambassador grinned.

Lt. Katy looked at the Ambassador. She frowned. Then, she looked at Sentar, Maru, B'ani and Galen. "What are they talking about? Who are these people?" she thought. She looked at the Ambassador again and shook her head. "You aren't an ordinary Ambassador, are you?" she asked.

The Ambassador smiled like a Cheshire cat getting ready to disappear and shook her head. "No. I'm not," she said.

They all laughed. No one in that room was ordinary. Not a one.

FRIENDS FROM FAR AWAY
THE DIPLOMATIC BRIEFING ROOM ON THE MAGELLAN

The Ambassador sat down next to the Doctor.

Captain Logan stood up to continue the briefing. He walked to the front and switched the display to show a station in deep space. "This is the Theta Alpha station. We will have about two weeks to complete our basic preparations while we are in transit. The Alliance has arranged all four of our Lewis-class ships to join us. They are similar to the Magellan. They can carry a number of close-range cruisers and anything else we think will be needed. As we work through the details, you will each have briefings on your ships and their capabilities. We will start those tomorrow," he said. He looked at Galen, Sentar, B'ani, and Maru.

Kell arrived and stood in the doorway. He waited for Captain Logan to pause. "If I may, Captain," he said stepping into the room.

Captain Logan blinked a few times. "This is unusual. Kell is always ready to answer any questions and fill in the details, but he doesn't usually volunteer to say anything," he thought. "Of course," he said.

Kell walked towards the front of the room. "Captain, I would like to offer my appreciation for the charts and details you have shown here today. I have been in that region. It has many navigation challenges. We should all spend time studying these charts in detail. Knowing where we have defensive positions could be important," he said.

Captain Logan nodded. "Thank you, Kell," he said. He started to continue then stopped.

Kell stood very still. He looked around the room. He nodded to Captain Logan. He smiled and nodded to the Ambassador. "Ambassador, you asked me about something. The answer is yes. They will meet us at Theta Alpha," he said.

The Ambassador sat up straight. Her eyes got big. She shook her head. She was smiling a huge smile. "Yes? They said yes? Really? Yes!?" she asked.

Kell grinned and nodded. "Yes, Ambassador." He sat down.

The Ambassador sat back in her chair.

Galen pursed his lips and turned his head. "Were you going to share, or no?" he asked.

Sentar shook his head and shrugged.

"What are you talking about? Who are they?" Maru asked looking first at Kell then at the Ambassador.

The Ambassador took a deep breath and bowed to Kell. "Niyé pilamayaye. Thank you," she said.

Kell bowed.

"Give," B'ani said.

The Ambassador smiled. "I asked Kell if there might be four of his friends with his level of skill who would agree to come with us. There are. Each of you will have an Aldaran pilot," she said.

Everyone was silent. They looked at Kell and then at the Ambassador. They knew this could mean the difference between success and maybe not coming back at all; between avoiding encounters or being detained. There was no better pilot to have in a difficult situation than an Aldaran.

"Micha, it seems there is more to you than even we know," Galen said. He smiled and nodded quietly.

Kell nodded to the Ambassador. "We know this will be difficult. We have decided we will do whatever we can to help protect the local neighborhood. We have many good friends here," he said. He looked hard at N'amani and nodded to him.

N'amani smiled at Kell and nodded. "Thank you," he whispered.

Kell took a deep breath. "I don't normally talk much. But this needs to be said and all of you need to hear it. I'm not speaking only for myself now. If my people can provide some advantage, we will. Ambassador Lawrence has shown us time and again that she will not ask my people for frivolous or trivial things. She doesn't ask anything for herself alone. She has courage and a great, caring heart. My people respect her. There's always someone she's trying to help. Now, we will help her," he said.

The Ambassador bowed her head humbly at the compliment. She looked up and smiled. "Thank you, Kell. Captain, it seems we need to modify the briefings," she said.

Captain Logan grinned. "Just a little, maybe?" he said. He turned to Kell. "I don't know what to say. Thank you," he said.

"We will do what we can do," Kell said. He stood taller, the warrior in him matching Captain Logan's question.

Captain Logan nodded and smiled, acknowledging the simplicity of his statement and his resolve. "I'm very glad you and your people are willing to help," he said.

The Ambassador sat back in her chair. "This will change everything," she thought. She shifted a little and winced.

Galen looked at her arm. "Time's up," he said.

The Ambassador smiled and then frowned. She winced again.

"Doctor," Galen said.

The Doctor nodded. "I need to get something from my quarters. I will meet you there," he said.

Galen got up and went over to the Ambassador's chair. "Let's go," he said. He reached out his hand to help her stand up.

The Ambassador tried to smile. "It hurts now," she said.

Galen nodded. He led her out of the room.

N'amani stood up. "We should all get some rest. Now that we all know what we're doing here. Maja and I will prepare some briefing packets for you. We can start again in a day or two," he said.

Captain Logan nodded and stood up. "Thank you, N'amani" he said. He nodded several times to Kell as he walked out.

Commander Brandon and Lt. Katy got up to leave.

Beth followed N'amani and Kell out the door.

Sentar, Maru, and B'ani sat there for a minute.

Sentar scratched his head.

Maru and B'ani shrugged.

"Let's go get something to eat," B'ani suggested.

Sentar smiled, stood up, and headed for the door.

B'ani grinned at Maru. "No need to ask him twice," she said.

Maru stood up and followed Sentar out the door. She walked up beside him grinning. "Are you still hungry all the time?" she asked.

Sentar looked at her and smiled. "Not so much all the time. But right now, yes. We skipped dinner, remember?" he said.

"We did, didn't we?" B'ani said. She walked up on his other side.

Sentar grinned. "So that means I get two plates, right," he said.

B'ani and Maru shook their heads and laughed.

SOUVENIRS
THE AMBASSADOR'S QUARTERS ON THE MAGELLAN

Galen walked the Ambassador to her quarters. Her arm had started to hurt. The door opened and the lights came on as they entered the room.

"Galen, it's getting worse," the Ambassador said.

"Did you expect it would be getting better?" Galen asked.

The Ambassador looked down and frowned a little then looked up at him and smiled. "Why yes I did," she said.

Galen grinned and walked her over to the center table. "Sit. I have to take that scarf off," he said.

"Can't it wait?" the Ambassador asked.

Galen nodded then shook his head "For now. It will have to come off. Your arm needs to be scanned and properly set. What I did was field medicine. You need more," he said.

The Ambassador held up her good hand. "Marc has the Jewel of Aron," she said quietly.

Galen smiled and sighed with relief. "Then you will be fine," he said.

The Ambassador nodded.

The door chime sounded.

The Doctor came in. He set his bag on the table. "How is she?" he asked Galen.

"She is in pain, Doctor," the Ambassador replied.

Galen and the Doctor both laughed.

"You are a Keeper of Water?" Galen asked.

"You are a Keeper of Wood," the Doctor said.

"You can tell?" Galen asked.

"Yes. It's one of my gifts," the Doctor replied.

Galen smiled.

The Ambassador looked up at them. "Guys?" she said.

The Doctor grinned, reached into his bag, took out a small packet, and unwrapped it. He'd brought Jewel of Aron. He slipped the ring over his middle finger and held the jewel in his palm. The jewel radiated pink with a golden glow. He began moving his hand along her arm. The jewel turned a dark red. He frowned. He slipped it off and put it down.

"She did more than fracture it in three places, didn't she?" Galen asked.

The Doctor nodded. "Part of the bone in her elbow is shattered," he said.

"Can you repair it?" Galen asked.

The Doctor nodded. "I can clear the debris. I have a program that will regenerate the bone. Yes, I can do it. But it will take several hours. First, the fractures have to be set," he said.

"Do you have something for the pain?" Galen asked.

The Doctor picked up the jewel again. "This will only last a few minutes, Micha. Then, it's going to hurt worse until it heals. I will give you something to make you sleep so you won't feel it," he said. He moved the jewel along her arm again. This time, it glowed bright red.

The Ambassador relaxed her shoulder. "Much better, Doctor. Thank you," she said.

Galen smiled.

The Doctor shook his head. "I still have to set your arm," he said.

The Ambassador smiled at him. "Give me a minute if you would please? I'm enjoying the moment," she said.

The Doctor and Galen both laughed.

"How many were there?" the Doctor asked.

The Ambassador chuckled. "Four. I got two. Galen got the other two," she said.

Galen grinned and turned his head to one side. "But I didn't break anything," he said.

"Yes, you did," the Ambassador said.

Galen laughed. "Not mine," he replied.

The Doctor shook his head. "You aren't as young as you were. You can't keep doing these sorts of things, Micha," he said.

"No options, Doctor," the Ambassador replied. A bit of the fighter came out in her voice. "I wasn't going to stick around so the Olmeri could take me to Olm for a nice, long talk. Vice Chancellor Jarvis had arranged that for me. They would have taken Galen, too," she said.

The Doctor took a deep breath. "I appreciate the need, Micha. But you can't do what you could do back in the day. You may still think you can," he said.

The Ambassador looked at him harshly. "Think?" she asked.

"Ok, ok, yes. You can still do what you could do. But your body isn't the same. You bruise too easily. Using external force is not your best skill anyway," the Doctor said.

The Ambassador grinned. "That is true. Thanks Marc. I really do appreciate your concern," she said.

Galen turned his head and looked at the Doctor. "She said something about body armor," he said.

The Doctor smiled and shook his head. "She does have a knack, doesn't she?" he asked.

Galen nodded. "We still need to set her arm," he said.

The Doctor nodded. "You wrapped it," he said.

Galen stepped behind the Ambassador's chair. "Lean forward just a little," he said. He nudged her away from the chair. He began gently unwrapping the scarf.

The Doctor moved the table closer. "Rest her arm here," he said.

Galen moved the Ambassador's arm onto the table and finished unwrapping it.

"Such a lovely shade of purple," the Doctor said.

The Ambassador looked down at her arm. It was swollen and the bones in her forearm weren't quite where they should be. She relaxed her shoulder. "Go ahead," she said.

The Doctor took hold of her arm just so and moved the bones back to their correct position.

"You have a gift for that too apparently," Galen said smiling.

"It's easy for me to see the connections," the Doctor said. He took hold of the Ambassador's shoulder. "One more," he said. He shifted and the bones moved into place. He picked up the jewel again and moved it along her arm. This time, it turned a dark orange. "Much better. Everything is where it should be. Now, hold still. We need to wrap your arm. You have to keep still for the next few hours," he said. He slid the jewel off his hand, took several medical wraps out of his bag, and handed two to Galen. He slid one under the Ambassador's forearm and closed it snugly.

Galen wrapped her upper arm.

The Ambassador looked up at both of them grinning. "Can I have my lolly now?" she asked.

The Doctor took a small packet out of his bag and put it on the table. "Your arm is going to start hurting pretty soon. Take this. It will make you sleep. Maja, please change the lighting around Ambassador Lawrence's sleeping area to my medical preset A97," he said.

The lights in the sleeping area repointed themselves so they were all directed at where she slept. They started to pulse ever so slightly, changing through shades of orange and pink then fading to blue and starting again. It wasn't bright or garish. The lights were subtle and dark with a penetrating glow. They made the room feel quiet and calm.

"Nice," Galen said.

"It took me a few tries," the Doctor replied.

Galen shook his head and smiled. "Pretty sure it was more than a few. It's quite good," he said.

The Doctor nodded and picked up his bag. "Get some rest, Micha. I will check on you in the morning," he said.

The Ambassador smiled at him. "Thank you, Marc. I wouldn't," she said.

The Doctor grinned. "Yes, you would. But I'd rather you didn't need to find out. Now, go to sleep and let the lights do their work. You really messed up your arm. It's going to take a few hours," he said.

"Yes, Doctor," she said grinning. Then more quietly. "I appreciate everything you do for me, for all of us," she said. She really didn't know what she would do without him. He kept her and the whole team together.

The Doctor nodded gently. "It's nice to be appreciated. Now get some rest," he said.

Galen smiled at him. "Thank you, Doctor. Seems we are going to have some very interesting conversations," he said.

"Yes indeed," the Doctor replied. He smiled as he walked out.

Galen sat down at the table. "Micha, this is quite something you've gotten me – all of us -- into. Why didn't you tell me when we were on Procyon 5?" he asked.

The Ambassador exhaled. "You can still opt out, Galen. Captain Logan won't be coming all the way with us. You can stay on the Magellan or he can arrange transport for you," she said.

Galen shook his head. "That's not what I meant, Micha," he said.

The Ambassador looked down. "I'm sorry. I shouldn't have snapped at you like that," she said.

Galen nodded. "I get it. You're hurt. And this really is a big deal. We aren't simply attempting a rescue or diverting some local pirates. Look, I'm happy to help you and I'll do everything I can to make this mission a success. But what you are asking.... Well, it isn't trivial," he said.

"I know, Galen. I wanted to tell you, but I couldn't. That's why I was insisting on having the briefing. You all needed to know what we're up against and what I'm going to try to do. This is the first time that we've all had a briefing. Kell and I did some planning and I talked with Captain Logan, but none of the others knew anything until just now. I had to keep it quiet. There are too many spies about these days," the Ambassador said.

"Chancellor Jervis?" Galen asked. He held up his sleeve.

The Ambassador nodded. "I'd suspected him for several months," she said.

Galen nodded. "I've been wary of him, too. He seemed just a little too interested in some of my research," he said.

"We've got a lot to cover," the Ambassador said. She sat up and winced.

"Time for you go to sleep," Galen said. He picked up the packet, got a cup, and emptied the packet into it. He poured some warm water from a thermal bottle into the cup.

The Ambassador smiled.

"Bed is that way," Galen said. He pointed to the bed. He held out his hand to help her get up.

They walked slowly.

The Ambassador sat down on the bed.

Galen handed her the cup. "Here, drink this. Marc is very good. This should put even you to sleep," he said.

The Ambassador laughed. She took the cup. "Smells like flowers," she said.

Galen nodded. "Sleep. I'll see you in the morning," he said. He turned to leave.

"Thank you. For everything," the Ambassador said softly.

Galen smiled, nodded, and walked out the door.

The Ambassador finished what was in the cup and put it down. She carefully laid down on the bed. She was exhausted. Her arm hurt. She fell asleep almost instantly.

GOOD MORNING
THE AMBASSADOR'S QUARTERS ON THE MAGELLAN

The Ambassador was sleeping. Maja had kept the medical lights on, delaying the normal light cycle. The room had a dark, pleasant orange glow.

The comm link chimed.

"Ambassador? Good morning. How are you feeling?" the Doctor asked cheerfully.

The Ambassador turned over and sat up. "Is it morning already? Can I have another 10 minutes?" she asked.

The Doctor grinned.

The Ambassador gingerly raised her arm "I'm much better, thank you. I can move my arm again. It's still sore, but I can move it. You are a miracle-worker, Doctor," she said.

"No deification please. But thanks ever so for the ata boy. We still have some time before the briefing. Are you going to get breakfast?" the Doctor asked.

"I really do need a few minutes. You and the others go on without me. I will see you at the briefing," the Ambassador said.

"Ok. See you there," the Doctor said.

The Ambassador closed the comm link. "I have the most excellent team," she thought. She put her head down again and closed her eyes. She half-dozed for a few more minutes. Then, she sat up and swung her legs over the side of the bed. Most of the bruising around her knee was gone. She took the wraps off her arm. It looked good too. She took a shower, got dressed, and started toward the dining hall. She went the long way, through the arboretum. The clean scent of dirt from the trays of new sprouts reminded her of the garden on Ras 2.

BREAKFAST IN THE GARDEN
THE DINING HALL ON THE MAGELLAN

Sentar, Galen, B'ani, and Maru were sitting at a table in one corner of the dining hall finishing breakfast. Several empty plates and cups were scattered on the table.

The Ambassador walked in.

"Micha!" Sentar bellowed.

The Ambassador looked over at him with a big smile and waved. He so reminded her of Master Tai. He used to do the same thing. Extending his energy to fill the room and give the person entering a sense of being the most important person there, at least for a moment.

"Coffee," the Ambassador said. She pointed to a table of cups.

Sentar smiled back at her and waved.

The Ambassador picked up a plate and put some fruit and bread on it. She wasn't that hungry. She got a cup of coffee and went over to where they were sitting. "We have quite a bit to cover in the briefing this morning," she said.

Sentar grimaced. "More than yesterday? That was already too much," he said.

The Ambassador nodded.

B'ani frowned impatiently. "I thought we were done with the group things," she said.

The Ambassador smiled apologetically. "Em, these individual briefings are in addition to not instead of," she said.

"Ah, I see," B'ani said. She took a deep breath, looked down, and frowned.

Maru shook her head. "What have you gotten us into, Micha? You know B'ani and I like a good adventure. But we were just talking about that briefing. This seems like way more than an adventure," she said.

The Ambassador looked down. "It is. It's a lot more. But you don't have to do anything. It has to be your decision. I need your help. And I know what I'm asking. It's ... well, if you don't want to," she said.

"We are all willing to help you Micha," Sentar said. "But we need to have some idea of what you actually want us to do. Taking some ships out into the Perseus Transit will be dangerous all by itself. We really have no idea what we're up against," he said. He looked at Maru, B'ani and Galen.

They all nodded.

The Ambassador nodded to them. "I'm not entirely sure of that either, Sentar," she said.

"Think fast. We have a briefing in a few minutes," Galen said.

The Ambassador smiled at him and shook her head. "Not going to happen," she said.

"The briefing?" B'ani asked hopefully.

"No. My having a working plan in the next ten minutes," the Ambassador replied.

They all laughed.

"Let's go. We might as well finish our conversation in the briefing room," Sentar said. He stood up.

"Is that coffee table still in the briefing room?" Galen asked.

"Yes, yes it is," the Ambassador replied. She smiled at the thought.

THE PLAN
THE DIPLOMATIC BRIEFING ROOM ON THE MAGELLAN

Beth and N'amani were adjusting the controls on one of the wall screens. Lt. Katy and Cmdr. Brandon were reviewing a 3D model with Maja when Captain Logan walked in.

"How are the preparations coming along?" Captain Logan asked.

Lt. Katy, Commander Brandon, and Maja turned to attention. "Good morning, Captain," they said more or less in unison.

Captain Logan nodded. "As you were," he said.

"Almost ready, Captain," N'amani said.

Beth nodded.

The Doctor and Kell came in.

"Good morning, Doctor, Good morning Kell," N'amani said.

"Good morning, N'amani. Good morning, Beth," they said unison.

Beth smiled.

Sentar, Maru, B'ani, Galen, and the Ambassador arrived.

Sentar, Maru, B'ani, and Galen went to sit on one side of the table with the Doctor and Beth. Captain Logan,

Commander Brandon, and Lt. Katy sat on the other side. Kell took the end chair, opposite the Ambassador. Maja stood in the back next to Kell.

"Everything is ready, Ambassador," N'amani said. He handed her a small controller and took a seat next to Maru.

"Thank you, N'amani," the Ambassador said. She smiled. "He just gets things done. I don't have to think about whatever it is; I don't have to give him instructions. He just got it done, perfectly, impeccably. And it isn't so much that he always succeeds. He doesn't. But he always lets me know what is going on and he is always there for me. Whatever we need, he is always ready to try. I'm was going to need his competence and quiet courage on this mission," she thought. She took a deep breath and looked around the room. She grinned at Sentar, then Kell. "Good morning. Yesterday, I went over the basic ideas: why we are here, what my plan is, and what we want to accomplish. That was the what. Now we have to work out the how. Thanks to Kell, we have a lot more flexibility. First, let's talk about why we are here. Maja, if you would, lights please. Screen," she said. She sat down.

The room lights dimmed and a screen activated.

B'ani had been listening carefully. She leaned towards Maru. "She doesn't have a plan, does she?" she whispered.

Maru shook her head. "I don't think so, not yet," she whispered.

B'ani shook her head. "Oh great. We're out in here wherever that is and," she said.

Maru grinned and shrugged. "Sit back and enjoy the show?" she asked.

B'ani leaned back in her chair and held out her hand. "Where's the popcorn?" she asked.

They both giggled.

Maja appeared next to the screen. She started a video montage. "These images show the ecosystems of planets as they were before and after the Olmeri arrived. What used to be productive farmland is desert, the lakes and rivers have been polluted beyond use, and huge swaths of land have been converted into these mega cities. We don't know how many of the native species on these planets have been wiped out. We suspect most of them," she said.

N'amani looked down. His shoulders were shaking. "My people would not fare well. It would mean the end of our entire way of life. Everything my family has worked for. It takes generations to grow a forest. It would all be gone. For what? For what!" he said. He pressed his hands on the table and lowered his chest.

Maru slowed her breathing, reached out her hand, and touched his arm gently. She was going to use her skills as a Keeper of Water to calm him. "We cannot do anything about that which we do not know. We must know. Quiet. Be still. Quiet," she thought. She didn't say anything. She smiled at N'amani with a deep kindness and an understanding that was more than empathy.

N'amani looked at Maru. He stopped shaking. He could feel her calmness reach into him. She was so very quiet and still, like midnight after a snowfall. Nothing moving, not even the wind. So quiet. He could feel something more. Something deeper. Something she didn't want him to see.

Maru took her hand away

"Thank you," N'amani said softly.

Maru nodded.

The Ambassador touched a control on the table. It opened a 3D model of the local neighborhood and nearby star systems. The stars appeared at various heights and were spread out across the display as if she'd somehow managed to miniaturize part of the galaxy.

"Nice!" Kell said.

"Thank you," Maja, Beth, and the Ambassador all said at once.

Captain Logan nodded. "It really is quite a display," he said.

The Ambassador looked at her old friends then at Captain Logan and her team. She pointed at the display. "The Olmeri have begun forays into this area near the Hyades Cluster. Traders with the Alliance have had occasional encounters with them as have the Aldarans. We met them near Ka'len, here. As far as we know, this is the closest they have come to actually entering the Orion Arm. What do your people know about how the Olmeri advance, Kell?" she asked.

Kell took a breath. "My people avoid them. They start by appearing outwardly humble. They offer to help with this or that. As soon as they gain a foothold, their attitude changes. They start making demands and issuing orders, as if they are the rulers and everyone else is a servant. They have long disputed this characterization. But it is in fact, their view and their goal. My people have seen it repeatedly. Up to now, they've mostly left us alone. We have not seen them be this aggressive before. They seem to be skipping the outwardly humble phase and going straight to the 'we are here to rule you' phase," he said.

Beth nodded. "The Alliance is getting the same information from our traders. We think that is their way of testing to find out what level of resistance there is going to be to their invasion," she said.

"Invasion?" Sentar asked.

"You have a better word for it?" Captain Logan asked.

Sentar shook his head and frowned.

Beth went on. "We have some new images from one of our traders that show the damage and how it progresses. I haven't seen them all yet. But I warn you that they are disturbing. This is the third planet in the Tau Ceti system as it was before the Olmeri moved in. Notice the pretty blue color with large water bodies and groups of land masses. If we move in a little closer, we can see various population groupings. These are mostly small cities and towns. We don't see much technological development. Next, we see images taken by the same trader three years after the Olmeri moved in. Notice the color of the water. It is almost black. We can barely distinguish the water from the land masses. As you can see, the planet now has almost no organic life," she said. She turned her head away. Her hands were shaking.

The Ambassador walked over and put her arm around Beth's shoulder. "Shusss. Calm yourself. We have to know. We can't look away. It hurts. I know. I know," she said. She patted Beth on the back gently.

Beth felt an unexplainable calm reach through her. It seemed as if all the pain she just felt was gone. She knew she still hurt. But she didn't feel it anymore.

"Go sit down. Close your eyes and focus on your breathing for a minute," the Ambassador said.

Beth sat down next to N'amani.

N'amani smiled at Beth and took hold of her hand.

"Maja, would you continue please," the Ambassador asked.

Maja started another series of images. "The civilizations on Tau Ceti 3 were not advanced enough to fend off the Olmeri. At first, they didn't realize they should. The Olmeri offered technologies and engineering – what Terrans call shiny new toys and pretty beads. The Olmeri said all they wanted in return was a little bit of space to set up a few remote outposts for their traders. Nothing much, just a small area, somewhere out of the way. But once they got started, they had to bring in more Olmeri to supply the outposts. Then, they needed to expand their farms and needed Olmeri workers to manage things. Next, they needed to do some mining. They needed building materials, didn't they? Next, they needed to rechannel a few rivers to divert water for the mines and the camps of workers building the cities. Nothing to worry about. Just a small change. As they brought in more and more workers from Olm, their home world, the people who originally lived on the planet were quickly displaced. The Olmeri began insisting everyone learn the Olmeri language and customs. At first, there were confrontations. But dissent was quickly quashed and the original people were pushed to the outlying areas. The Olmeri promised to take care of everything. They did. Most of the original life forms on the planet, plants and animals have become extinct. Many areas have been so poisoned by the Olmeri's activities they can't sustain any life at all. The Olmeri dump massive amounts of solid and liquid waste into the surface waters. They use sub-strata engineering to extract ground water for their massive synthetic food processing facilities. By the time they finish, there is nothing of the original world left," she said.

N'amani had been gripping the arm of his chair as he watched the images. "There is no respect for life in what they do. So much is gone," he said. He was not able to hold back tears any longer. He bowed his head and started sobbing.

Beth tightened her grip on his hand. "N'amani," she said. She tugged on his hand like a little sister.

Maru reached out to touch his hand again. "You are not alone. I am here," she said quietly so only he could hear.

He felt her voice again. It was so quiet, so calm. He stopped shaking.

Galen looked at Maru. "Do you need...?" he asked
Maru shook her head.

Sentar sat still. His jaw tightened as he watched.

B'ani narrowed her eyes in anger.

The Doctor looked down.

Captain Logan and his officers shook their heads.

"What a waste," Commander Brandon said sadly.

The Ambassador looked around the room. "Maja, please
stop the images," she said quietly. The screen went dark. She
walked over and put her hand on N'amani's shoulder. "You
are in very good hands, N'amani," she said. She patted his
shoulder gently and nodded her thanks to Maru.

The Ambassador started pacing. She wanted them to
watch her, not think about the images. "Let's review the
pattern. First, the Olmeri make a few forays into a sector to
find out, well, basically to find out who lives there and what
their capabilities are. They look for less-developed worlds
with lots of raw materials. Sometimes it seems they want
minerals. Sometimes it seems they want whatever the targeted
ecosystems provide. They start by trying to develop
benevolent relationships with those worlds. They offer goods
and technologies in exchange for raw materials. Then, they
find something that must be done that can only be done by
Olmeri workers. Building new docking ports for their ships,
for instance. They need special technical skills. So, they need
to bring specialists from Olm. Those workers have to live
somewhere. They would like to eat familiar Olmeri food, not
whatever the locals have. As more and more work needs to be
done by Olmeri, more and more Olmeri arrive. They consume
more of the planet's natural resources to build more megacities so they can bring in more Olmeri. Whatever benefits
were promised during the negotiations are always delivered,
the Olmeri are good about that. But they never benefit of the

original inhabitants. The cities are always only ever built to benefit the Olmeri," she said.

Sentar nodded. "I see the problem," he said.

The Ambassador sighed. "We used to hear stories occasionally from trade ships who had encounters with them. Over the past 3 years, we've heard more and more stories. Right now, our information puts the Olmeri generally in this area, just outside the Sagittarius arm. We know they are moving. We have recent reports from long-distance traders about problems in these five systems near Arcturus. Recently, we've heard some very quiet reports that not all Olmeri are in favor of the destruction. They want to stop it. We've not made contact with them," she said.

Galen grinned. He looked around the room. "Three guesses where we're going," he said.

Everyone in the room laughed. Then, they all looked at the Ambassador with a bit of skepticism and the realization that she had just told them exactly where they were going and what they would be doing.

The Ambassador nodded, confirming what they were thinking. "Ok, then. Here's the plan. We want to lead them away from the Orion Arm and redirect them towards this sector in the Perseus Transit. Notice this asteroid belt. We're going to seed it to bring them in. They will think they have found a massive new source of minerals. Then, we create a trail of mineral readings and planetary signatures that will lead them to these systems with mineral deposits. The other systems nearby have enough natural resources to keep them occupied for we hope, at least a few years," she said.

Kell grimaced a little. "We're going to do what we did with the asteroid belt near Ka'len? I'd rather not," he said.

The Ambassador shook her head and smiled broadly. "This time, you stay outside the belt. We don't want to confuse them," she said.

Kell grinned. "We want them to find the breadcrumbs," he said.

Sentar smiled, looked over at Galen, nodded, and shrugged.

Galen shrugged and nodded. "Might," he said.

The Ambassador grinned at Kell. "Exactly. We want to lead them through this empty corridor, here. We'll put the EM projectors along an arc along this corridor. As the Olmeri ships come thru, they will have a few minor instrument failures as we tag them and upload a virus. The virus will let us feed them false readings and wipe parts of their navigation logs. But if the virus can't get them to turn back or go somewhere else, we have a fallback. Any ship that gets past this point will trigger the array to emit a directed EM pulse. It will disable all but their local drive for a short time. They will have to turn back. When they do, the virus will scramble their logs so they won't know where they were and can't avoid the area," she said.

Kell smiled. He'd written that part of the virus.

"We know they will figure it out eventually," the Ambassador continued. "We're counting on having seeded enough worlds that they will call for more Olmeri and be so distracted by the wealth they are going to have that they don't notice it's not real until it's too late. We're hoping it will be at least a year before they figure out what's going on. By blocking these corridors – here, here, and here – we cut off the most direct routes to the Orion Arm and to the Central Alliance systems. We would like them to bypass the Orion Arm entirely," she said.

Captain Logan looked closely at the pattern she was setting up. He nodded. "It could work," he said.

The Ambassador stood taller. "Our mission, if you choose to accept it," she said grinning at the cliché and knowing they had already accepted, "is to find out what the Olmeri are doing in these five systems, find and make contact with the resistance, and lead as many of the Olmeri as possible to their new home," she said.

Lt. Katy once again had a puzzled expression on her face. She was capable and a quick study. But she was quite young. She still did not understand what it meant to be a Keeper or what an Adept could do. "But, Ambassador, how can we do all that? It's going to take," she said.

Captain Logan shot her a look that said 'shut up now.'

The Ambassador frowned. "You have much to learn and you should shut up and do it," she thought. "Yes, Lieutenant. It's going to take all our skills and quite a bit of luck. For now, I'd like to ask Beth and N'amani to load the reports they have collected. After lunch, Captain Logan will review the Magellan's special features and we'll have a look at the ships we'll be using. Then, we'll spend some time with the maps and various routes. Kell, would you help me work on some alternative planning? Since your people are coming to help, we have some options we need to discuss and we must reconsider how to prepare," she said.

"Of course, Ambassador," Kell said. He stood up to leave with her.

"What's for lunch?" Maru asked. She stood up and patted N'amani's shoulder. "Come join us," she said.

N'amani nodded and smiled a 'thank you' to her. "As soon as we get the reports set up," he said.

"Yangroutang," the Ambassador replied over her shoulder as she and Kell left the room.

Sentar and B'ani doubled over laughing.

The Doctor got up. "I'll make something. Not yangroutang," he said.

Galen smiled. "I'll come with you. I'd like to have a look at what's available on board," he said.

Sentar grinned. "We're going to have a good lunch today!" he said.

B'ani laughed and took Sentar's arm. "Let's go," she said.

Maru laughed. "We will meet you in the dining hall," she said to N'amani. They walked out.

Captain Logan, Commander Brandon, and Lt. Katy followed them out the door.

N'amani and Beth set up the reports so that each of the five would have quick access to what they needed. It didn't take them long. Then, they went to join the others in the dining hall.

ANOTHER TIME
THE AMBASSADOR'S QUARTERS ON THE MAGELLAN

The Ambassador had invited her old friends to have a private dinner in her quarters. Several plates with the remnants of vegetables, pies, and a whole fish were scattered on the table. There were a few empty wine bottles, too.

"You know why I asked you here?" the Ambassador asked. She looked around the table.

"Dinner and drinks?" Maru asked.

"Wine tasting?" B'ani asked.

"Yes, a wine tasting!" Galen said. He raised his glass.

"Let's have more!" Sentar bellowed, maybe just a little too loud.

They all laughed. They knew.

"We have something to do," the Ambassador said, beginning the invocation.

"It will take all of us..." Maru joined in.

"...and all our skills," B'ani finished.

"We do not know what we must do," Galen said.

"We must succeed," Sentar said, completing the refrain. "Micha, we have not tried to do anything like this many, many years. And I'm not particularly fond it," he said.

B'ani looked at Maru then at Sentar. "We do it all the time! It's not that intrusive and it can be extremely helpful," she said.

"I'm good with the helpful part. It's the intrusive part I don't like," Sentar said.

Maru smiled. "I don't know what B'ani is thinking specifically. It's more a sense of what kind of thoughts, what kind of feelings she is having. If she's in trouble, I know it instantly," she said.

"But it would be all of us," Sentar said.

"Well, yes. That's the point," B'ani said.

"We haven't done this since training," Sentar said.

"I know. There will be a lot to sort through," the Ambassador said.

Galen nodded. "It's the best way, Sentar. We won't know what we will need until we get there. At least, if we have to, we can draw on all our skills," he said.

"Not ideal," Sentar said.

"Y'think?" B'ani quipped.

"You have a better idea?" Maru asked.

"Whatever we are going to do will be risky," Galen pointed out.

"No! Really?" the Ambassador asked.

"That's my point," Sentar said.

"Each of us has a gift and an element we keep. When we share, it makes us stronger," Maru said.

"We didn't practice that so much. I'm not sure," Sentar said.

Galen smiled at Sentar. "Now is a good time to practice. We need to do this," he said.

"What if we just do a little now? Ten seconds? Would that be ok?" Ambassador suggested.

"That would be ok," Sentar said. Then, he smiled and shook his head. "You always were a good negotiator," he said.

The Ambassador grinned and extended her hand to Sentar. "So, we begin..." she started.

"I know the path," Sentar said. He reached for Maru's hand.

"I see the changes," Maru said. She reached for Galen's hand.

"I form the bridge," Galen said. He reached for B'ani's hand.

"I carry the light," B'ani said. She reached for the Ambassador's hand.

"I keep the balance," the Ambassador said. She lowered her head then sat upright to extend her energy in both directions, to Sentar on one side and B'ani on the other.

The others all sat a little straighter and extended their energy in both directions.

"We are different and the same. We return to one and become one." they said in unison.

The joining was complete. They could see each other and keep their own separate thoughts. But they could also sense what the others were feeling. They were all breathing together, as one.

Master Tai had insisted they learn this merging skill. He didn't explain. He just told them they were going to learn it.

Much later, they found out that this skill was one of the most treasured skills in all the Ancient Arts. Every one of the Masters wanted students who could learn it. The problem was finding five students who could form the group. Master Tai had seen their potential and selected them.

"In the center there is balance," the Ambassador said. She released her hands.

"And new beginnings," Sentar said. He released his hands.

"We start," Maru said. She released her hands.

"We continue," Galen said. He released his hands.

"One becomes many," B'ani said. She released her hands.

"We are many," they said in unison. They sat back to look at the table and each other.

"That wasn't at all what I remembered from practice." Sentar said with a hint of a smile. "It was actually sort of nice. It seemed as if I was twice as strong as I normally am," he said.

"Maybe we should hold off on that? You are already stronger than three of me," Galen said.

"We helped. We've been practicing," Maru and B'ani said in unison.

"We were able to sort out most of the confusion." B'ani said. "When we were learning, we didn't have the discipline to keep quiet for very long," she said.

"To keep our thoughts quiet," Maru said.

"Yes," B'ani smiled at Maru. "To keep our thoughts quiet. Just now, we shared that skill with all of you," she said.

Sentar sat forward. "That's what seemed so nice! There was a moment when I was quiet and I could still feel all of you. But it wasn't noisy or intrusive. It was like…," he said.

"Sitting at a table having a quiet dinner with old friends?" the Ambassador asked.

Sentar nodded. Then, he sat very still. "You...?" he asked.
The Ambassador grinned and nodded.

Sentar shook his head and grinned as he realized what she'd done. He walked over to her chair, picked her up, hugged her, and set her down.

The Ambassador put her arms around his neck, hugged him, and smiled.

"More wine!" Galen called out. He raised his glass.

CHAPTER 7:
ENDINGS AND BEGINNINGS
PART 3: GOING HOME

Wanderer, look to your footsteps
The road will follow you and lead you home

DO YOU REMEMBER?
THE DINING HALL ON THE MAGELLAN

The Ambassador, Sentar, Maru, B'ani, and Galen were sitting in the back corner of the dining hall. The table was littered with creatively stacked small plates. Some had a few remaining items. Several empty bottles of jiu, a clear alcohol from Ras 2 with a somewhat floral aroma and the kick of a mule, were scattered among the dishes.

They had spent the past two weeks in strategy meetings or in the ship's simulators working on their evasion and fighting techniques. This would be the last time they'd have to relax together until after the mission was over. Once they docked at the station, they would go to their respective ships.

"Do you remember that time when we were staying in the mountain cabin and Micha came up the stairs," B'ani started.

"As if she had somehow appeared out of nowhere? And the two fellows who had been standing at the top jumped and ran off?" Maru finished.

The Ambassador almost dropped her cup laughing. "I don't think I will ever forget the look of bewilderment on their faces. Not only were they not expecting anyone, they were most definitely not expecting someone like me to be coming up those stairs," she said.

B'ani chuckled. "They were so frightened. We could see it on their faces as they ran past us," she said.

The Ambassador grinned. "I wasn't trying to scare them. I was just practicing," she said.

B'ani winked and smiled a knowing smile. "How did you do that, by the way?" she asked.

The Ambassador grinned and lowered her head. "I told them to look for me coming down the stairs behind them," she said.

Being able to misdirect then counter was a skill Master Tai had required they all learn. It took some concentration to plant the misdirection. The counter was easier, as long as the setup was complete.

Sentar nodded to B'ani then looked at Micha. "Her skills at being quiet are pretty good, too. Helps with surprises," he said.

Maru nodded and smiled. "We all had to learn that. Moving quietly is one of the essential skills," she said.

B'ani raised her glass. "Only in quiet..." she said.

"Can we hear the wind." Maru finished as she raised her glass.

Galen smiled at Micha and raised his glass. "To being quiet," he said.

They all drained their glasses again.

Galen turned his head to the side. "Do you remember the first time Master Tai tried to teach us that lesson?" he asked.

Sentar laughed. "I absolutely remember that. Micha asked directly "Is that some kind of riddle?" he said.

The Ambassador pouted. "And I learned never to do that again," she said.

Sentar looked down a little and smiled. "The look on your face when Master Tai came around the table was priceless," he said.

The Ambassador shook her head. "I am never going to forget that. I was already upset over being scolded about the garden. I muttered something about him always talking in riddles. He was all the way over on the other side of the room. The next thing I knew, he was standing in front of me. "How could you hear me?" I asked. "I was listening. You are loud. You must become quiet." Took me a full year of practice to understand what he was talking about," she said.

"Only one?" B'ani asked grinning.

"How long did he make you clean the pigeon coops?" Maru asked.

The Ambassador looked down, frowned, shook her head, then smiled a little. "Three months. And every day, he came to make sure I did a good job," she said.

Sentar nodded. "He is still a task-master. He insists on perfection and if it's not right..." he said.

"Do it again!" Galen, Micha, Maru, and B'ani shouted all together. It was Master Tai's favorite phrase and his answer for everything.

Galen stood, picked up one of the bottles of jiu, and poured for everyone. "Cheers to Master Tai!" he said raising his glass.

They grew quiet.

Sentar smiled, stood, and raised his glass. "Quiet the mind, quiet the heart. Listen to the stillness. Then, we can hear others. When we can hear others, we can learn what is in their hearts. And, we can choose to let them hear us – or not," he said.

Maru nodded to Sentar, stood, and raised her glass. "From the Second Book of the Ancients. There can be no movement without stillness. If the mind and the body are not quiet, the energy cannot flow. In the blink of an eye, we find the changes," she said.

B'ani also stood up and raised her glass. "Within stillness, movement is born. When the Tiger and Dragon join together, the true Spirit will emerge," she said.

The Ambassador stood up and raised her glass. "First, we must learn to be quiet," she said.

Galen looked up and then lowered his head sadly. "That took me a long time," he said.

Sentar nudged Galen's shoulder. "You had a lot to deal with. Give yourself credit," he said.

Micha smiled sympathetically. "Indeed," she said.

"We wouldn't be who we are otherwise," Maru said.

B'ani offered another toast. "To who we were! Bottoms up!" she said.

They all drained their glasses again.

These were teachings they had lived by. They had long ago become part of each of them. They weren't separate things. They were joined with who they were.

The Ambassador looked around the table. She didn't have to say anything. They all knew it was time. "We have tomorrow to rest. Take advantage of it. We rendezvous with the other ships at the space station and meet the Aldarans in two days," she said.

Galen leaned forward. "This was a very nice dinner, Micha. As always. You managed to have more than enough but not too much," he said.

Sentar looked at the table sideways. "I'd like to remember the stacked plates. We are still very creative at plate stacking," he said proudly.

"Were you offering to do dishes?" Micha asked.

"No, I was just admiring our balancing skills," Sentar replied.

They all laughed and got up to leave.

WHICH WAY TO GO
THE DINING HALL ON THE MAGELLAN

The Ambassador hung back a bit and watched the others leave. She walked over to look out the large observation windows. There wasn't much to see. She didn't care. She wasn't really looking out. She was looking at her reflection.

Maru turned back and went to stand with her. "Micha? Are you okay?" Maru asked.

"Do you remember that cove we used to go to?" the Ambassador asked. She looked up. She didn't turn. She looked at Maru's reflection in the darkened window.

"For early morning practice? Of course." Maru said. She looked at Micha's reflection in the window.

The Ambassador smiled wistfully. "It was always cool at that time of day. The sand was dark and the ocean always made sure we knew it was present. It was constant. Some days, it would barely creep ashore. The water lapped the sand so quietly. There were no waves. The ocean seemed to be some sort of indigo glass, reflecting even the birds as they flew overhead," she said. A tear ran down her cheek, then another, and another.

"Oh Micha, what' is it?" Maru asked. She touched the Ambassador's arm gently and turned towards her.

"Tonight reminded me of all the times before. The time the five of us first met each other. Our training together, the adventures we had, Master Tai, all of it just came rushing back. So many memories. I miss those days," the Ambassador said. She stood quietly and stopped trying to hold back the tears. One ran down her cheek, then another.

Maru nodded. A tear ran down her cheek, too. "Sometimes, so do I, old friend. So do I. For tonight let's remember the smiles. Let's remember we were all here. Together again," she said. She tucked her arm through the Ambassador's and pulled her close.

The Ambassador hooked her arm and pulled Maru closer, too. The tears were still streaming down her cheeks.

They stood there, side by side, arm in arm, looking at each other in the window, not saying anything.

Maru patted the Ambassador's arm then let go. "We've been through a lot. None of it was easy," she said.

The Ambassador smiled. She turned into the room and started pacing. "We still have more to do. It has to be done," she said.

Maru shook her head. "That's not really what's bothering you, is it?" she asked.

The Ambassador lowered her head. "You see it, don't you? Thank you. Are we doing the right thing, Maru? Am I doing the right thing? What I'm asking of you, of B'ani, Galen, Sentar, of my team. It's not going to be easy. We could fail... or worse," she said.

Maru walked over to face Micha, put her hands on Micha's shoulders, and looked straight at her. "What you are asking of us is that we be who we are. Do you honestly think that we would let you do this alone?" she asked.

The Ambassador smiled quietly. "No. You wouldn't. That's why I hesitated to ask," she said.

Maru frowned and turned her head with a slight smile. "Who else you gonna call?" she asked.

The Ambassador laughed.

Maru smiled. "That's better. We're always going to be here for each other. You have more than just the four of us, Micha. I can see the love and respect everyone on your team has for you. They wouldn't let you go out alone, either," she said.

The Ambassador nodded humbly. "I remind myself how grateful I am for them every day. I'm worried about what we are going to try to do. There are so many things that could go wrong," she said.

Maru shook her head. "What about what can go right?" she asked.

The Ambassador started pacing again. She walked back over to the windows. "I don't worry too much about that. We know what that might look like. What I'm having trouble with is the alternatives. What if this, what if that. What are the choices?" she asked.

Maru turned her head and rolled her eyes. "I've seen your plans in more detail than I want, Micha. We've talked through I forgot how many strategies and scenarios. There aren't a lot of options and none of them are good. We're going to go roll the dice and hope we get lucky," she said.

The Ambassador raised her eyebrows, pursed her lips, and narrowed her eyes. She smiled a little. "We've always been lucky," she said.

Maru looked up and frowned. "Skill," she said.

The Ambassador smiled and nodded. "That too. But that's the problem. If we knew what would stop them, we could figure out what skills we need to make it work. But we don't know. We need to find a weakness, something that we can use against them," she said.

Maru looked at her carefully. "Your plan will also show their strengths. You know that right? We still have to find that out, too. Right now, we are standing outside. We see what they are doing. We are trying to find a way to stop them," she said.

The Ambassador frowned. "Yes, that's true. What's your point?" she asked.

"We are outside," Maru said.

The Ambassador shook her head. "What do you mean? I'm not following you," she said.

Maru smiled. "You want to find a way to get inside," she said.

The Ambassador shook her head again and frowned. "Well, yes. The Olmeri won't talk to us. So, we can't just ask them what they are thinking or find out through conversation," she said.

Maru smiled. She walked over to the windows and turned around. "We are only looking at this from our point of view. We see the destruction. What do they see?" she asked.

"I'm still not following you," the Ambassador said.

Maru looked out the windows again. "Perspective. Remember? Look inward to see what is true. Look outward to see the reflections. How do the Olmeri see what they are doing? What's their perspective? What do they think? Your plan, risky as it is, gives us a chance to find out," she said.

The Ambassador went over to stand next to the windows with Maru. "Well, yes. If we want to stop them, we need to find out what motivates them," she said.

Maru turned to look at the Ambassador. "There's something else we are going to find out," she said.

The Ambassador frowned. "What's that? I thought I'd covered everything we needed to find out," she said.

Maru grinned. "Oh, this isn't something we are going to try to find out. But it is something we are going to find out," she said.

The Ambassador grinned and bowed. "Thank you, Master Tai," she said.

Maru frowned and took a deep breath. "We are going to find out how they respond," she said.

The Ambassador stopped and grew quiet. "You are right. Whatever we do, the Olmeri are going to respond. They don't like us. We already know that," she said.

Maru took a step back and shook her head. "Not what I meant and you know it. Whatever we do, they are going to do something in response. We're absolutely going to find out what that is," she said.

The Ambassador took a deep breath and nodded. She smiled and turned towards Maru. "All the scenarios, all the plans, all the possible outcomes. Yes. Yes. Whatever they do will tell us something too. The shape of the form comes from what is there," she started.

"Usefulness comes from what is not." Maru finished.

"Maru..." the Ambassador said. She wanted to say thank you but it really wasn't necessary.

Maru grinned. "I know," she said.

The Ambassador nodded. She started pacing again. "We do have an advantage. The Aldarans. But after the first encounter, the Olmeri will know the Aldarans are helping us. We only get one chance," she said.

Maru shook her head. "Maybe, maybe not. You are making a big assumption. Why do we have to let the Olmeri know the Aldarans are helping us?" she asked.

The Ambassador frowned. "The Olmeri are destructive but they aren't stupid. Once they see how the ships are maneuvered, they'll know. Nobody can pilot a ship like an Aldaran," she said.

Maru tilted her head back a little and smiled. "Why can't they? Maybe we can misdirect them on that, too. It would give us at least one, maybe two more opportunities," she said.

The Ambassador turned her head sideways. "They know I have an Aldaran pilot. They don't know more Aldarans are joining us. So maybe Kell has been giving flying lessons? Is that what you are thinking?" she asked.

Maru shrugged and nodded. "It's not that much of a stretch. And with a little help," she said.

The Ambassador grinned and stopped pacing. "It might just work. It might.... It might just work. What if the Aldarans actually do the flying, but somehow, we arrange for the Olmeri to see someone else in the pilot's chair. The Olmeri don't even need to know the Aldarans are on board. If we can convince the Olmeri that whoever is in the pilot chair can do what an Aldaran can do that would give us an even bigger advantage. It could also make the Olmeri a lot less inclined to look at Alliance properties for their development activities. You were always so good with tactics. Maru, this is brilliant!" she said.

Maru smiled with humble pride. "Thank you. I try. But you know what the biggest problem with this idea is, don't you?" she asked.

The Ambassador sighed and nodded slowly. "The Olmeri have to be allowed to see who is sitting in the chair. That means we have to get really, really close," she said.

"Close is an understatement. And then there's what you're asking of the Aldarans," Maru said.

The Ambassador nodded thoughtfully. "I'll speak to Kell first. Asking them to just 'step aside' isn't something we can do, not when we are asking them to use their piloting and navigation skills to help us," she said.

"Don't you dare frame it like that," Maru said.

The Ambassador blinked.

Maru shook her head. "The Aldarans are helping us? Really? That's not the perspective you want to present and it's certainly not something the Aldarans should expect to do. We are not asking them to help us. We are asking them to stand with us. Big difference. We need to find a way to stop the Olmeri from coming into the local neighborhood. The Aldarans could be the key," she said.

The Ambassador bowed. "Thank you, Master Tai. Keep reminding me," she said.

Maru smiled. "Every chance I get," she said.

The Ambassador smiled. "That gives me an idea. I have something that would make our appreciation clear," she said.

Maru turned her head slightly. "The Aldarans don't value objects so much. They don't like medals, awards, or showy things. What do you have that the Aldarans would consider had that much value?" she asked.

"Regulan Star Coins. I can give one to each of the pilots," the Ambassador whispered.

Maru's eyes got big. "You have what? How did you?" she asked.

"A private trade group I escorted to Epsilon Indi many, many years ago. I told them it was too much, but they insisted," the Ambassador replied.

Maru ginned. "They got the deal?" she asked.

The Ambassador smiled. "Oh yes," she said.

Maru nodded. "That should do it. Those coins are such a big part of Aldaran history. The early traders used to pay the Aldarans in Star Coins. I can't think of anything that would better show our appreciation for their help now and for their culture," she said.

The Ambassador took a deep breath. "It seems I need to arrange a recognition ceremony for the Aldarans. I feel better now. Thanks!" she said.

Maru grinned. "Glad I could help," she said.

The Ambassador grabbed her shoulders and gave her a hug. "Old friend, you have done so much more. Thank you," she said.

Maru smiled and winked at her. "Let's get some sleep. Tomorrow is going to be a long day," she said.

"Tomorrow is always a long day," the Ambassador replied.

They linked arms and walked out together.

COMING INTO THE STATION
CAPTAIN LOGAN'S QUARTERS ON THE MAGELLAN

Captain Logan was at his desk in his quarters, reviewing the charts and plans. He was still having a bit of trouble seeing how this was going to work. Oh, he understood the plan and the tactics and what they hoped to accomplish. But he wasn't sure it was going to be enough. The Olmeri were persistent and formidable. They weren't going to be deterred easily.

"Captain, I have Station Commander Lucas for you," Commander Brandon's voice came through his comm link. She had the watch.

"Put him through," Captain Logan replied.

The comm link lit up.

Commander Lucas appeared on the screen. "Good morning, Captain Logan. We've been expecting you," he said.

"Commander Lucas. It's good to see you again. It's been a while," Captain Logan said.

"Eight years, isn't it?" Commander Lucas asked.

Captain Logan nodded. "About that, I think. We'll have to catch up later. There are a few things we need to discuss," he said.

Commander Lucas chuckled. "Y'think? Some of your friends have already arrived and we have four starships docked and waiting for something. We might have a few things to go over. Just a few," he said.

Captain Logan laughed. "Mushrooms, Bob. Mushrooms," he said.

Commander Lucas laughed out loud. "Indeed, Alex. That we are. So, you called. What did you need me to do that you can't tell me about?" he asked.

Now it was Captain Logan's turn to laugh out loud. He composed himself and took a breath. "I have a request from Ambassador Lawrence," he said.

"Does she want the dinner special or the lunch plate?" Commander Lucas asked.

Captain Logan laughed. "Oh, you are so very close. So close. She'd like a formal reception to recognize the help we are getting from the Aldarans. Everyone in full dress for a formal presentation," he said as quickly as he could trying to get it all out at once.

"Well. That's quite a tall order on short notice. Does she understand what it's going to take to pull off any reception, let alone a formal one in ... how far out are you?" Commander Lucas asked.

"About twelve hours. I can make it fourteen if that helps," Captain Logan answered.

Commander Lucas laughed and shook his head. "Ok sure. Two more hours would be great. Thanks. This is going to be a tough thing to pull off. We've got our regular duty and quite a bit to get done for your excursion. I'm assuming she wants compliments from all four ships, too," he said.

Captain Logan nodded. "She knows it's really big ask. Trust me. I've been transporting her for a few months now. I've seen her pull off what should have been impossible more than once. She's good at it. If she thinks it can be done, it's possible. Highly improbable is something she does regularly," he said.

"But you just said she's not asking for just my people. She wants everybody. That means a full crew compliment from each command and each ship along with a presentation table and reception. Why does she need a big formal reception? Couldn't we do something smaller, less formal?" Commander Lucas asked.

Captain Logan shook his head. "Not for this," he said.

Commander Lucas shook his head again. "It's a lot of work for a little recognition ceremony," he said.

"Bob," Captain Logan said. He looked at the screen and stopped. "Maja, priority encryption, level 9, full scramble, your record only. Both channels," he said.

Commander Lucas shook his head. "That's way above my pay grade, Alex," he said.

"You need to know, Bob. Maja," Captain Logan said.

"Yes, Captain," Maja said.

The screens blurred then became clear again.

Captain Logan looked directly at the screen. "The Aldarans have agreed to pilot for us. That much you know. What you don't know and I'm not telling you right now is that she doesn't want the Olmeri to know that the Aldarans are with us. She wants the Olmeri to believe that maybe the Aldarans are teaching us. So, she's going to arrange it so the Olmeri can see a Terran in a pilot's chair," he said.

"She's nuts! Does she know how close she will have to get?" Commander Lucas said.

Captain Logan smiled and nodded in agreement. "I have thought that exact thing several times myself. But she has a way of pulling off things that seemed impossible. One of the keys to her plan is the piloting skills of the Aldarans. She's counting on them to be able to do it. And Bob, I am here to tell you, I've seen what Kell can do. Her confidence is well-founded. He's a magician in flight," he said.

Commander Lucas nodded. "Okay. Now I get why she wants the reception. We're counting on the Aldarans for their expertise and we're going to insult them by asking them to step aside and pretend a human can do what they can do? Right. Even with a nice reception, how is she going to pull that off without insulting them?" he asked.

Captain Logan shrugged. "I don't know. But you're right, that's why she wants the reception," he said.

Commander Lucas shook his head. "Alright. I'll take care of it. Give me as much time as you can. What's she going to present?" he asked.

Captain Logan turned his head with a puzzled frown. "Huh?" he said.

Commander Lucas smiled. "She wants me to set up a reception for a formal presentation. What's she going to present?" he asked.

Captain Logan laughed. "I don't know. She didn't say. I hadn't thought about it," he said.

Commander Lucas nodded and grinned. "Mushrooms, Alex," he said.

"Thanks Bob," Captain Logan said. He closed the comm link, sat back in his chair, and frowned. "What is she going to present?" he thought.

SHORT NOTICE
THE STATION COMMANDER'S OFFICE

The station was remote. It was not tethered, so there wasn't much in the way of planetary decoration. Only a few potted plants were set out along the corridors. The loading area was busy. Central Alliance cargo ships had mineral dust and other supplies that had to be sorted, separated, and loaded on each of the five star ships.

The Ambassador stepped off a transport platform onto the Station. She walked down a wide hallway then up a flight of stairs to the Commander's Office. She stopped at the open door and knocked.

Commander Lucas looked up, stood, and waved to her to come in. "I'm pleased to welcome you to Theta Alpha, Ambassador Lawrence. It has been a long time," he said.

The Ambassador grinned as she walked into his office. "It has been a long time, Bob. You weren't a station commander then," she said.

Commander Lucas grinned. "And you weren't an ambassador," he said.

They both laughed.

"I have quite a few memories of the days you flew transport for the trade missions I was assigned to escort," the Ambassador said.

Commander Lucas nodded. He gestured to a chair and went back to his desk to sit. "The reception will be ready in about three hours. It's the best we can do. My staff have been working non-stop since I spoke with Captain Logan. They are putting the final touches on the side tables now. Once that's done, we'll notify everyone to assemble and bring out the food for the main table," he said.

The Ambassador smiled and looked at him closely. "I appreciate the effort, Bob. My apologies for the late notice. Captain Logan said he told you. It's important that..." she said.

Commander Lucas held up his hand to stop her. "Ambassador, yes, he told me. I get it. I only meant that we could do better with more time. I've asked my chefs to include some Aldaran foods plus some fruit we've grown here on the station and add their own specialties. It will be a nice table," he said.

The Ambassador smiled. "It sounds perfect, Bob. I really do appreciate the work it takes to put something like this together at the last minute. If it wasn't important, I wouldn't have asked. Thank you and please extend my thanks to your staff for their hard work and efforts," she said.

Commander Lucas nodded. "I will do that. We're happy to support your mission. Having the Aldarans' bring their skills to the effort could make all the difference," he said.

The Ambassador took a deep breath, smiled, and stood up. "Thank you, Bob. I should go to get ready," she said.

Command Lucas stood up and nodded to her. "You're welcome, Ambassador," he said.

The Ambassador took the long way back to the transport platforms so she could have a look at the reception area.

RED ENVELOPES
THE AMBASSADOR'S QUARTERS ON THE MAGELLAN

The Ambassador was sitting at the table in her quarters on the Magellan. She had almost finished getting dressed for the reception. She had asked Beth to get a small box from her shuttle. She kept several large cases with small bags and boxes that she might use during a trip. Some were personal items. Others were gifts for those they might meet.

The door chime sounded and the comm panel lit up.

"Come in," the Ambassador called out.

Beth came in smiling with a small box in her hand. "I have the things you wanted," she said. She walked over to the table and put the box on it. She took a step back, still looking at the box.

The Ambassador smiled. "You'd like to know what's in the box?" she asked.

Beth nodded. "Yes, please. It has an odd feeling to it," she said.

"Come closer," the Ambassador said. She raised the lid. Small lights flickered from inside the box.

Beth leaned over and peered cautiously into the box. "What are they? They're beautiful," she said.

Inside the box were several small coins unlike anything she had seen before. They glistened and glimmered. There were carvings on them. They looked like tiny mirrors. But the twinkling lights weren't reflected. They were coming from within the coins.

The Ambassador gestured for her to sit down and turned the box so Beth could see inside. "These are Regulan Star Coins," she said.

Beth peered into the box. She looked up at the Ambassador. "Where do they come from? How are they made? How did they get the little lights to shine from inside? Where do the lights come from?" she asked.

The Ambassador sat back a little, smiled, and nodded. "You ask good questions. These are very old coins. They come from Regulus 2. We only know they are made of palladium and ionized silicon fused through radiant fire and frigid water. The process is described in the Ancient Archives. But the art of actually making them was lost centuries ago," she said.

Beth frowned and sat back in her chair. "That's too bad. What are the carvings?" she asked.

The Ambassador smiled, nodded, and took a few of the coins out of the box. She handed them to Beth. "The carvings on the backs reference historical eras. The front depicts the Ancient Leaders of Aldebaran," she said.

Beth's eyes got bigger. She looked at the coins and turned them over. She looked up not quite able to close her mouth. "No way! Wait, you were serious! What are you going to do with them?" she asked.

The Ambassador grinned. "Where are the envelopes I asked you to bring?" she asked.

"Here," Beth said. She took a small packet of red envelopes out of her pocket.

The Ambassador took the packet and pulled out five. "To answer your question, I'm going to put one of these coins in each of these envelopes. I'm going to present them to the

Aldaran pilots at the reception," she said. She put one of the coins in each of the envelopes.

Beth blinked. "Your personal seal is on those envelopes. Ambassador. I thought you were just going to recognize their efforts with a nice reception and a speech," she said.

The Ambassador nodded and smiled. "Well, yes, I'm going to do that. Please bring both archive cameras," she said.

"Ambassador? We only use the archive cameras for treaty signings," Beth said.

The Ambassador smiled and nodded. "Ask N'amani to help you," she said.

Beth looked puzzled. "This isn't just a reception, is it?" she asked.

The Ambassador grinned like a Cheshire cat just beginning to appear and shook her head. "No," she said.

Beth smiled and nodded. "Wow. Whatever it is must be really important," she thought.

The Ambassador picked up the box and the envelopes. She handed them to Beth. "Thank you. Would you please put these back where they were? I will meet you in the reception area. Let me know when you and N'amani are ready," she said.

Beth nodded and started for the door. "Yes, Ambassador. It should only take a few minutes," she said.

The Ambassador nodded. "Thank you, Beth. I'll see you shortly," she said. She watched Beth leave. "Oh, she is a treasure! How many others would have seen those coins and wanted them? She thought they were pretty. She didn't want to keep them," she thought.

The five envelopes were spread out on the table. They weren't sealed. The little lights from the coins peeked out from around the edges.

PRESENTING THE SUN
STATION PROMENADE

A large projection screen on the side of one wall would let everyone see the presentation. The table was beautifully set and arranged with fruits, baskets of breads, several types of cheese, and small plates with pies and cookies. Two colors of punch gave the table a festive appearance. Everyone was dressed in a formal uniform or formal attire.

Sentar, Maru, Galen, and B'ani stood near the front and just to one side. They were dressed formally, but not in their full colors. When they graduated from the program on Ras 2, the Council of Nine had cautioned them about appearing together in their full colors. They were the Five Elements and that was absolutely not something to be revealed lightly or without consideration. For today, only the Ambassador and the Doctor wore their colors.

The Ambassador walked into the receiving hall. She was pleased. There weren't any open spaces.

N'amani and Beth had arrived and were set up on each side of the room. One camera would focus on the Ambassador's presentation. The other camera would focus on the room.

Beth waved to the Ambassador and pointed at N'amani.

The Ambassador waved back and nodded to N'amani. She shook her head to let them know to wait. She spotted Kell standing with four Aldarans near the reception table. She walked towards them.

Kell noticed her coming. They all turned to wait for her to extend their greetings.

"Welcome" the Ambassador said. She crossed her arms, extended her palms, then lowered them. "Pilamayaye hihúŋni. I thank you all for having come here," she said.

The four Aldarans were surprised. They looked at Kell.

Kell nodded approvingly. "Ambassador Lawrence, please let me introduce Pak, Rai, Xora, and Beel. We have known each other since we were children," he said.

The Ambassador bowed. "I'm very pleased to meet all of you. We've arranged this reception to acknowledge what your being here means to all of us," she said.

Pak stepped forward. "We understand the seriousness of this problem," he said.

Kell nodded to him. "Pak is the oldest among us. He has the most experience. He is the best navigator in the galaxy," he said.

"But you are the best pilot," Pak replied nodding to Kell.

Rai frowned a little at their banter. "Thank you for arranging this reception, Ambassador," she said.

Xora stepped up behind Rai. "We're not going to be on display, right? It will only be a few minutes on screen," she whispered.

The Ambassador smiled gently. "No, you won't be on display and yes, it will only be a few minutes. I will say a few words. You don't have to say anything. You can if you like, but you don't have to. Should be no more than two minutes, maybe three. Then, we will go eat. You saw the table, didn't you?" she asked.

Xora grinned and nodded.

The Ambassador looked around the room. She nodded to Beth and N'amani, signaling them to start recording. Then she walked to the center of the floor. She stood there quietly then turned and gestured for Kell and his friends to come stand with her.

The Aldarans formed a line next to her. The room became quiet.

The Ambassador looked up through the windows then around the room, acknowledging where they were. "Thank you. The view from here is exceptional. I appreciate all of you being here today. I'd like to start my remarks by saying thank you to Commander Lucas and his staff for their work on this reception. Commander, on short notice, you have arranged an elegant table with baskets of fruits, plates of small pastries, pies, and a variety of cheeses that were all produced on the station. We thank you and your staff for your efforts and this amazing table today," she said. She extended her hand in a broad sweep towards several of the station staff in duty uniforms standing along the wall.

They all stood just a little taller.

"Today, we have something to celebrate. As you all know, the Alliance has asked the Aldarans to stand with us to defeat the Olmeri and protect the local neighborhood. They have agreed. These five Aldaran pilots will fly with us. We honor our historic defense agreement with Aldebaran today," she said. She turned and bowed deeply to the Aldarans.

The Aldarans bowed to her. This had all been planned.

The Ambassador bowed again to the hall. "In appreciation, I have a small token of thanks which I would like to present," she said. She walked towards the Aldarans.

This was not planned.

Everyone began to applaud.

The Ambassador stepped in front of each of the Aldarans. One by one she took one of the red envelopes out of her pocket and with both hands presented it to the Aldarans. Kell was last. She stood next to him and turned to face the room. She looked at Beth and N'amani.

Beth knew that look. Something was about to happen that she needed to record. She checked her camera and signaled N'amani to check his. She nodded to the Ambassador.

The Ambassador stood quietly and looked around the room for what seemed a long time. It was as if she was looking at each person, one by one, and asking them to remember what she was about to say. That's exactly what she was doing. Finally, she smiled and nodded. "In addition to the thanks of the Central Alliance, I extend my personal thanks to each of our Aldaran friends. I am in your debt," she said. Her voice seemed to fill the entire station. She crossed her arms, extended her palms, brought them down, and bowed deeply to the Aldarans.

Beth almost dropped the recorder. For a First Contact Ambassador to say something like this was a really, really big deal. She was telling the Aldarans and everyone in the room and anyone who might ever see this archive that she was giving them a marker they could call in whenever they needed it.

The Ambassador turned slightly. "There is one more thing. Kell, would you please empty your envelope into your hand?" she asked.

Kell looked puzzled. He shook his head slightly.

"Please," the Ambassador said. She smiled and nodded to encourage him.

Kell held out his hand and turned the envelope over. The coin fell out. Its lights flashed rainbows across its face and his. "Oh, oh, my. It's.... it's...a Star Coin," he gasped. Tears began streaming down his cheeks. He looked at his friends and nodded. "It's a Regulan Star Coin!" he said quietly. The joy in his voice echoed through 500 years.

The others crowded around Kell and the Ambassador. They turned their envelopes over and let the coins fall into their hands.

Kell looked up at her. "Ambassador, how? These are among the most precious, the most revered artifacts of our people. For generations, our people were paid in Star Coins to escort travelers," he said.

Pak stepped closer and held out his coin. His hand was shaking. "Ambassador Lawrence, this is my ancestor. How did you? This is more than we could possibly have imagined," he said.

The Ambassador nodded to him. "You deserve much more. We can talk later," she said quietly. She turned to the room. "Once again, my deepest appreciation to all of you. Now, let's all enjoy some of the fine foods Commander Lucas has put on these tables," she said. She extended her hand towards the tables, signaling Beth and N'amani to pan the tables then stop recording.

The room began to break up.

The Doctor, Sentar, Galen, Maru, and B'ani already had plates in hand and were looking for a place to sit. Several lines had formed around the food tables.

Kell moved closer to the Ambassador. "This is the most amazing, most wonderful, most...," he said.

The Ambassador smiled. "I'm happy you are pleased," she said.

Kell looked at her again with maybe just a bit of reverence. Then, he saw something in her eyes. "She understands. She really does know. She knows," he thought. He knew his friends had seen it too. They saw the coins. They definitely saw the coins. But the coins weren't as important as what he saw in her eyes. He didn't know how, but she knew. She could see them, who they were and who their ancestors were. And she cared. It mattered to her that they existed, that they were who they were. She was a warrior who would defend them. And because of that, he would follow her.

The Ambassador nodded to him and pointed at the food tables. "You should get something to eat while you can," she said

Kell grinned at her, motioned to his friends, and pointed.

They nodded to him and started towards the tables.

"Ambassador, we won't ever forget this," Kell said. He hurried to catch up with his friends.

The Ambassador watched them for a minute then walked up to the mezzanine to get a better view.

Commander Lucas was standing just outside his door. He had been watching. "Nicely done, Ambassador. Very nicely done," he said as she came up the stairs.

"Thank you, Commander. I meant what I said. They deserve more," the Ambassador said.

Commander Lucas smiled. "I'll see what I can do while you're gone," he said.

The Ambassador grinned. "I'd appreciate that. Thank you, Commander. By the way, the tables you set were quite exceptional. They will be icons," she said.

"What do you mean, icons?" Commander Lucas asked.

The Ambassador smiled her Cheshire cat grin. She paused, trying to break the news as gently as possible. "Commander, the reception you arranged for us today is now part of my formal treaty archive and will be referenced as such. It celebrates our new mutual-defense treaty with Aldebaran. Congratulations. You, your staff, the station, and the tables you set for us are going to be part of Alliance history. I'll ask Beth to send you a copy of the footage as soon as she has it ready," she said.

Commander Lucas' eyes got bigger and his mouth dropped open. "Alliance archives? Treaty with the Aldarans? You were recording? The Central Alliance has been trying to get the Aldarans to agree to any kind of mutual-defense treaty for longer than I can remember. They always said no. What, what did you do?" he asked.

The Ambassador nodded. "I reminded them that they were out here long before we were and that we were not asking them to defend us in the sense of being cannon fodder. We are asking them to show us how to defend ourselves and to lend their considerable skills to the fight," she said.

Commander Lucas shook his head. "I don't get it. You didn't ask them to help defend us?" he asked.

"No, Commander. I didn't. I asked them to defend themselves," the Ambassador said.

Commander Lucas nodded. "You really are good," he said.

The Ambassador smiled. "I had help, Bob," she said.

Commander Lucas nodded and grinned. "Thank you, Ambassador. I will let my staff know. We're going to be in the history archives," he said. He was still trying to come to terms with it.

"You set a nice table, Bob. Very nice." the Ambassador said with a big smile. She stood up, nodded, and walked out the door.

"We're going to be in the history archives," Commander Lucas muttered.

SOMETHING TO DO
THE AMBASSADOR'S QUARTERS ON THE MAGELLAN

The Ambassador had invited her classmates to her quarters for dinner. They would be leaving for their respective missions in the morning. They had practiced drills and run scenarios until they couldn't come up with any more possibilities. They knew what they each might need to do. They had finished eating and were lingering around the table. None of them wanted to go.

"This was nice, Micha." Galen said. He put down his glass, pushed his plate aside, and leaned back in his chair. He smiled and rested his hand on his stomach.

The Ambassador grinned happily. "Thank you, but I didn't do it. The Doctor said he wanted to practice. What he can do with simple foods is impressive, isn't it?" she asked.

"He's very good," Sentar said. He nodded approvingly as he picked up another pie.

"High praise coming from you!" the Ambassador said.

They all laughed.

Sentar finished the pie and looked around the table. "Are we ready?" he asked.

B'ani nodded.

"I think so," Galen said

"Yes," Maru replied.

The Ambassador looked at each of them and nodded. "We have something to do," she said, beginning the invocation.

"It will take all of us," Maru joined.

"And all our skills," B'ani added.

"We do not know what we must do," Galen said.

"We must succeed," Sentar said completing the refrain.

The Ambassador reached for Sentar's hand. "So, we begin..." she said.

Sentar reached for Maru's hand. "I know the path," he said.

Maru reached for Galen's hand. "I see the changes," she said.

Galen reached for B'ani's hand. "I form the bridge," he said.

B'ani reached for the Ambassador's hand. "I carry the light," she said.

The Ambassador bowed her head. "I keep the balance." She looked up.

"We are different and the same. We return to one and become one. We become one. We are one," they said in unison.

The Ambassador gripped Sentar and B'ani's hands. "In the center there is balance," she said. Then, she released her hands.

"And new beginnings," Sentar said. Then he released his hands.

"We start," Maru said. Then she released her hands.

"We continue," Galen said. Then he released his hands.

"We remain," B'ani said. Then she released her hands.

"We are one," they said in unison.

They sat quite still for a long time. Only their eyes moved, from one to another.

Then, Sentar sat back.

So did the others. They looked at each other with a new sense of familiarity.

"This is going to be interesting. You??" Maru said, looking at Micha.

"I told you I was open to other suggestions," the Ambassador replied, grinning at her.

"It will be fine. We will be fine. I will be fine," Galen repeated, only half joking.

"You will be fine, Galen. I've got you," Maru thought. She didn't say anything.

"You are so calming. Thanks!" Galen said aloud, smiling at her. "Wait, how did you...?" he asked.

Maru laughed.

B'ani smiled at Galen. "You will need a few hours to get used to us being in your head, Galen. Maru and I are accustomed to each other and the changes we need to make. With all of us, it may take a day or two. Then, we become more like side dishes. Available if you are still hungry, but not the main course," she said.

They all laughed at her analogy.

Sentar smiled and looked over at B'ani. "Well, that's different. I didn't need to hear you laughing. I felt it," he said.

"That's the idea. We'll be joined like this until we get back," Maru said.

Galen shook his head solemnly. "Or not. If one of us falls, we will all know," he said.

"We're not going to fail. We will have what we need. We will all return," the Ambassador said quietly.

Maru smiled. "Your confidence is very appealing. Thanks!" she said.

"So, what are we having for dinner when we meet back here in three weeks?" Galen asked.

The Ambassador grinned playfully. "Yangroutang?"

Galen shook his head and laughed.

"Great idea!" B'ani said with a huge grin.

Maru sat back in her chair and grinned.

Sentar looked calmly around the table. "Let's all come back," he said.

The Ambassador raised her glass. "To our reunion dinner. Here. Three weeks," she said.

They each picked up their glasses. "Three weeks!" they said together and drained their glasses.

PREPARING THE GROUND
THE FLIGHT DECK ON THE MAGELLAN

The screens on the bridge of the Magellan showed the four other ships and the station. Sentar was with Pak, Maru with Rai, B'ani with Xora, and Galen with Beel. They were ready to depart. The feed was also being sent to the large view screen on the station.

The Ambassador looked at her team, Captain Logan, and his crew. She took a deep breath. "Today, we will write a new chapter in the history of the Central Alliance. Our courage, our honor, our ingenuity, and our friendships will be tested. Let our descendants look at us and say with pride, 'Those were my ancestors,'" she said. She grew quiet. Then she spoke in the old language, "Go siúlfaidh cuimhní agus biotáillí ár laochra in éineacht linn isteach amárach. May the memories and spirits of our heroes walk with us into tomorrow," she said. She stepped closer to the screens showing her four friends, bowed her head, then looked up. "So we begin," she said.

They nodded to her and to each other. "So we begin," they echoed in unison.

The comm links to the ships faded.

The comm link to the station was still active.

The Ambassador looked at the screen and smiled. "Commander Lucas, we're planning to come back this way in a few weeks," she said.

Commander Lucas grinned at the reference. "We'll keep the lights on for you, Ambassador! See you soon!" he said.

The comm link faded.

The ships pulled away from the station one by one, each in good time.

GOING TO FIND OUT
SPACE

The star ships moved away from the space station and fanned out toward their respective destinations. As soon as they were clear of the station and each other, they engaged their star drives. Short range cruisers had been prepped and were in the hangers on each ship. The Aldarans would use them to take Sentar, Galen, Maru, and B'ani to their target systems. Each of the five star ships dropped off the cruisers then turned toward the Perseus Transit.

It would take them a few days to get there, even with the star drives. They would be seeding or ecoforming planets and setting up barriers. Each ship had a region and a set of targets. They'd practiced so many times they were clocking times without a clock. They were supposed to return and pick up the cruisers in two weeks. Then, head back to the space station.

Everything went smoothly.

The star ships completed the seeding, terraforming, placed the sensors, and got the EM barriers set up without encountering any other ships. There wasn't much out there. It was mostly just a really long ride.

Sentar and Pak had taken the furthest system of the five. It would let him get a sense of that region of the galaxy. They were going to try to find out how the Olmeri were moving so at least they might be able to predict where they were going to go next.

B'ani and Rai went to the left. Maru and Xora went to the right. The Council had reports of some sort of resistance in both those systems. They were hoping to get more information about Olmeri culture and make contact with their resistance.

Galen and Beel were going to the closest system. It was the newest system to be taken over by the Olmeri. Galen wanted to see first-hand what was going on. He was also going to look for weaknesses.

The Ambassador was going to the center, the one that seemed to have the largest concentration of Olmeri. It was the riskiest of the sectors they had plotted. It was also their best chance to lure as many of the Olmeri as possible into their trap.

LET'S GET CLOSER
KELL'S CRUISER

The Ambassador, Beth, N'amani and the Doctor were on Kell's Cruiser. They were going to what looked like a central system for the Olmeri.

Kell swung around yet another asteroid.

The Ambassador smiled. "You make that seem so easy and smooth, too," she said.

Kell smiled. "Thank you, Ambassador. We are coming up on our target system. First, we'll make a pass or two around the outside. Then, we'll do a fly-by of the four outer planets. We want to get close to the fifth planet," he said.

The Ambassador looked around. "Doctor? N'amani? Beth? Are you ready?" she asked.

"Yes, Ambassador. We're ready," they all chimed in together. They were going to be taking the bio and eco readings as they passed through the system.

Kell started a series of twists and turns that he hoped would make them appear to be a wandering comet or large asteroid. It was part navigation, part being able to feel the gravity fields, and part intuition. When to speed up, when to slow down, when to turn. He'd learned to disguise his craft's movements to match his current surroundings when needed. That skill was another of the reasons Aldaran pilots were legendary. "So far, so good, Ambassador. They haven't noticed us," he said.

They saw a few Olmeri ships heading towards the inner planets.

Kell kept close to them when he could. His cruiser was too small to be noticed by long range sensors. He showed up as just another Aldaran cruiser on local sensors. "Ambassador, we're approaching the fifth planet," he said.

The Ambassador got up and went to out the main viewer.

There was more activity around this planet than around all the other planets combined. Dozens of ships were moving in and out of orbit. Several large ships that could be space stations were clustered in orbit. They each had a broad circular crown and a long pylon below.

The Ambassador leaned forward and pointed at the pylons. "Wonder what those are?" she asked.

N'amani shook his head. "Some sort of fueling station maybe? The smaller ships seem to hover then fly off. The larger ships look like they are tethered somehow," he said.

The Ambassador straightened and looked at Kell. "Can we get closer?" she asked.

"If you sit down," Kell said. He turned just a little and looked up.

The Ambassador grinned. "I'm going. I'm going," she said. She took her seat and strapped in.

"Please make sure your seatbelts are fastened and your seatbacks are in the upright and locked position," Kell said.

Beth settled into her seat. "My recorders are active, Ambassador," she said.

The Doctor and N'amani set their recorders to auto and checked their seatbelts.

The Doctor looked over at N'amani.

N'amani nodded.

"We're ready!" the Doctor said.

Kell looked at the Ambassador.

The Ambassador nodded. "Take us in," she said.

Kell maneuvered so they were in the shadow of a small transport. Then, he took a position just underneath one of the larger ships. "Their sensors won't pick us up and they can't see us here," he said.

"Could they see us from those windows?" Beth asked. She pointed at an array of windows just below what looked like a docking clamp.

"It's possible," Kell replied.

"What's are those lights for? They keep repeating some sort of cycle," the Ambassador said. She pointed at a series of lights next to the clamp.

Kell looked at the lights and the pattern. "They look like charging lights. Old fashioned charging lights," he said.

Beth quickly turned to watch the lights. "No way! Even our most basic ships have fusion drives. The core might need some adjustments from time to time. But they last what, 300 – 400 years or so?" she said.

The Ambassador shook her head and looked at Kell. "Maybe. But they have long-range ships. For that, they need a stable fuel supply," she said.

N'amani pointed at one of his screens. "Ambassador, I'm definitely showing some sort of signal flowing from the pylon to the ships that are tethered. Several of the smaller ships are receiving it as well," he said.

The Ambassador smiled. "Get as much data as you can. Whatever it is, this could be very useful!" she said.

Kell hovered under the larger ship.

The Doctor, N'amani and Beth collected readings.

THROUGH THE LOOKING GLASS
KELL'S CRUISER / OLMERI STATION

The flashing lights next to the clamp began to slow and become steady. A figure appeared in the window on the Olmeri station.

The Ambassador was standing behind Kell watching the lights. She looked up to see several Olmeri at the window, jumping and pointing at their ship. "Oh crap. Kell, they've spotted us," she said.

Kell nodded and started setting a course.

The Ambassador started back to her seat. She turned. "Wait, we need to do something first. Beth, quickly!" she said.

Beth unbuckled her seatbelt, hurried to the pilot's chair, and strapped in.

Kell ran to Beth's seat. He closed the panel they had rigged to conceal Beth's seat. From the front and the sides, the chair looked like a component cabinet.

The Ambassador rested her hand on Beth's shoulder. "Turn the ship and move us just a little closer so they can see us clearly through the windows. N'amani, can you open a video comm link to that screen?" she asked. She pointed to a screen inside the window.

N'amani grinned. "Yes, Ambassador. I can most definitely hack their system. Give me just one second. Okay. You're on," he said.

The Ambassador stood up straight, smiled, and waved. "Hello. So nice to see you today. This is Beth. Beth is my pilot," she said. She patted Beth's shoulder.

Beth smiled and waved. "Hi, I'm Beth. Very pleased to meet you," she said.

"Hi, I'm Doctor Grey. How are you?" the Doctor said. He waved and smiled.

N'amani shook his head. He couldn't help but laugh. Why did the Ambassador think taunting the Olmeri was a good idea? She had an uncanny ability to taunt their enemies without actually doing anything more than being polite. She was good at it, too.

Several more Olmeri had gathered around the screen. A few more were visible in the window. They were shaking their fists at her ship and jumping up and down angrily.

The Ambassador could hear them yelling through the comm link. She took a step away from Beth's chair and turned so she was facing another screen to redirect their attention. She took a fighting stance. "I am Ambassador Micha Lawrence. I was told you were looking for me," she said. She stood still. She looked at the screen. Then, she shifted forward and started waving at them again. "I'm so happy I had the chance to meet you today. We'll be going now. See you soon. Bye!" she said. She cut the link. "Kell..." she called out.

Kell was already at the pilot's chair waiting for Beth to unstrap.

Beth ran back to her seat and strapped in.

The Ambassador did the same.

"Seats please," Kell said. He started gradually moving towards the outer planets. "Ambassador, your invitation appears to be working better than we thought it might. They are definitely going to follow us. Several groups of smaller ships are massing near one of the larger ones. The largest one is no longer tethered," he said.

The Ambassador grinned. "Don't lose them. Remember they are supposed to be able to follow us," she said.

"How easy should I make it?" Kell asked.

"Not too. Make them work for it," the Ambassador said.

The Doctor grinned and tightened his seatbelt. "Excellent! We're going for a ride!" he said.

N'amani looked over at Beth. They both laughed.

Kell continued moving quickly toward the outer planets. He deliberately made mistakes. As he came around a small moon, he got a little too close. He made two more mistakes to avoid some large asteroids. He wanted the Olmeri to see him make mistakes. It was part of their plan.

The large Olmeri ship had started accelerating towards them as they approached the outer planets in the system. The smaller ships stayed close to the larger one.

N'amani pointed at the clusters on the sensor. "Look at that. Do the smaller craft have a range limit? They're sticking real close to the larger ship," he said.

Kell shook his head. "Range limits won't help us if they get close. There are too many of them. I can outmaneuver the larger ship. That's easy. There are too many of the smaller ones. It'd be like trying to fly through a meteor shower. We're going to get hit," he said.

The Ambassador nodded to Kell. "Let's not let them get that close. Can you make it seem like we are getting away, but something happens and then they might catch us? We don't want to actually get away. We want them to follow us," she asked.

"Should we leave some meat pies for them, too?" N'amani asked.

The Doctor grinned. "Can we have some too? Beef or chicken?"

They all laughed.

FOLLOW ME, FOLLOW ME, ALL THE WAY HOME
KELL'S CRUISER

The Ambassador, Beth, the Doctor and N'amani were strapped into their seats.

Kell was playing interstellar cat and mouse with the Olmeri. He tried to make the ride smoother when he could, but it wasn't a smooth ride. He would accelerate to get a good lead on the ships then come around a large asteroid too close and brake, giving them a chance to catch up. Just as they got almost close enough, he'd lose them again only to make another deliberate mistake so they would believe they could catch him again.

Beth looked at the short-range screens. "They seem determined. They're still with us," she said.

Kell nodded. He looked at the navigation screens. "We're almost at the outer barrier," he said.

"Ambassador, I'm showing the sensors are all in place," N'amani said

The Ambassador took a deep breath. "Very well. Let's hope this works. Take us through, Kell," she said.

Kell slowed down to let the large ship get closer. He wanted to make sure it followed him. The smaller ships started to extend their range to close in on him. "This could be a chance to eliminate some of those smaller ships, Ambassador," he said.

"If you have to, but don't try. That's not our goal," the Ambassador said.

Kell nodded. "Understood," he said.

"Make sure you are securely strapped in," the Ambassador said.

The Doctor grinned. "When do we get to go up? I like roller-coaster rides," he said.

Beth shook her head.

Kell chuckled. "Soon, Doctor. Very soon," he said. He adjusted their course so they would just skirt the inside of the asteroid belt. He'd be dodging asteroids and the Olmeri. He was more worried about the asteroids. It worked. Several dozen of the smaller ships that had been closing on him followed him into the asteroid belt. They didn't last long. He tried to make it seem as if he was just very lucky. He used the ships lasers to clip some of the asteroids so it looked like they had hit the ship. He brought the ship out of the belt and turned back towards the Olmeri who hadn't followed him. He flew straight towards them as if he hadn't been paying attention to where they were. Then, he banked hard and turned toward the first of the systems they had planned to seed. Some of the smaller ships came out to intercept. He turned and flew back towards the asteroid belt, leading the Olmeri through a large, stable gap.

The Olmeri took the bait.

The star ships had set up the gap so Kell could bring the Olmeri through without triggering an EM pulse. The plan was for them to activate it on their way back.

Kell slowed down to make sure the Olmeri followed him. He looked over at the medium and short-range sensors to track their positions. He saw a large Olmeri ship pass through the belt and move towards the closest of the systems they'd seeded. "Ambassador. It seems to be working. They are following us," he said.

The Ambassador looked at an array of charts. "Take us into the upper atmosphere over the seventh planet. We targeted it for extensive ecoforming. It should be very hard for the Olmeri to resist," she said.

Kell maneuvered the cruiser so the Olmeri could track where he was going but would not be able to catch him. He entered the atmosphere and took a low orbit around the planet's southern axis. The Olmeri wouldn't be looking for them there. They waited.

N'amani sat up and leaned forward. "The Olmeri are here. The large ship has stayed in high orbit. A handful of smaller ones are in the atmosphere. It looks like they are landing? They don't seem to be looking for us anymore," he said.

The Ambassador smiled. "Exactly what we wanted. Let's give them a little more time. It's a long way back to the space station and I'd rather not have company," she said.

Kell nodded.

More and more of the Olmeri craft landed on the planet.

The Ambassador sighed. "Okay. I think we've seen enough. Kell," she said.

"Make sure you are strapped in. I can out-maneuver the larger one. But if we get too close, the smaller ones could overtake us. It would be a problem," Kell said.

The Ambassador frowned then smiled. "We are going home, Kell. You've got this," she said.

Kell turned and grinned at her. "Can I?" he asked.

"Yes," the Ambassador said smiling at him.

"Let's go home then," Kell said. He set the controls to full manual and took the ship out of orbit. The forward motion changed slightly as he disengaged the automated controls. He pulled up and sent the cruiser into a graceful sweep around the planet, using its gravity to propel them back towards the asteroid belt. Thanks to that, they were moving quite a bit faster than normal.

The Olmeri were caught by surprise. They couldn't power up the large ship fast enough to pursue them.

Kell evaded the few smaller ships that tried to catch him. They weren't fast enough. They seemed to lose interest and turned back. He started to relax a little. Then, he looked at the forward sensors. "Ambassador. We have more company," he said.

They'd been so busy leading the one Olmeri ship to the planet and watching what happened with that ship that they had not paid attention to what the other ships they'd seen around the planet were doing.

The Ambassador looked at the sensors. "Oh dear. I count three of their large ships on this side of the barrier. This is both a good thing and a not so good thing. They've seen us, haven't they?" she asked.

N'amani nodded. "Yes Ambassador. They are increasing speed and spreading out. They have definitely seen us," he said.

The Ambassador pouted. "Oh phoo. Not again. I would rather not be their guest for dinner. Well, Kell, it seems we are going to have a chance to field test a few more of your upgrades after all," she said.

Kell nodded. "I can think of no better time, Ambassador. Make sure your straps are tight!" he said. He changed his trajectory to tack left and down as if he was going to try to slip under the Olmeri ships and accelerated. Several of the small ships turned to follow. He kept going, waiting for the large ship to commit, then pulled up hard and turned sharp to the right. It was too big to change direction that fast. The smaller ships had started grouping at different points, looking for where they could get out in front of him or where they could come in from the sides. They made some test runs, then stared in earnest.

Kell turned and twisted the ship into pretzel shapes that only his mother would appreciate. He did a forward back arc with a twist that took out five of their craft. They were trying to follow him but they all flew into each other. It was a thing of beauty. The Olmeri were like a swarm of mosquitoes that couldn't quite get a bite because their intended food was moving too fast. He skipped past four more and headed into the asteroid belt. He twisted and turned, bringing the ship out on the other side. The Olmeri that had tried to follow him through the belt had been destroyed or had given up and rejoined to the larger ship. He leveled off. "We should have a smooth ride the rest of the way back," he said.

The Ambassador smiled. Her eyes were wide open and she had just a tinge of green in her voice. "Kell, you are amazing. I have a great deal of appreciation and respect for your skills. However, there are those times when I wish you didn't need to exercise all of them at the same time," she said.

Kell looked at her and grinned.

"I'm going to second that," the Doctor said.

Kell smiled at him." I didn't expect to hear that from you, Doctor. You do look a little unwell," he said.

"I have my days," the Doctor replied. He grimaced just a little.

"Ambassador, you need to see this." N'amani said. He patched the video sensor through to the main screen. "That's the fifth Olmeri ship to have come through the gap," he said.

Kell frowned. "How many more are there? We need to close that opening before we leave this sector," he said.

"That appears to be the last one. I don't see any more on the long-range scans." N'amani answered.

"Close it. Let's get out of here," the Ambassador said.

Kell fired two short blasts into the clumps of asteroids on each side of the gap, breaking them up. With gravity and a little magnetic help, the pieces began distributing themselves across the gap. Then, he turned the cruiser towards their rendezvous coordinates with the Magellan. They weren't followed.

The Ambassador sat back in her chair. "How many did you say, N'amani?" she asked.

"Five," N'amani replied.

The Ambassador shook her head in disbelief. "They all followed us? All of them?" she asked.

Beth sat forward. "Ambassador, I've been monitoring their comms. I can't understand everything, but your name keeps coming up. They are very unhappy with you. More than just unhappy. They are enraged that you would do such a thing," she said.

The Ambassador, Kell and N'amani all doubled over with laughter. "What's so funny?" Beth asked.

The Ambassador sat up and tried not to laugh. She grinned. "We just counted coup at one of their worlds and their leadership knows it. Of course they are not happy. Wait until they find out they are stuck here. Kell, can we swing around and make it so they have less chance of finding that gap?" she asked.

Kell chuckled. "Yes, Ambassador," he said. He touched a control panel as he swung around and under the asteroids. "That does it. The gap is now littered with minerals, other asteroids, and a few random viruses. They won't be coming back this way again," he said.

N'amani grinned. "Random viruses? Nice touch! They are going to be so not happy. So very not happy," he said.

Beth smiled. "Ambassador, I'm hearing a lot of chatter about the new planet. They are sending messages that they've found it, and that they have mineral readings from three of the other planets we seeded," she said.

The Ambassador grinned. "That's exactly what we were hoping for! So they get to rant about me as a bonus. I'm good with that," she said.

"This is going to make a fantastic story!" the Doctor said.

"Who's going to believe it, Doctor? Maybe a few people on the station would enjoy it," the Ambassador said. She winked at him.

'Tm enjoying it. Is there more?" the Doctor asked.

The Ambassador nodded. "Yes. There's more. Let's go meet the Magellan. We have a dinner to go to," she said.

There were going to be lots and lots of stories and many dinners with friends. They were going home.

CHAPTER 8:
ORIGINS

Wait in stillness.
Listen for the quiet.
Before the beginning,
Dreamers dream dreams.

HOW DID WE GET HERE?
THE AMBASSADOR'S QUARTERS ON THE MAGELLAN

The Ambassador was in her quarters trying to sort out what she needed for her report to the High Council. They had asked for a preliminary report as soon as they arrived on Dagon. She paced back and forth. She looked down at several screens she had on her desk. Each had a different archive and a different collection of footage. She switched a wall screen on then off. Finally, she went over to the comm link. "Beth? N'amani? Could both of you please come to my quarters and help me sort out this report? We got quite a bit more than I thought," she said.

"Do you want me to bring the small recorder? It's good for collecting notes," Beth asked.

"I'll bring my notepad," N'amani said.

"Yes, Beth. Thank you, N'amani. That would be super. You have such a knack for making me stick to the main points," the Ambassador said. She closed the comm link and sighed in relief. She really didn't like writing reports. At least with Beth and N'amani helping, it wouldn't take nearly as long. She put on a fresh pot of coffee.

She was happy they had gotten so much data and more than a little intimidated. It was going to take weeks to sort through all the visual recordings they had made and do a full analysis. They had even more data from the spectral sensor readings.

The door chime sounded.

"Come in," the Ambassador called.

Beth came in. She set the small recorder on the table with the Ambassador's screens. She looked at the different screens and then at the Ambassador. She frowned.

N'amani followed Beth into the room. He pointed to the screens. "Were you trying to watch all of them at once?" he asked.

The Ambassador shrugged. "Sort of. It was just too slow to go through them one by one. But it wasn't working. That's why I called you," she said. She and grinned her Cheshire cat smile.

N'amani chuckled. "Of course you did," he said.

The Ambassador laughed. "Would you like some coffee, Beth?" she asked.

"Yes please. I've gotten quite fond of coffee," Beth said.

"N'amani, would you..." the Ambassador asked.

"No. I would not. Thank you," he said emphatically. He cringed.

The Ambassador laughed. "I have tea and fresh orange juice. The trees in the arboretum have fruit now," she said.

N'amani smiled. "Thank you. Orange juice. I'm sorry to be so quick but that coffee drink is not to my liking. Not at all," he said. He wrinkled his nose.

The Ambassador grinned. "I remember," she said. She poured a glass of orange juice and handed it to him.

"Thank you. This really is quite nice," N'amani said. He took a sip, kept the glass under his nose, and smiled.

The Ambassador started pacing again. She picked up one of the screens then put it down and picked up another one. "The Council wants a preliminary report. I've been looking at what we collected this time, our previous reports, and what we know about the Olmeri," she said.

N'amani reached out to take the screen from her hand. "Ambassador, the Council is expecting a trip report, not an encyclopedia. Why are you looking at these archives? Some of them date back to the founding of the Alliance," he said.

The Ambassador sighed. "I need to put what we have in perspective somehow. There are so many things we don't know and don't understand about our own history. How can we look at what the Olmeri are doing? We don't know that much about their society, their culture, or their history. Why are they destroying whole systems? What do they gain?" she asked.

Beth shook her head. "Can't we just start where we are? We have sensor readings. We have our own logs and the logs from the other ships. Isn't that enough?" she asked.

The Ambassador shook her head. "If I don't put some perspective on it, the Council members will add their own. They are going to slice and dice whatever I give them. I want to start with something they won't be able to pick apart quite so as easily. There are still some who consider it might be better to find a way to get a deal with the Olmeri, even offer some concessions to get a treaty," she said.

N'amani shook his head emphatically. "They can't be serious! A treaty with the Olmeri?" he asked.

The Ambassador nodded. "There are those on the Council who would consider it. They won't advocate for it. But if they could find a way to see it as an option, they'd take it," she said.

Beth shook her head. "That's hard to believe. Don't they understand what the Olmeri are doing?" she asked.

The Ambassador looked at Beth then N'amani, straightened her shoulders, and grinned. "They will after they read my report," she said.

N'amani lowered his chin and looked at her. "Ah yes, the report that hasn't been written yet," he said.

The Ambassador smiled at him. "Somehow, we need to make it crystal clear that what the Olmeri are doing is not benevolent," she said.

"You couldn't just show them the footage?" Beth asked.

"Not without perspective. I agree with you. It's horrible. But why did they do it? What's the background? There has to be some context," the Ambassador said.

N'amani nodded. "She's right, Beth. The images we have make me sick. All that destruction for what? Shiny cities with skyscrapers? But if we only show the destruction without talking about the patterns of incursions, the impact on the existing civilization, and all the rest," he said.

Beth nodded and smiled. "Ok. I get it. But, then where should we start? What the Olmeri are doing has a connection to every planet in the Alliance. It's not just minerals or grain crops that are at risk. It's everything," she said.

The Ambassador looked at her. "Yes. That's where I was when you came in," she said.

N'amani laughed.

Beth looked down, shrugged, and smiled.

N'amani took a few steps back then turned around. "Ambassador, your perspective is important for this. It's hard to argue with the perspective of an ambassador anyway. The way you frame the situation affects everything, from the way we present the report to the decisions that the High Council might make. They are not out here with us. The only way they know what is going on is from the reports they get," he said.

The Ambassador shook her head. "It's not quite that stark. They look at other things," she said.

N'amani turned his head to one side. "Really? Then why am I here? Hmmm?" he asked.

The Ambassador nodded. "Point taken. Thank you. Alright then. How do I get from "we went there, did stuff, came back" to something that will make sense? Something that's coherent?" she asked.

N'amani and Beth looked at each other, shrugged, and shook their heads.

"Maja, would you join us?" the Ambassador asked.

Maja appeared in the center of the room.

"I'm trying to put the situation with the Olmeri in perspective for a report to the High Council. I'm stuck. Could you give us a synopsis? How did we get here? I mean, as a civilization, how did we get here? Just the highlights though," the Ambassador said.

"Of course, Ambassador. Where would you like me to start?" Maja asked.

"When the first Terrans left the Sol system. How did we migrate?" the Ambassador asked.

Maja frowned. "That's a little early, don't you think?" she said.

The Ambassador smiled. "Humor me? Just the short version," she said.

Maja nodded. "When the first Terrans left the Sol system, they migrated erratically at first, choosing the closest systems not necessarily the most promising, mostly because they couldn't get any further. Their craft were limited in speed and distance. Two, almost simultaneous discoveries gave them the ability to go further. First, they developed what would become our light drive. Then, they developed a more advanced version of their existing fusion engines with a stable radiant core. The ability to stabilize, aggregate, and focus that energy, along with developments and discoveries in the material sciences gave them the capacity to build faster ships. They were still quite slow compared to our current interstellar ships," she said.

N'amani shook his head. "That seems like too much information about things that aren't really connected to our report. Do we need to include how we developed our ships?" he asked.

"Does it help us understand how they developed their ships? Do we have anything to connect this to the information we have about the Olmeri? Some progression of development? Do we even know how they build their ships, Maja?" the Ambassador asked.

"Unsure as yet, Ambassador. I have only stored what you brought back. It's quite a lot. It's going to take time to tag and process," Maja said.

N'amani made a note. "That is a good point, Ambassador. If we understood more about their ships, we might have a better idea of how to stop them," he said.

"Okay. Maja, please continue," the Ambassador said.

Maja started again. "As the Terrans learned to build better ships, they began traveling to nearby systems. They started with the Alpha Centauri system and moved out to Sirius and Procyon, the closest systems to Sol. As they developed ships with greater range, they moved into the Vega, Eridani, and Fomalhaut systems. They found many planets around minor stars, some occupied, others not. They looked for places they could establish trade, create alliances, and of course, more settlements. They established the first galactic central government on the planet Dagon in the Fomalhaut system during the second millennia of outward expansion," she said.

Beth looked at the Ambassador. "This seems like it could be relevant to what we are seeing with the Olmeri," she said.

The Ambassador nodded. "Maja, please tag this passage for the report," she said.

"Yes Ambassador. Should I go on?" Maja asked.

The Ambassador nodded. "A little further, please," she said.

Maja continued. "During the Great Expansion, the Central Alliance sent traders to many worlds. Some of those they met were friendly. Others were not. Some preferred to be left alone. Some welcomed the Alliance. Others became interested in what the Alliance could offer for the taking. The High Council decided they needed a better understanding of what was going on and a better way to address threats. Treaties weren't enough. The Alliance knew the assessments they needed weren't something they could send spies to do. A military team could not do it nor could a trade negotiator. They needed someone who could negotiate a treaty and read the room. Someone who could blend in with different cultures and different situations. They didn't want spies to report secretly nor did they want someone who would only follow orders. They needed emissaries who could tell them what their position should be, help change things when necessary, who could actively build the Alliance. They needed ambassadors," she said.

"Stop there please, Maja. What comes after this?" the Ambassador asked.

"The development of the ambassador program on Ras 2," Maja said.

N'amani frowned. "Maja, would you scan that entire period. Is there anything in that part of Alliance history that seems relevant to what we are facing with the Olmeri?"

Maja was quiet for a moment. "I can't find anything. Most of that period is concerned with trade alliances and working with the Masters on Ras 2 to create the training program," she said.

The Ambassador shook her head. "I'm not sure that's relevant. The Olmeri are definitely going out to colonize other planets, but they don't seem interested in treaties or any sort of cooperation. The training program on Ras 2 was created to help facilitate trade and cooperation, not takeovers," she said.

"That might be an important difference," N'amani suggested. He made a note.

"True," the Ambassador said nodding.

"Ambassador, Could Maja continue just a bit? I'd like to hear more about how the ambassador program got started," Beth asked quietly.

"I'd like to hear more, too," N'amani said.

"Of course," the Ambassador said. She smiled and nodded to Maja.

"During the Early Years of the Great Expansion, the Alliance and the Council of Nine at Ras'alhague came to an understanding. The Ras'alhague sector was to be left alone. Trade would be limited to keep traders from spending too much time on their worlds. Casual travelers were not welcome on Ras 2. Only the original people on their worlds would be allowed to develop any new settlements. The Masters valued their way of life and were determined to protect it. What the Alliance did not know was that the Masters were quite a bit more advanced than they let on," Maja recited.

"Like the Kora?" N'amani asked.

The Ambassador looked carefully at them. "More. The Masters of Ras'alhague have exceptional fighting skills and an uncanny ability to assess the true character of a person. That's why the Alliance contacted them. They wanted a program that would both reveal the character of the person and prepare those who could complete it to become ambassadors," she said.

Beth pulled back, a little in awe. "This is the program you went through? And your classmates?" she asked.

The Ambassador smiled at Beth. "Yes. Maja, just a little more please," she said.

Maja nodded. "The Masters decided who they would accept into the program. A person could have the qualifications to apply, wait years, and still not be chosen. Their selection process remains well-guarded to this day. Both the Central Alliance and the Masters benefitted from the exchange. As the years went by, the Masters became less reclusive and more open to trade. They started allowing a few casual travelers to promote cultural exchange. Study with the Masters of Ras'alhague became a requirement for any trade negotiator post in the Alliance," she said.

The comm chime sounded.

The Doctor's voice came through the comm link. "Ambassador, we're planning dinner for 7 pm. Everyone is invited. I'm preparing a few special selections. It's going to be a very nice table. I'm making truffles, too!" he said.

The Ambassador laughed. "No space barnacles, ok?" she asked.

The Doctor laughed. "No, no thank you. Not today," he said.

"I'm here with N'amani and Beth trying to sort out this report. I'll try to be there a little early, maybe 6:30?" the Ambassador said. She sighed and rested her head on her hand.

The comm link closed.

"You don't look very happy, Ambassador," N'amani said.

"It could be quite some time before my old classmates and I have dinner together again. They will be going home soon," the Ambassador said. It had been great catching up with Sentar. Maru and B'ani were still the same. And Galen, well, he always made her smile. The Doctor reminded her a bit of Galen. They had the same playful, boyish charm and quick wit.

"Did you want me to continue, Ambassador?" Maja asked.

"No, thank you, Maja. I think we've narrowed things down quite a bit. It looks like it's going to take another few days to sort out what to put in the report. It's not going to get done today," the Ambassador said.

Maja faded.

N'amani looked at the Ambassador. "I'd like to hear more about your training program. Your skills are pretty amazing," he said.

Beth nodded with an eager smile.

"You would? Both of you? Are you sure?" the Ambassador asked. She was surprised and wary. It wasn't casual conversation. It would be their introduction to the program and all it represented.

They both nodded.

The Ambassador smiled. "Very well. But not right now. I'm not saying no. Just not right now. Thanks to both of you, I've just figured out how to start my report. I need to draft it while it's fresh. We can talk about some of it at dinner, if you like," she said

"With your classmates?" N'amani asked. He smiled a huge smile.

The Ambassador nodded. "Why don't you two go get ready for dinner and then see if there's anything you can do to help the Doctor," she said.

N'amani smiled a mischievous grin. He picked up his notepad and started out the door. "I'd like to help with the truffles. We'll see you shortly, Ambassador," he said.

"I could help with those, too!" Beth said. She quickly picked up her recorder and followed N'amani out.

The Ambassador went back over to the table and sat down. She looked around the room. Her quarters on the Magellan were quite nice. Not opulent or pretentious. But nice. There were always a few things she wanted to change.

This could be better. That could be different. But she was content with what she had. It was one of the lessons Master Tai taught them. Be content with what you have. It wasn't that they should be resigned to not having something better, but they should avoid paying too much attention to wanting whatever it was they didn't have. That was the key. What we have or don't have isn't what matters. It's "wanting what we don't have" that creates the problem. So then, if we don't have a nice bowl of soup today, we can spend the day thinking about how nice it would be to have that soup and bemoaning our fate that we don't. Or, we can accept that today we don't have the soup and try what we can so that tomorrow, maybe we can have the soup. Or, we could decide that we don't want soup. "Wanting" makes us uncomfortable or discontented. That longing gives rise to jealousy, greed, lust for power, and more. It's destructive. At the same time, striving for what we don't have, gives us courage, determination, and something to work for, something more to achieve. It's creative. She turned on one of the screens and began recording. "The Olmeri are not content with what they have," she said, starting her report.

FRESH DIRT AND THE SMELL OF FLOWERS
THE ARBORETUM ON THE MAGELLAN

The Ambassador had finished drafting her preliminary report. She decided to take a detour through the Arboretum on her way to dinner. Being there reminded her of her time on Ras 2. She liked the smell of fresh dirt and the way the air smelled clean just after the sprinklers had stopped. She was looking at one of the racks of small sprouts.

Beth came around the rack. "Ambassador, the Doctor said he thought I might find you here," she said.

"It's not time for dinner yet, is it?" the Ambassador asked.

"No, not yet. I wanted to find a way to ask Maja to tag the recordings and the data we collected. It's good that we brought back all this information, but I don't know how to even start to catalog it so we can find anything. There's so much," Beth said.

"We did get quite a lot, didn't we?" the Ambassador asked.

Beth nodded. "Yes. But I'm used to dealing with our archives. They are extensive. They've been tagged and there are all sorts of tools we can use. Trying to tag all this raw footage is much harder. With our trips, I was there, so I know what to do. For these, I really don't know where to start," she said.

"We were all looking for different things, weren't we? What if you use our teams? Tag everything we did with my name. Do the same for Galen, Sentar, Maru, and B'ani. That would at least let us know who the source is for that information the location, and the perspective," the Ambassador said.

Beth's face brightened. "That's so much easier than what I was trying to do. Thank you!" she said. She turned to leave. "Now, I'll be finished before dinner. I've already got a script written and Maja," she said under her breath as she hurried out the door.

"You're welcome. Come back when you're done," the Ambassador called out after her. She began slowly walking around, looking at the plants, and smelling the air. The Arboretum wasn't small. They'd created paths that wound through the racks of plants that made it seem like a much larger space. A few of the trees were in flower. The scent carried through the air. Racks above held vines covered with gourds in various stages of growth. Grapes trailed across a lattice. Tomatoes and peppers were just sprouting on the lower rows.

She came around one end where they had planted spices and herbs. She took a leaf from one of the basil plants and broke it just under her nose. "So nice. Fresh picked. There's nothing like it," she thought. She stopped to look at the small beds of freshly planted lavender and sage. Little shoots were just starting to poke above the dirt. She nodded. "They will need time to grow," she said. She smiled, sat down on a small bench, and dozed off.

PLANTING THE GARDEN (RECALL)
THE GREETING COMPOUND ON RAS 2

Micha Lawrence had just arrived on Ras 2. She was standing near the gate at the reception compound. It was still too early for daylight. Several other recruits stood around looking at each other and waiting. She'd gotten in late, been assigned to a room, and told to report to the front gate before daybreak the next day. Not much of a welcome.

"Do you know what we're doing here?" Micha asked a young man near the gate.

He frowned at her. "Selections. Weren't you here for orientation?" he asked.

Micha shook her head. "No, I was delayed. I got in last night," she said.

"I'm Sentar. Welcome to Ras 2," he said grinning.

"My name is Micha," she replied smiling up at him.

Just at daybreak, nine Masters arrived. They each wore robes of different colors. They stood at a distance and talked among themselves. Then, they split up and walked over to where they were standing. Each Master pointed at a few of the new students and motioned for them to follow. They all walked off in different directions.

Micha had known from childhood that she wanted to become an ambassador. She read all the stories and watched the history archives over and over. She never thought about doing anything else. But attending the special academy that would prepare her hadn't been possible. Her grandparents couldn't afford it. It wasn't their fault. They had raised her after her parents were killed in an accident. They'd done their best. They'd tried to discourage her. They wanted her to accept a clerk's job. It would be safe and reliable, they told her. She couldn't stand the thought. She wanted to be an ambassador, not a clerk in some back office somewhere. She had spent years doing physical training, learning languages, studying history. She'd worked hard at all of it. Finally, she had received her invitation letter.

She had been selected by one in gold and rust colors who introduced himself Master Tai Aragon. It wasn't until after selections that she learned Master Tai was the Master of the House of Tu (Centering) and a Keeper of Earth.

The Keepers of Earth worked with solids, especially the soil used for growing things. Master Tai had mastered the Three Arts of Centering – finding the middle way, standing still, and becoming one. He was an Adept of the 9th Order in the Ancient Arts. He had selected five of them. Sentar, Galen, Maru, B'ani were the others. She was glad Sentar was in her group. As with most things, she would not understand why they had been selected until much later when they would be asked to choose which element they would keep: Metal, Water, Wood, Fire, or Earth.

Galen and B'ani were from the Vega system, her family's home system. Sentar came from the Eridani system. Maru was from the original home system, Sol.

Micha liked Galen immediately. He was outgoing and friendly. He had a boyish quality and an insatiable curiosity.

Maru and B'ani became friends almost on sight. They were so very different. Maru was calm and quiet. B'ani was not. Micha liked both of them immensely.

Sentar had seemed a little distant at first. But soon showed himself to be warm, generous, and quite protective of all of them. He came to be the most loyal friend any of them could possibly want. He was the one they could go to when there was something hard to do or something they were trying to work out. He had the uncanny ability to cut directly to the core; to ask the hard questions. And he would always, always tell the truth, even when it might hurt. He was destined to become a great teacher. They all felt it.

The five quickly became fast friends. They shared a table in the dining hall and had more than a few spirited conversations.

THEY WILL NEED TIME TO GROW (RECALL)
THE GARDEN AT THE TRAINING COMPOUND ON RAS 2

Micha was on her hands and knees planting 30 seedling peppers in the garden. She had dug out the plot but then Master Tai changed where she should plant. She had to do all the work over again. It took her all day. Then, she had to plant the peppers. She had just finished putting the last ones in the ground when Master Tai reappeared.

"They will need time to grow." Master Tal said. He looked down at her. "You must tend to them so they grow well," he said.

She looked up at him with a puzzled expression. "Ok, how am I supposed to do that? What kind of training is this? I didn't come here to learn farming. All this Master Tai wants me to do is dig in the dirt," she thought.

She had been trying to keep calm, but she was about to give up. She'd expected to be attending classes and doing physical training. Maybe attending some lectures on philosophy and taking some language classes. But for weeks, all she'd done was work in the garden. Shoveling and raking and turning the soil. Making and repairing the fences to keep the small animals out of the beds. Potting mint and peppermint to put around the outer edges of the garden to keep other animals away. Every day, Master Tal found some part of what she'd done needed 'something more' so she had to do it all over again.

Today, Master Tai came to get her an hour before sunrise. He stood in the doorway. "Come along. It's time to plant," he said.

"But Master Tai, it's still too dark. We can't see anything," Micha complained. She sat up on her cot. It was a simple wooden frame cot with padding. Not the most comfortable thing she'd slept on. She'd started to get used to it. Like everything else, most things on Ras 2 were primitive compared to what she'd had at home.

"Come along. Come along. It's time to plant. Come along," Master Tai said. He chided her as he turned and started walking toward the garden.

Micha shook her head. She'd tried asking him about several things. But most of the time, all he said was "come along, wait and see." It made no sense. So, she gave up asking. It was easier to just wait and see. She could see him outside waiting for her. She got up, put on her shoes and jacket, and went out to follow him.

Master Tai led her to the garden patch she had been working the day before.

She'd broken up most of the big clumps. The fresh turned dirt was clean and fine. It was ready to be planted. Her tools were still there, ready for the plants.

Master Tai looked around. Then, he pointed to a section of land on the other side of the yard from where she'd been turning the dirt. "Over there is good. We will plant there. Make sure the soil is broken into small pieces. I will go to bring the plants," he said.

"But Master Tal. I've already prepared this area. Every day, I turned the soil like you showed me. This spot is ready. That one is not. I will have to do all of this work again," Micha said.

Master Tai frowned a little. He looked back and forth at the two areas thoughtfully. "Yes, that is true. However, I see that you have become very good at turning and breaking up the soil. It will not take you long at all to make that section ready. I will go to get the plants. You prepare the soil. I will come back later," he said. And just like that, he left.

Micha sighed and picked up her tools. There was no point in arguing with him. Once he decided something, it was impossible to change his mind. She walked over to where he had pointed and started digging. The soil was harder than the area she'd finished. She looked back at the section she'd already prepared. "How can we plant anything here? What's wrong with him? Why didn't he tell me he wanted this area and not that one? Seems like he's taking advantage of me, making me do all this work. Sure, if the peppers grow, we'll all have some. Why do I have to do all this work? He didn't help at all. He just pointed and told me what to do. He should be here helping me. He's the one that wants a different spot now. He couldn't even stick around to help. He just walked off and left me here to do all this, again," she muttered.

It took her the better part of an hour to calm down. She reminded herself that whatever was going on, she had signed up for it. Whatever it was, whatever the training was going to be, she might as well get used to it. "Besides, we have to eat. If growing some peppers will help put food on the table, I can do my part," she thought.

She stopped to take a break just before noon. Just as she was getting ready to sit down, Master Tai appeared out of nowhere. "It is time to plant. It is not time to rest. The seedlings will not wait for you. It is time to plant," he said.

She got up and started in again. It was early evening when she finished, not yet dusk. She was standing off to one side, resting on the rake handle, when she saw Master Tai approaching with a large tray of seedlings in his hands. She'd planted the seeds right after she arrived. She'd been surprised at how well they had sprouted and how quickly they'd grown.

"Let's get started," Master Tai said. He put the tray on the ground.

Micha sighed. She picked up the tray and started to turn it over to dump out the seedlings. "He didn't mean that. He's not going to help me do this," she thought.

Master Tai stopped her. "No. Not that way. One at a time. Be careful not to break the stems. Don't crush the leaves," he said.

Micha took hold of a stem and started to pull one of the seedlings out of the tray.

Master Tai stopped her again. "If you do that, you will break the stem. It is too small to hold. You must start from underneath," he said.

Micha looked at him again and took a breath, trying to contain herself. "Okay fine. He's picked at everything else I've done. Why stop now?" she thought.

"Use this," Master Tai said. He handed her a small, flat, rather dull knife.

Micha looked at it for a minute. She was tired and hungry and this really wasn't making any sense. She couldn't hold back. "What am I supposed to do with this, Master Tai. I thought you wanted me to plant these seedlings?" she asked.

Master Tai smiled. "The shape of the bowl is determined by what is, it's usefulness by what is not," he said quietly.

Micha looked up at him. "Oh great. More riddles. I'm too tired for this. He isn't making any sense. A dull knife and riddles? What do I do with this?" she thought. She knelt down next to the tray. Each of the seeds had been planted and the sprouts cultivated so there was space between them. That gave each one a better chance to grow big enough to plant. She looked at the neat rows of plants in the tray. "What is not?" she thought. Then she saw it. Each of the seedlings had some space between the others. She used the knife to cut in behind one of the seedlings, lifting it from underneath so the roots and some of the soil came up too. Then, she used the back of the knife to set the roots into the ground and closed the dirt over it with her hand. She looked at Master Tai. He seemed to have a little bit of a smile. It was hard to tell. Sometimes he smiled and a smile was not really what he intended.

Master Tai nodded. "Do it again," he said. He looked at the tray. Then, he walked away.

The work went slowly.

Micha had to be careful not to break the stems or damage the tiny leaves. She figured out that if she kept her hand soft around the new seedling and her fingers strong to move the dirt out of the way she wouldn't damage them. One by one she set each into the ground. By the time she finished, it had gotten dark. She could barely see what she was doing. She had to feel her way along the rows. She gathered the tools. Tired did not begin to describe how she felt. She'd been up since before sunrise and had worked all day without a break. Every time she stopped to rest, Master Tai appeared. "It is time to plant. It is not time to rest," he'd say and walk off. Finally, she finished and sat down. "I'm tired. It's late. I'm done," she said.

And, as if on cue, Master Tai appeared.

She stood up. "Now what?" she thought.

Master Tai stood there and looked at her for what seemed to be a long time. Then, he looked at the garden. "They will need time to grow. You must tend to them so they grow well. Now, it's time to rest. We will start again tomorrow," he said. He turned to leave.

Micha picked up her tools. She thought she saw him smile. "Yes, Master Tai," she said.

Master Tai did smile. He had already seen that she was pretty amazing. Her dedication and perseverance were admirable. She didn't quit. That was what he liked the most about her. She was stubborn. She worked hard. She was quick. She was good at solving problems and puzzles. "Yes. She might be able to do it. She might be able to center all five for the joining. But she has much to learn," he thought. He smiled a little more.

TENDING THE GARDEN (RECALL)
MASTER TAI'S HOUSE ON RAS 2

Micha had gone back to Ras 2 for a visit after she graduated. She was sitting with Master Tai in the garden. They were talking about the next group of students and how the Masters selected who to train.

"Master Tai, what was it that made you choose me?" Micha asked.

"At first, I felt you," Master Tai replied.

Micha shook her head. "I don't understand," she said.

"I knew you were there before I saw you. I felt you," Master Tai said.

Micha nodded in recognition. He'd taught her this skill. It was more a sense of knowing that there was someone there and what they wanted.

"Then, I watched you," Master Tai said.

Micha grinned. "That is true. It seemed like every time I turned around, you were there. I got used to it. What did you see?" she asked.

"I saw you," Master Tai said.

"I don't understand," Micha said.

"I saw you," Master Tai said again. He smiled. "I saw you get up every day to turn the soil in the garden. I did not have to tell you to fetch water or mend the fences. You took care of what needed to be done. You listened to me, even though you were angry and thought it was beneath you to dig in the dirt," he said.

Micha blushed. "You knew that's how I felt?" she asked.

Master Tai nodded. "I also saw how quickly you learned, that you would follow, but not without question. You had the will and the stamina to finish the planting, no matter how tired you were or how long it too. You took special care with each one of the plants, tending the soil, carrying water for them. Making sure they were safe," he said.

"I tried to keep them all alive. But two of them didn't take root and three more were damaged by a rabbit that got through the fence," Micha said.

Master Tai patted her hand gently. "Micha. We had a very good harvest from those twenty-five plants. Do you remember?" he asked.

Micha smiled proudly. "Yes, Master Tai. We had plenty and enough to share with others," she said.

Master Tai lowered his head then smiled at her. "I'm not sure you understand what you did," he said.

"I grew some peppers?" Micha asked.

Master Tai looked at her and smiled. He shook his head. "You did more. Much more. I would normally not talk about this, but it seems I need to tell you. We didn't expect so many of those plants to survive and bear fruit. We never expected twenty-five would survive or that we would have such a harvest. The soil where I told you to plant was not good," he said.

Micha sat forward. "Then why? How?" she asked.

"We wanted to know that too. It seems you have a gift for growing things," Master Tai said.

Micha shook her head, puzzled. "All I did was pay attention to them and try to give them what they needed," she said.

Master Tai smiled approvingly and nodded. "Yes, you did. Yes, you did," he said.

Micha had learned to tend the garden. Other than what Master Tai told her to do, she had to rely on her intuition and instincts. She'd never tried growing anything before. If there wasn't enough rain, she had to pump water from the well and bring the buckets to the garden. Master Tai showed her how to carry two buckets, one on each end of a long pole. After several days of very sore shoulders and legs, she could get most of the way to the garden without spilling too much. She got better at managing the buckets and stronger day by day. The plants grew tall. They had fresh peppers for weeks. Master Tai had given her the mithril shirt shortly after that first harvest. At the time, she didn't know that the Masters had never before accepted anyone for inside training before their first year was complete. She also didn't find out until much later that the Masters had all suspected from the first day that she might have some special skills or that Master Tai had chosen her first.

"Tend to them so they grow well," Master Tai said. She could still hear the encouragement in his voice.

SEEDLINGS
THE ARBORETUM ON THE MAGELLAN

Beth went back to the arboretum to get the Ambassador for dinner. She found her dozing on a bench next to a rack of new herbs.

Beth smiled. "She looks almost fragile," she thought. She touched the Ambassador's arm lightly. "Ambassador?" she asked.

The Ambassador was smiling just a little in her sleep. She opened her eyes. She smiled up at Beth. "Seems I drifted off," she said.

"Are you okay?" Beth asked.

"Yes, I'm fine," the Ambassador replied, noticing her concern. She looked at Beth closely. "I need to be sure," she thought. She slowed her breathing, crossed her arms briefly as if preparing to close her outer cloak, and extended her energy.

Beth felt a gentle warmth. She looked around to see if the grow lights had come on. That wasn't it. Then, it was over. She felt an odd sense of peacefulness.

The Ambassador smiled a little more. "I was just thinking about the history we were reviewing, my own history, about Ras 2, and about gardening. Have you ever tried to grow something from seeds, Beth?" she asked.

"No, Ambassador. We always had synthesizers. I didn't learn much about agriculture or seeds until I joined your delegation. I enjoy learning how things grow. N'amani said when we got the chance, I could go with him to visit his farm," she said. She smiled broadly.

The Ambassador turned her head sideways. "Do you want to learn how to grow things?" she asked.

Beth looked at her quizzically. "Now?" she asked.

"Why not? Now is a good time," the Ambassador said.

"Well, sure. Of course I want to learn. All the times I've helped the Doctor pick different plants and make different preparations, I want to learn how to do that, too. And all the foods he can make. I wish I knew how to make the soup he made for us last week. It was so good," she said.

The Ambassador smiled her Cheshire cat grin. "It starts with the seeds," she said.

"But there weren't any seeds in the soup." Beth said before she realized that wasn't the question.

"Were there vegetables in the soup?" the Ambassador asked.

"Well, yes," Beth replied. She was still trying to make the connection.

"Then there were seeds in the soup," the Ambassador told her.

Beth looked sideways at her and frowned.

"Where did the vegetables come from?" the Ambassador asked.

Beth shook her head.

"Come with me," the Ambassador said. She got up and walked down one of the paths between the racks of seedlings. She stopped in front of a rack and turned to face Beth. "What do you see?" she asked. She pointed at a tray.

"Dirt and some little green things," Beth replied scrunching up her nose.

"Those little green things are seedlings. They just sprouted. In a few weeks, some of these seedlings will have grown into tomato plants. A few weeks after that, they will bear fruit," the Ambassador said.

Beth shook her head. "Those are tomato plants? How can you tell?" she asked.

"Seedlings often don't look the same as mature plants. We watch them grow. We cultivate them. And we have to wait for them to develop," the Ambassador said. She was watching Beth closely.

"How can you tell which ones are which? I mean, how do you know these are tomato plants and not carrots or something else?" Beth asked.

The Ambassador nodded and smiled. "That's a very good question. First, you have to look. But you must also know what you are looking at. When you can see clearly, then, you can distinguish. Look at the shape of this leaf and the way it is pushing up through the center. See the edges on it. Now look at the stem, how it holds the small leaves on both sides. Use your fingers to pinch the tip from one of the small leaves," she said.

Beth reached out to pinch the leaf of one of the tiny plants. She uprooted it. "Oh no! I'm sorry. How do I put it back?" she asked.

"It can't be put back. It is too small," the Ambassador said quietly.

Beth looked down sadly. "I didn't want to ..." she said.

"You feel sad that you can't put it back so it can grow?" the Ambassador asked sympathetically. She wanted Beth to pay attention to the feeling.

Beth nodded. "Yes," she said.

"Then why did you uproot it?" the Ambassador asked. Her tone became stern and sharp.

"I wasn't trying to uproot it. It was just so small. It just seemed to come up by itself," Beth said.

"Would it have moved if you had not touched it?" the Ambassador asked.

"No," Beth replied nervously.

"Then it was your action," the Ambassador insisted.

"Yes. Yes. Alright. It was my action. But I didn't want that to happen," Beth said. Her hands were shaking and she was trying not to cry.

"Really? If you did not want that to happen, why did you do it? Why didn't you stop it?" the Ambassador demanded.

Beth started crying. "I wasn't trying to do it. I wasn't. I'm sorry, Ambassador. I'm really sorry," she said. "The Ambassador has always been so kind to me. But now, she is being very sharp and so much more demanding. There is no sympathy, no kindness, none of the usual empathy in her voice. She is hard and cold," she thought.

The Ambassador shook her head. "But you did. You did it. When you reached out to pinch that leaf, you did not see how fragile those small plants are. You did not pay attention to how tiny the leaves are nor to how much force you were using. So instead of taking a tiny pinch of a leaf, you uprooted the entire plant. Now, that plant won't ever grow," she said.

"I'm sorry I'm sorry," Beth said over and over. She wanted to run away, but she couldn't.

The Ambassador wasn't having it. "This is not about you being sorry. It's about you not doing it next time. You must understand what you are doing. You must be ready to bear the consequences of your actions," she said.

Beth looked down. She was ashamed and embarrassed. Then, she stopped crying. She shook her head. "I don't deserve this. I wasn't trying to harm anything," she thought.

The Ambassador saw the change in Beth. She smiled. "You said you wanted to learn, didn't you? Did you think the lessons would be easy? They are not. None of them are easy. That's the point," she said.

Beth looked up, raised her eyebrows, and shook her head. She was not quite sure what she was hearing. The Ambassador still wasn't being sympathetic, but there was understanding in her voice again, not harsh judgement.

The Ambassador smiled quietly. "If you want to learn, you must be prepared for many lessons. Some will be easier than others. Some will be extremely hard. You will fail. From failure, you will learn much more than you will ever learn from success," she said.

Beth smiled at the irony.

"That's better," the Ambassador said.

Beth looked at the Ambassador, blinked, and took a deep breath. Her tone had almost returned to normal. "Ambassador, you weren't inviting me to learn about growing tomato plants, were you?" she asked.

The Ambassador shook her head and smiled like a Cheshire cat on a porch swing. "No. I wasn't," she said.

Beth couldn't quite contain herself. It was hard to say it. It was more than she had dreamed. She wanted so much to learn. "You, you? you were inviting me...?" she asked.

"Yes. I will teach you," the Ambassador said. She smiled as a tear welled up in her eye.

"Yes, of course I want to learn. Ambassador, I never dreamed ...." Beth said. She started crying again.

The Ambassador patted her shoulder. "You need to learn to dream bigger dreams. You must learn to see with your heart. Then what you dream will change," she said.

She was not going to tell Beth what she had seen when she looked into her heart. There was much she would not be telling her any time soon. "Maybe one day," she thought.

Beth looked at her puzzled. "I don't understand," she said

The Ambassador smiled. "Seeds need time to grow," she said.

Beth shook her head. "I still don't understand," she said.

The Ambassador nodded. "You will," she said.

Beth looked up and caught a glimpse of one of the timers. "Ambassador, we are late for dinner. The others will be waiting for us," she said.

The Ambassador smiled. "We are not late. We will arrive at precisely the time we are supposed to arrive," she said.

"But we were supposed to be there 20 minutes ago. They will all be waiting for us," Beth said.

Ambassador raised her eyebrows. "That is true. But if we had been there 20 minutes ago, we would not have been here. Was there nothing here we needed to do?" she asked.

Beth shook her head and frowned.

The Ambassador smiled gently. "You must learn to consider everything, not just one thing. If we were destined to be at dinner now, we would be there. What we have done here is what we needed to do in this time, in this place. It could be no other way. Now, it is time to go. Do you understand?" she asked.

"I was only thinking about...," Beth said. She stopped, realizing that was the point. Her face brightened. "Yes, Ambassador. I understand," she said.

"Now we can go," the Ambassador said. She walked to the door. She turned to wait for Beth. "Are you ready?" she asked. She held out her hand.

"I think so," Beth said stepping forward.

The Ambassador linked her arm with Beth's. "Come along then. It's time," she said.

They walked through the doorway together.

THE AMBASSADOR

About the Author

TERRI MORGAN

I'm a writer, internet pioneer, computer programmer, linguist, international champion martial artist, grandma, and foodie. I've been a space fan since I was nine. Growing up, I climbed trees, played baseball and basketball, learned to swim and play music. I studied writing, theatre, and dance in college.

I've spent most of my professional life in technology. I've promoted events, been an invited performer and speaker, and organized classes, workshops, and seminars. For almost 30 years, I traveled between the US and China. In 1995, I was listed in the World Who's Who of Women. I've written dozens of technical manuals and edited more than a few. Besides keeping wudang.com online for 25 years in English and Chinese, I've published several articles and a few books.

My latest work is THE AMBASSADOR series and the old-time radio drama I'm producing via Channel 15 radio dot com. We're going for a ride. Come with? And bring the family.

The Ambassador Series

Sci-fi/Adventure/Martial Arts/Hopepunk
The Ambassador presents a grounded vision for a hopeful
future and who we could become.

The Ambassador
An accomplished older woman leads a tight-knit team to
protect the Local Neighborhood. Together, they must find a
way to stop the invading Olmeri.

The Ambassador: At Ras'alhague
An adventurous young woman joins an elite training
program on a primitive world. To succeed, she must learn to
trust herself and her four new friends.

The Ambassador: A Fragile Alliance
Book 1 of The Alliance Trilogy
An accomplished older woman and her team look for ways
to protect the Local Neighborhood. Together, they must find
a way to stop the invading Olmeri.

The Ambassador: The Olmeri
Book 2 of The Alliance Trilogy
An accomplished older woman brings the next generation
into her close-knit team to look for ways to protect the Local
Neighborhood. Together, they must find a way to stop the
invading Olmeri.

The Ambassador: Tomorrow
Book 3 of The Alliance Trilogy
An accomplished older woman and her team begin training
the next generation to protect the Local Neighborhood.
Together, they must find a way to stop the invading Olmeri.